M000196447

PRAISE FOR VIVIAN AREND

"If you've never read a Vivian Arend book you are missing out on one of the best contemporary authors writing today."
~ *Book Reading Gals*

"The bitter cold of Alberta, Canada, is made toasty warm by the super-sexy Coleman brothers of **Six Pack Ranch**."
~ *Publishers Weekly*

"Brilliant, raw, imaginative, irresistible!!"
~ *Avon Romance*

"This story will keep you reading from the first page to the last one. There is never a dull moment..."
~ *Landy Jimenez*

"I definitely recommend to fans of contemporaries with hot cowboys and strong family ties.."
~ *SmexyBooks*

"This was my first Vivian Arend story, and I know I want more! "
~ *Red Hot Plus Blue Reads*

"In this steamy new episode in the "Six Pack Ranch" series, Trevor is a true cowboy hero and will make any reader's heart beat a little faster as he and Becky discover what being a couple is all about."
~ *Library Journal Starred Review*

ROCKY MOUNTAIN ROMANCE

SIX PACK RANCH: BOOK 7

VIVIAN AREND

ALSO BY VIVIAN AREND

Six Pack Ranch

Rocky Mountain Heat

Rocky Mountain Haven

Rocky Mountain Desire

Rocky Mountain Rebel

Rocky Mountain Freedom

Rocky Mountain Romance

Rocky Mountain Retreat

Rocky Mountain Shelter

Rocky Mountain Devil

Rocky Mountain Home

Thompson & Sons

Ride Baby Ride

Rocky Ride

One Sexy Ride

Let It Ride

A Wild Ride

A full list of Vivian's print titles is available on her website

www.vivianarend.com

This is a work of fiction. Names, characters, places, and incidents either are the product of the author's imagination or are used fictitiously, and any resemblance to any persons, living or dead, business establishments, events, or locales is entirely coincidental.

Rocky Mountain Romance
Copyright © 2014 by Arend Publishing Inc.
ISBN: 978-1500815509
Edited by Anne Scott
Cover by Angela Waters
Proofed by Sharon Muah

All rights reserved. No part of this book may be used or reproduced in any manner whatsoever without written permission except in the case of brief quotations.

For my cousin Pat, who does her own type of wrangling in the law courts of Alberta. I'm glad these books make you smile.

1

*O*f all the stupid, idiotic...

Melody Langley stared at the warning light taunting her from her dashboard and cursed the reckless urge that had prompted her to take the back route into Rocky Mountain House.

Curiosity killed the cat.

It was the only reasonable explanation why she'd left the main highway, and instead of driving straight to the veterinary clinic where they were expecting her, she'd pointed her poor, abused Ford onto washboard gravel.

The good part was there should be not a lick of rust left on her undercarriage.

The bad parts? The orange warning light blazing like an evil Cyclops' eye, plus the temperature gauge shooting higher by the minute, heading into the danger zone at a rapid pace.

"Come on, baby. Ten more minutes, and you can take a break."

She patted the dashboard in encouragement, laughing in

spite of her concern, when a wet nose poked her in the back of the arm as Lady sniffed in curiosity.

Melody moved her hand over the dog's small head, pausing to rub behind her soft ears for a moment in reassurance. "No, this time you can't do anything to help. You sit and be a good girl."

The elderly Bichon settled on its haunches, nestling into the small space left open on the passenger seat.

A loud *pop* rang out, followed by the engine stuttering for a moment, and Melody jerked her full attention forward, both hands back on the wheel as she made her way down the narrow gravel road running parallel to familiar land. In the fields beside her, the first couple lines of cut hay lay in long, extended rows, while a slow-moving tractor dragging a disc-mower was briefly silhouetted against the distant Rocky Mountains.

Coleman land. She was some kind of a fool to have wanted a glimpse. Although—maybe it *wasn't* foolishness. Maybe it was wisdom to prepare for the first time she ran into Steve.

Not like he'd broken her heart or anything, but if she was prepared, maybe she wouldn't have quite as strong an urge to punch in his pretty face when their paths crossed.

Punch him or jump him, because as crazy as their baggage was, she still wished things had worked out differently between them.

The rattle under the hood grew louder, the temperature gauge buried in the red, and Melody debated the wisdom of pushing her truck to finish the last part of the journey.

The decision was made for her as another firecracker-like sound snapped, the wheel shaking under her hands right before the engine died altogether. Melody swore and threw open her door, stepping onto the gravel. She paused and grabbed a rag from under the driver's seat before stomping forward to work the hood release.

Even through the fabric, the heat scalded her fingers, and

she'd barely gotten the hood open before a third explosion snapped in her face. She fell to her knees, narrowly escaping a scalding burst of steam that shot overhead. Steam that turned to black and coiled upward like a cry for help.

She scrambled to vertical, circling back to the driver's door, desperate to grab Lady in case things got dicier. A low rumble pulled her attention to the field beside her, a tractor jerking to a stop on the other side of the barbed-wire fence. There was no time to look—just an impression in her peripheral vision of a jean-clad man dropping from the cab to the field.

Her focus was on more important things as she stood in the driver's side doorway. "Come on, Lady, come here."

The dog had burrowed under the pile of stuff she'd crammed into the cab, and not a single spot of furry white fluff could be seen.

"Come, Lady, I got a treat for you," Melody lied, but it was no use. That last loud noise must've been too much for the dog, and she would have to be dug out for her own safety.

Melody crawled onto the driver's seat and shoved boxes aside even as she tried to sound reassuring and calm. "There's a good doggie. Come on, sweetie, we need to get out of here. *Oh—*"

A loud gasp escaped as she was dragged backwards, a rock-solid arm wrapped around her waist. She flung her arms to the side and clutched at the doorframe.

Her protest lasted about two seconds before her grip slipped and she was manhandled away from her vehicle.

"Get away from the truck," a familiar masculine voice ordered in her ear, her body held tight against what could have been a wall for how unyielding it was.

At that moment, Melody wasn't thinking about anything but saving her dog, and instinct kicked in. She jabbed back hard with one elbow, driving it into the man's ribs with as much force as she could muster. And while she barely got a grunt in response, the surprise was enough his grip loosened. She lifted her feet off the ground and put her full body weight on the arm around her waist, twisting away as soon as she'd gained the room. "My dog is in there," she shouted, wriggling from his grasp then racing around the back of the truck.

An ominous sound accompanied the smoke. Considering the engine was no longer running, there was far too much noise issuing from under the raised hood of her vehicle.

"Your truck is on fire."

Melody jerked open the passenger-seat door, heaving objects out and tossing them into the ditch behind her as she frantically searched for Lady. "Brilliant observation."

She was ready to hit the ground to check under the seat in the hopes that was her dog's hiding spot. Instead, she was whirled on the spot to face a familiar pair of blue-grey eyes and a determined expression. Steve Coleman caught her by the shoulders and physically pushed her away. "Move. Now."

"My—"

He was no longer looking at her. Instead, *he* had dropped to his knees and was peering into the vehicle, the fire extinguisher he'd been holding discarded to the ground.

"I'll get your dog." He glanced up, jabbing his finger toward safety. "Keep walking," he ordered before reaching under the seat with one big hand.

So much was happening at once she didn't know what to look at first as she shuffled away, gaze locked on the drama unfolding before her. Smoke continued to rise as she backed down the road, hands clenched at her sides in helpless annoyance.

Steve swore loudly then shot to his feet, running toward her at top speed, the growling white ball of fury that was Lady grasped in one hand. Three shotgun-like sounds rang out, and Melody didn't protest when Steve caught her by the hand, damn near dragging her down the road.

Once they were far enough from the crackling firebomb, Steve stopped. He held the complaining dog against his chest, pinned in place with one arm, and she reached to rescue them both.

"It's okay, Lady. It's okay."

She laid a hand over the shaking animal's head and made soothing noises until the animal stopped trying to leap from Steve's arms.

Only then did she look into his face.

He was staring, his expression midway between disbelief and amusement. She was curious what he'd say. Some smartass comment no doubt, or perhaps something laid-back and noncommittal. Typical responses she'd come to expect before she'd called things off between them the previous September.

He opened his mouth, but she never got a chance to find out which path he'd choose, because that's the moment her engine decided to go up in flames.

Somewhere between the mind-boggling boring task of cutting hay and this moment stolen out of an action-adventure movie—somewhere *between* the two was where Steve would've preferred to be reunited with Melody.

As he twisted them to the ground, attempting to put his body between her and the truck while simultaneously protecting her from the road, his brain raced through a whole lot of other situations that would've been a lot more fun and reasonable.

Having her show up to help deliver calves. Maybe running into her in town at the café. Or what he always thought would've been the worst possible scenario—coming across her unexpectedly one night at Traders Pub where the last time they'd met she'd thrown the contents of a pitcher of beer smack dab in his face.

Even with the history behind them, exploding trucks seemed a little melodramatic.

Okay, it wasn't exploding, but it *was* on fire and had just made enough noise to scare birds off the overhead wire. Maybe dragging her away was being too cautious, but he was trying to be heroic.

Instead, what he got was a short drop with a sudden stop. Sharp road-crush dug into his shoulder as he protected Melody from smacking the ground and still maintained a grip on the furry beast using him as a chew toy.

"Holy cow." Melody pushed up on one arm, twisting back toward her truck. A stream of creative curses flowed from her lips, but he was far more interested in the hand pressed palm down against his chest. In the way their legs tangled together, her hips resting over his. Familiar and yet brand new—it had been far too long since she'd touched him.

Too long since those pale-blue eyes had stared into his with anything other than frustration or anger.

Melody's blonde hair was long enough she'd pulled it up, curled into a loose bun held in place by a coloured contraption. Between the streak of dirt on one cheek and the tendrils of hair that had worked loose from her bun tumbling around her face, she looked delightfully disheveled.

He curled himself up, the animal in his grasp shaking violently as it attempted to crawl through his body and escape. "Help me with your dog," he suggested as mildly as he could in spite of the claws raking his shoulder.

Melody scrambled off him, wrapping her hands around the trembling ball of fur. "Poor Lady. She hates loud noises."

Steve brushed the gravel off his jeans, his attention back on the burning vehicle. "If you've got a good hold of her, I'll go use the fire extinguisher."

"My things are in the—"

"Don't go back to the truck. Promise, or I'll stay right here and let it burn." She stiffened, but he didn't give a damn. "I'll sit on you if I have to. This is not up for discussion."

She gave him the evil death-glare usually reserved for the more ornery beasts she'd meet while visiting the ranch. "I just meant you should hurry up."

Fair enough. Steve set out for the truck at a jog, wondering when someone would jump from hiding and laughingly exclaim this was all a setup.

It didn't take long for him to grab the small fire extinguisher he'd dropped in his urgent rush to get her to safety. By the time he was done using it, the billowing black smoke had faded, rolling into the sky with a final burst of strength. Metal hissed in protest as white foam covered the charred remains of her engine.

Melody joined him, cautiously moving closer. "Is it safe?"

"It's dead. Both the fire and your truck, I'm afraid."

She stepped beside him, sighing as she stared into the busted carcass. "Poor Myrtle. I should never have pushed her that hard."

Steve glanced sideways to see her wrinkle her nose in that familiar way. The one that always made him wonder what crazy thing she was about to do next. Lady wiggled in her grasp, trying to get to the ground.

"Myrtle?"

Melody jerked to attention, and he realized she hadn't been staring at her truck, she'd been checking him out. He was dressed for haying, with old work boots and well-worn jeans, so there wasn't much to impress her. Not the way he'd always hoped to impress her when they finally met again.

Her lips twisted. "My poor abused truck. She's given up the ghost on me a few other times, but she's always managed to pull through in the end." She patted the sidewall fondly, careful to stay away from the overheated section and the extinguisher foam as she moved toward the driver seat. "I have a new truck on order, but I thought this one would get me here in one piece."

Steve gave the engine one final inspection to make sure it was safe before joining her at the door. He'd been working to save the dog, but even distracted it'd been impossible to miss that the vehicle was filled to the brim with boxes and bags, furniture and more boxes in the back. "You're traveling on the heavy side."

He brushed against her as he avoided a pothole, and she breathed in suddenly, the sound sending a shot through him.

It was difficult to keep from blurting out everything he wanted to say. He walked toward the passenger door, glancing back to note the way her jeans clung to her hips, a plain T-shirt tucked in at the waist curving up over her amazing pair of—

"*Woof.*"

Steve jumped to avoid kicking Lady, stumbling over his feet and swinging his arms to regain his balance. The dog sniffed his boots, and he stood still to allow himself to be inspected. "There's nothing we can do to fix Myrtle right now. Can I call you a tow?" he offered.

She nodded. "Please. I can't leave it at the side of the road."

Steve reached for his cell phone, cueing up the local garage number as he glanced at Melody, casually checking her out without *looking* like he was checking her out.

She straightened the bottom of her shirt, smoothing the material over her stomach before she leaned in the open driver's door.

Steve's gaze dropped to her butt.

It might've been nearly a year since he saw her last, but they'd been together for a long time before that. There wasn't an inch of her he hadn't gotten up close and personal with.

It was shocking to be near her without that intimate relationship between them.

"Anywhere in particular you're headed?"

As if he didn't already know.

"Veterinary clinic. I'm moving into the on-site living quarters." She faced him, a small notebook in her hand. "Tow truck can take me there, right?"

He nodded, holding up a hand as the connection went through to the Thompson and Sons garage. "Hey, Mitch? Steve Coleman. Can you come out and do a tow? Corner of Moonshine and Jackson's, then head west about half a kilometre."

He listened to Mitch's response, but his attention remained on Melody. She'd moved to one side and was attaching a body harness and lead to her dog. The fluffy beast wasn't the type of animal he'd ever thought she'd get. The realization made him uncomfortable.

Did he really know her that little after all?

He hung up, focusing on what he *did* know. They'd had something special once, and he hoped they could again. And the best way to at least aim in that direction was to talk to the woman. "Someone will be out within half an hour. You want to wait in the tractor with me? It's got air-conditioning."

She shook her head, reaching behind the driver seat for a small bowl she filled from a water bottle, waiting as the dog lapped eagerly. "I'll take Lady for a walk."

"I'll go with you," he offered. He caught a quick glimpse of her face, her expression full of questions, but she didn't outright turn him away. They were only a few paces from the smoky heap before he spoke. "Back in town for long?"

Her shoulders stiffened, and her chin lifted. "I'm back for good. I'm full time at the vet clinic working for Mathis."

He'd already known she was coming home. He'd heard

months ago, both through the grapevine and through a little circumspect digging he'd done.

Not the time to let Melody know that, though. They had other bridges to cross first. "Well, now, that's a surprise. I thought when you left for school last fall you said you were never coming back."

Melody turned far enough toward him he couldn't miss her exquisite expression. Distaste and *are you kidding me?* all at the same time. "I said I was leaving *you*. I don't remember saying anything about Rocky."

Damn, he'd pushed too hard. Steve held up his hands and backed off. "Hey, I have no beef with that. Fact is, I agree with everything you told me the last time we talked."

Her look of distrust tightened as her gaze narrowed. "The last time we talked I called you a lazy son of a bitch, along with other things."

Steve laughed. "You have a very good vocabulary, Melody. *Along with other things* encompassed quite a lot."

"And you agree with all of it?" She had her hands on her hips, the leash tangled in her fist while on the other end, her dog tugged in vain to reach the ditch where wonderful smells must have been taunting it.

He'd never get another chance to confess this straight out. "I don't know if this is the time or the place to talk about it, but yeah, I agree. I was a son of a bitch, and I'm sorry."

If he'd turned pink and sprouted wings, she couldn't have looked more astonished. Melody blinked a couple of times before shaking herself and shifting uneasily on her feet. "I don't know what to say."

Steve hurried to reassure her. "I don't expect anything right now. But I wanted to say it, and since you refused to answer my emails this is my first chance. With you back in town, we'll probably see each other around."

She nodded.

The shock of having her stumble into his day unannounced faded rapidly as the hopes he'd shoved aside over the past year galloped to the forefront. He was a lot smarter now than he'd been, so he knew better than to reveal his intentions too soon.

But there was nothing wrong with planting a few seeds, or at least that's what his father always told him. He had been too stupid before to understand.

Melody glanced back at the tractor stopped in the middle of the field. "You don't have to wait. I'll be fine."

Steve shook his head, pointing down the highway. "Let's walk the dog. I'm not leaving you stranded."

She turned reluctantly, moving closer to the road edge, much to Lady's delight. The dog shivered with excitement before plunging headfirst into the tall grass at the side of the road.

"Did I hear you right? The Thompson family still runs the garage?" Melody asked.

"Yep."

"Some things never change." She slowed her stroll to almost nothing to let the dog sniff.

And some people only change when they have to. Steve didn't say that part out loud, though. He held it in as myriad images and memories flooded through him. They walked in silence for a few minutes, Steve scrambling to come up with the next thing he needed to say to pave the way.

For two years they'd been together, him and Melody. Years he'd pissed away being that thoughtless son of a bitch she'd called him. By the time he'd woken up and *grown up* enough to know that she was something special, she was gone.

It wasn't a busted-down truck at the side of the road he'd seen today, it was a second chance, and damn if he'd let it slip through his fingers.

"How's your family?" she asked.

"Good. Mom and Dad are well, Trevor's a pain in the ass, and Lee is twice as bad." He grinned. "And Anna—you won't believe who she's seeing these days."

They talked about not much for a while. Small-town gossip. Ordinary conversation. It was exactly what they needed, and yet nothing at all what he wanted.

The tow truck approached from the distance, dust rising behind the solid metal frame.

"Thanks for staying with me," she said, offering him a hesitant smile.

He waited until the truck had pulled into place and Mitch joined them. Steve made sure she felt comfortable, but he shouldn't have worried. She was coming home as well—and whether she admitted it or not, Rocky was home.

The entire time Mitch worked to hook up Melody's truck, Steve helped, ignoring the questioning glances from the other man. He should have gotten back to his chores, but he couldn't bring himself to leave.

When he tugged open the passenger door for Melody, she finally realized he'd stuck around. "Thanks, Steve. I'll see you later."

He offered her a wave, and then stood until the tow truck rattled off down the gravel road, disappearing behind a veil of dust as they headed into town.

Melody was back.

Steve didn't have to think too hard about what he was going to do next. He'd screwed up a year ago. Scratch that, he'd screwed up *long* before she'd officially called them off. Now he could make things right, and Melody would find out exactly how important she was.

He hoped she'd enjoyed her time away, because this time, he wasn't letting her go.

2

Melody gazed around the familiar lab space, happily inhaling the pungent scent of antiseptic and cleanser. The tow truck had stopped by the small residence she'd be moving into, and Mitch Thompson had helped unload her gear before dragging the smoldering mess of her truck away.

She reeked of smoke, and everything she owned needed a washing, but considering how much worse it could have been, she wouldn't complain.

"It's good to be back," she said with a sigh as she settled into a chair, smiling across the room at her mentor.

"You do know how to make an entrance." Mathis Wisniewski grinned, easing his back muscles with a slow stretch. His dark hair had more lines of silver than before she'd left, age catching up with him in visible ways. His smile was still as broad, though, the lines by his eyes formed from frequent grins as well as years of work in the outdoors in all kinds of weather.

She wondered if down the road she'd have that as well—enough wear and tear to transform the baby-faced features she'd been cursed with.

In the meantime, she counted herself fortunate to get to work with the man. "You're lucky you were out on a call when I got here," she teased. "I could have used your help wrangling boxes."

"That's why I made sure I was wrangling chickens." He winked. "It's good to have you back. Did you have fun during your year away?"

"Fun?" Melody wrinkled her nose, thinking back to the hours she'd put in updating the large-animal license of her veterinary training. "Is that what we call it? Slogging through fields full of cattle shit and narrowly escaping being crushed against the sides of stalls by our patients?"

"Hell, yeah," the older man said, the twinkle in his eyes growing brighter the longer she spoke. "You know there's nothing else like it."

Her expression probably mirrored his, both of them fools for thriving on the utter joy they found in the midst of backbreaking labour. "You're right. Although I do wish the animals would try not to get sick in the middle of the night *every* damn time."

Mathis plopped onto the edge of his desk and settled in to catch her up on everything he'd changed over the past year.

The clinic was as up-to-date and modern as any that she'd worked during her practicum. She still couldn't believe her good fortune in having been taken on by Mathis. He'd built the practice from nothing, slowly gaining a solid reputation with the local ranchers so that he and Rocky Mountain Animal Care were the first place many turned for help.

Two other full-time employees and a handful of part-time rounded out the clinic staff. Tom Van Horne, a single man in his late thirties, had started on with the clinic a few years before Melody. Callie Hager worked the front desk and dispensed medication, and as a whole, they and the part-timers got along fine. Like a well-oiled machine, their different degrees of training allowed them to care for small-town pets and the bigger rural needs.

Melody enjoyed the challenge of both sides, although before she'd gone away, she and Mathis had been working together to handle most of the larger ranching jobs.

She listened intently as he caught her up on some of the major changes in local ranchers' situations. Who'd retired, who'd expanded their operations. It was fascinating to have him share information without glancing once at any kind of notes.

Mathis *knew* these people, and he cared for them like they were a part of his soul.

He rose and led her through the office into the small-animal area to show off the new equipment he'd purchased, and a sense of deep satisfaction struck.

This was why she'd come back. The familiar setting was the closest thing to a home she'd ever had. Memories from the years before she'd taken off for training rushed in, triggered by the meeting with Steve Coleman.

Out of all the people to run into on her first day back—although, if she was honest, she'd kind of been asking for it. Driving past Coleman land like she was looking for trouble. She shook her head for a moment as if to knock the cobwebs loose.

Mathis caught her, frowning as he paused in the middle of boasting about the great deal he'd gotten on a sterilizer. "Did you want to finish this tomorrow?"

She hurried to reassure him. "Sorry. Just a little distracted. I look forward to getting into the swing of things as soon as possible."

"I'll be glad to have you. The people I had in on relief were necessary, but they weren't you."

Her cheeks flushed at his compliment. "Go on with you, you silver-tongued devil."

Mathis laid a hand over his chest as if in shock. "Me? Oh, hell no." He shook a big beefy finger at her. "Don't you go running your skills down. You're one of the best. And if you aren't the best, I don't want to know about it."

Melody laughed. "I'm the best, that's right. Because I was trained by the best." She bumped him with her shoulder as she made her way to the sink to wash her hands. "You know I never would've gotten as far as I have without you. I appreciate everything you've done for me."

The older man shrugged. "Don't have any family to get involved in the trade, so I figure you're the next best thing. Someone who is just as close, but better because you choose to care."

He cleared his throat gruffly then switched the conversation. Melody hid her amusement at his deflecting from such an emotional topic.

"Melody?"

She and Mathis turned toward the door, Melody eased forward to offer a hand to Tom. "Hey. I hoped I'd run into you, but I thought you were done for the day."

"Just dropping off equipment." The dark-haired man hesitated, rotating his hand to show fingers covered with dirt. "I need to wash up before I go."

"Messy comes with the territory." She offered him a smile instead, pulling her hand back.

Mathis eyed his watch. "You have troubles out there today?" he asked. "I thought you'd have been done over an hour ago."

Tom shook his head. "Spent an hour doing a couple of extra jobs for Sean Dalton. He's been harping about how long he's had to wait lately, so I figured I'd drop by *before* he complained this time."

"Sean is always complaining about something," Mathis pointed out. "But good for you. Have to keep them happy, I suppose. Just make sure you charge him for your time."

He offered Melody a wink as he spoke, and she smiled. Mathis cared for the locals, but he didn't let them run ram-shod over him, either.

Meeting over, she breathed deeply of the warm June air as she wandered across the yard to her new home in the residence behind the veterinary clinic. Unpacking boxes gave her plenty of time to mull over their conversation.

The real reason she was back in Rocky was perfectly clear. Not just to work at the clinic, but because Mathis was family to her. She'd come to Rocky Mountain House and spent two years under his tutelage, taking what she learned in school and putting it into practice in a real, live, shit-on-your-boots ranching community. She'd loved every minute of it.

Of the work, that is.

So many memories. She laid another box on the kitchen table and opened it, emptying the contents as she puzzled over where to stash stuff in what amounted to a one-bedroom cabin. Having someone on site meant it was easier to keep track of emergency cases, or animals being observed overnight.

She smiled wryly. It also meant everyone knew where to track down the vet for those God-awful three-a.m. emergency moments, and yet even those heart-pounding moments she couldn't begrudge.

She pulled out another coffee mug and placed it on the shelf next to the ones she'd unpacked. Her fingers smoothed over the brilliant colours on her favourite ceramic mug as she thought back to the county fair where she'd found it, which of course triggered more memories of Steve.

She would have to deal with him at some point, but his out-of-the-blue appearance today, and his confession that she'd been right, was unexpected.

It changed *some* things—but not all. She'd learned that lesson. Steve Coleman was off her list for good.

"Hey, this is a private residence. What're you doing in here?" someone demanded loudly.

Melody's head shot up as she glanced toward the open door to discover another familiar face beaming back.

"Allison," Melody shouted. "Oh my God, it's been forever."

Her friend opened the door the rest of the way and rushed forward to offer a hug, squeezing Melody tight for a moment before she stepped back, her dark grey eyes examining Melody from top to bottom. "I can't believe you're home."

"I was going to call you as soon as I got settled. I'm done school, and yes, I'm home for good."

Allison cheered before brushing a strand of long dark hair behind her ear as she plopped herself down at the kitchen table, looking expectantly at Melody. "Spill. I know we talked a few times, but you really are terrible at keeping in contact. I want to know everything you did while you were gone."

"Everything?" Melody shook her head. "I don't know what you think was happening out in Saskatoon, but trust me, girlfriend, it's not some wild metropolis. I have no stories to burn your ears. You've probably had more excitement around here over the past year."

A rude noise escaped her friend as Allison picked up a magazine from the table and thumbed through it nonchalantly. "Rocky? Nothing exciting happens around here." She glanced at Melody, her eyes shining. "Well, maybe that's not true. We have *some* excitement, but it's also just... You know, *Rocky*. We don't want anything too out of the usual to happen."

That was the way Melody wanted it as well. She examined her friend closer, though, suspicions rising as Allison took care to keep her expression innocent.

"What are you not telling me?" Melody demanded.

The glow on Allison's face only got brighter. "I do have a bit of news. I was saving it to tell you in person—"

Melody waited, although she already had made a guess from the way Allison could barely keep still.

"I'm pregnant," her friend announced with a burst of delight.

A suitably excited noise escaped Melody's lips as she leaned forward to envelop Allison in another bear hug. "That *is* exciting. I'm so glad to hear it."

Allison sat back in her chair, beaming brightly. "I'm four months along. I didn't want to tell anyone earlier because I had a miscarriage back in the winter, so it's scary and exciting at the same time."

"I'm sure you'll be fine this time," Melody assured her.

"I hope so." She pulled an awful face. "If the old wife's tale about morning sickness is anything to go by, this kid is going to be extremely healthy."

"You've got it bad?"

Allison groaned. "Forget morning sickness, mine lasts most of the day, and by supper time when it finally goes away, I'm so hungry I eat nonstop between five and bed. I need to stop that soon or I'll end up with heartburn and no sleep."

"I'm sorry you're not feeling well, but I've heard every pregnancy is different."

"Exactly. Nothing's wrong, I'm just one of the lucky ones who gets sick for longer than usual." She flicked up two thumbs. "Go me."

Melody smiled as she leaned her elbows on the table and changed the topic. "Things are good with you and Gabe?"

Her friend didn't say a word. The sheer joy on her face was more than enough answer.

Melody waited for a flash of jealousy to strike. Across from her was a close friend who had so many things society said a woman had to have to be fulfilled—a partner, a family on the way. Melody didn't have those things and yet...

Nothing. No envy. Just pure happiness for her friend, and

the realization only made things sweeter. Melody laid a hand on top of Allison's and squeezed. "I'm glad everything is working out well for you."

"It's better than I'd ever dreamed possible. I thought taking off and getting my training was exciting, and I enjoyed my time living in Red Deer, but this?" Allison paused. "It's like I've found my way home."

"That's right. You moved away for a while."

Allison's expression softened as she stared into space. "I had left for good, I thought. Came back for my mom, and ended up setting down roots. Now I can't imagine living anywhere else."

Melody wondered if she'd ever come to the same conclusion. "I can live anywhere, you know. There's no family holding me back."

"Friends are family," Allison insisted. "And heaven knows I've got enough extended family. You're welcome to borrow some of them if you get the urge."

The comment brought Steve back to mind all over again.

She must've made a face because her friend frowned. "Or... not. If you want, I can chase them away and we'll pretend they don't exist."

"As if I could pretend the Coleman clan doesn't exist," Melody said, laughing. "Probably half of our business comes from looking after their stock."

"True, but isn't it good to know you don't have to put up with anything you don't want to?"

"Oh, I don't intend on putting up with anything, period."

Allison leaned forward, elbows on the table as she lifted her grey eyes to meet Melody's. "I like that about you," she confessed.

"My no-bullshit attitude?"

She was given a decisive nod followed by a warm grin. "I'm glad you're back, whatever that looks like. I missed you while you were gone."

The sentiment warmed Melody's heart. "Awww, I missed you too. And don't worry about that certain someone who pissed me off so badly before I left. I'm over Steve Coleman. In fact, he gave me a hand this afternoon when I ran into him."

Allison's expression changed to concern. "Which hospital did you send him to, or should I assume 'ran into him' wasn't meant literally?"

"He's fine," Melody assured her. "Just another Coleman living in Rocky Mountain House as far as I'm concerned."

"Good. That means I can invite you to the Coleman Canada Day picnic, and you'll come?"

Fools rush in where angels fear to tread. Melody deliberately smiled. "Of course. I'd love to join you."

She was surprised her nose didn't grow three inches.

STEVE PUSHED through his front door with his shoulder and came face to face with his brother.

"I hope that's supper." Trevor reached for the plastic bags hanging from Steve's hands.

"It is, but it's *my* supper," Steve growled, reluctantly letting go and following his brother into the kitchen area. "Why the hell are you here? Go home. You have your own place."

"My fridge is just as empty as yours was when I checked a few minutes ago." Trevor flashed a grin. "I swear I'll restock for both of us at Costco when I hit Red Deer this coming weekend. Invite me to stay for supper..." he begged.

Steve reached for the package of sausages after tossing an oversized cast-iron pan on the stovetop. "I thought Jesse was going to restock for everyone the last time he did the drive."

Trevor made a face, hauling eggs from the container in the fridge. "He forgot."

"Screw him," Steve grumbled.

The unmarried cousins were slowly dwindling, which meant there'd been changes in living arrangements across the board. The three youngest—all from different local Coleman clans— now occupied the rental that he, Trevor and friends used to live in.

The family who owned the house had moved into town years ago, and there was plenty of space for four or more, but Steve had had enough of the bullshit. He was over thirty, and sharing a place with twenty-year-olds with nothing on their mind but a good time had gotten old. Trevor agreed, and the two of them had moved out. Steve had built a bungalow. Trevor had hauled a trailer onto Moonshine land.

Still seemed as if Trevor ended up over at his place a hell of a lot.

He grabbed a couple of plates, putting them within easy reach to load when he finished cooking the eggs. "You notice there're a lot of things Jesse forgets?"

Trevor made a noise. "He has selective memory. I'll agree with you on that."

Steve didn't know that it had reached the point of making a big deal of it. Even though he wasn't living in the place anymore, their youngest brother, Lee, had moved into the rental, and Steve kept an eye on the kid. Or at least he had over the past nine months.

Another part of the *growing up* and *being more responsible* business.

Nope, Jesse was family, and so far he'd paid his portion of the rent on a regular basis without being too big of a pain in the ass. "Fine. If Lee complains, we'll intervene."

"Otherwise, let them learn, right?" Trevor looked far too pleased with the idea of the school of hard knocks whacking some sense into the younger crowd, and there were times Steve agreed.

Then he'd think back to how stupid he'd been only a short while ago, and have to reconsider.

Maybe if someone had given him a smack on the head he wouldn't have screwed up with Melody along the way.

Once their plates were loaded with sausage, potatoes and eggs, they made their way to the table, talking easily about the day's activities. The entire time, though, Steve was distracted by the large change in his agenda.

Trevor took advantage of a break in conversation to face him. "You may as well tell me what's wrong. You know I'll get it out of you before long."

"Ass... Nothing's wrong." Steve finished the last bites of his meal as he gathered his thoughts. "You ever made a huge mistake you wish you could take back?"

"Oh, man. This is going to be one of *those* discussions?" Trevor pushed his empty plate away then leaned his elbows on the table as he stared across at Steve. "People make stupid mistakes all the time. It's impossible to go back and fix them."

Truth. "So since you can't fix them, you have to look forward." Which was what Steve had been planning.

"Right. And try not to get caught doing the same stupid thing more than once." Trevor frowned. "Now you have me curious. You screw up on the job today?"

"No, nothing like that," Steve was quick to deny. "This is more like a huge mistake I made a million years ago. And I know I can't fix it, because too much time has passed."

He just had no idea how to go about getting what he very much wanted.

Trevor waited. "You have to give me a few more clues, because I'm lost."

"Melody's back in town."

Understanding dawned in his brother's dark brown eyes as he sat frozen in his chair, shock flooding his expression. Of course that was his *instant* response, and three seconds later, shock was replaced by amusement. "Oh, you are in for one hell of a time."

Steve ignored the jibe. "I'm going to get her back, Trevor."

"Masochist." Trevor was grinning now. "This is the woman who broke up with you by dousing you in beer. Then when you tried to talk to her outside the bar, she just about ran you over."

"That part was an accident."

"Whatever you say, bro."

A growl of frustration escaped. "You don't have to look like you're having so much fun. I'm serious about this. She's important to me."

Trevor shrugged, tilting his chair back to snatch up a new box of cookies from the counter behind him. He grabbed a handful, shaking his head as he passed the box to Steve. "Doesn't matter what you're serious about, does it? *She* was very serious about you being the last guy on earth she ever wanted to be with. I still don't know how you managed to get Melody that pissed at you."

And Steve had worked hard to keep the details of that stupid incident a secret. He'd never explained to anyone, and it seemed Melody had kept her mouth shut as well. "I was an idiot, okay? That's all you need to know. "

"For such an easygoing woman to dump you on your ass like that in public? You're more than an idiot. You're an idiot of epic proportions."

"Agreed," Steve said. "But that's in the past, and now that she's back, I'm going to change things."

Trevor carried their empty plates to the counter, stacking them to one side. "That's bold of you. I don't know who you knocked out, but somewhere out there is an optimist who wants his half of the glass back."

"Screw off."

"Only someone who thinks unicorns fart rainbows could imagine it's going to be a piece of cake getting back into her good graces. I don't know if you have a chance." Trevor folded his arms over his chest and looked thoughtful. "But maybe...?"

"What?"

His brother paced a few steps away before turning with a grin. "Maybe I should give a certain veterinarian a call. See how she enjoyed her time away."

Steve shot to his feet so fast his chair tipped over. "You keep the hell away from her."

Trevor waggled his brows as he beat a hasty retreat. "Lady's prerogative. If she's interested..."

He escaped from the room, laughing his fool head off.

Steve refused to chase after him like they were a pair of twelve-year-olds brawling around the house. It didn't matter anyway. There was only one Coleman Melody Langley was going to pay attention to, and that was *him*.

3

Steve crawled his way out from under the mass of preteen boys who had dragged him into an impromptu wrestling match, laughing as he disengaged the most enthusiastic combatant from his leg. "Enough. Don't you have someone else to torment?"

The shining white cast on Robbie's right arm wasn't slowing him down one bit. Seemed the kid was following in the tradition of ranch families everywhere. It was a rite of summer Steve remembered well—amongst the Coleman clan there had always been someone in a cast before school had been out more than a week.

"They told us to pick on you," Robbie admitted with childish honesty. "You and Uncle Trevor."

Steve glanced toward the main gathering at the Coleman Canada Day picnic, and laughed to see that one of the other boys was attempting to drag Trevor toward them. "Who is *they*?"

"Uncle Joel and my dad."

Figures. A quick glimpse to the side revealed cousin Daniel

from the Six Pack clan standing beside his wife, Beth, keeping an eye on his sons even as Robbie leapt and tackled Steve.

Steve let the boy take him to the ground again, laughing as he turned the wrestling into a tickling match, and suddenly the bodies crawling on top of him weren't just preteen boys, but a couple of petite girls with blonde pigtails.

There weren't that many kids in the clan yet, although from the looks of things, there would be a lot more added over the next couple of years. But whether it was kids or people joining the family through more grown-up ways, the Coleman party grew larger all the time.

He'd just scooped up Blake and Jaxi's two oldest girls, one in either arm, and was ready to change the game when a bell rang.

"I need the kids over here," Steve's mom called from beside the house. "Not you," she scolded Jesse as he slipped into the lineup next to Robbie who had raced up at a full-out sprint.

"I'm young at heart," Jesse protested.

"He is," Robbie agreed, linking his fingers through Jesse's. "He's like me."

Kate laughed. "What do you say, Jesse? You want to help us with the scavenger hunt? I was going to get Steve to volunteer, but if you want, you can stay."

Robbie leaned in and whispered loudly enough they all heard him. "You want to stay. There's always candy."

Jesse laid a hand over his heart. "For candy? Of course I want to help."

The family around them were still chuckling as Steve passed over the girls in his arms, the small group of kids heading to where Steve's mom had tables set up with supplies, including what was definitely a stash of candy.

"You timed passing off the rugrats well," Trevor teased.

Steve faced his brother, stealing the longneck out of his hands. "Never underestimate the power of preplanning." He took a drink before glancing over his shoulder to take in the crowd. "Nice to see Jesse show up at a family event."

Trevor nodded. "It looks as if we've got just about everyone. Thank goodness the Moonshine clan only has to host the picnic every four years."

"At this rate, four years from now there'll be a dozen more kids," Steve pointed out.

His brother shuddered. "As long as they're not mine, that's all I can say."

"Yeah, right. I bet you right now you end up with kids before I do."

Trevor stole his beer back. "You didn't see me in the bottom of that pile, did you? No, I was playing it safe and staying away from the kid cooties."

"Idiot."

"Ass." His brother winked. "Come on, Blake and Gabe said we could get some cards in before dinner. It's not poker, but it'll be fun."

"You go ahead. I've got a couple of things to do."

They marched in different directions, Steve drifting through small groups of conversation. Nodding politely at his aunts and uncles, and wondering at the sheer volume of noise the group generated.

When he'd arrived at the picnic, he'd left his truck back by the barns and walked to the house. He wasn't the only one—half a dozen trucks were parked in a row facing the nearby alfalfa field. With four families in the area, a gathering of the entire clan meant a whole lot of bodies.

Boxing Day and Canada Day were reserved for the family free-for-alls. They'd eat, take turns entertaining the kids, take turns entertaining each other with stories that had been told a million times before, and would be told a million times again.

He didn't mind any of it, but for a moment he wanted space.

He slipped away to the closest barn, heading for the ladder to the hayloft.

A sense of mischief struck, as if he were ten years old, hiding out when there was work to do. Or more often than not, he would've been the one to simply not notice it was time to do the next thing.

This was different, he reassured himself. He wasn't a distracted child at play, or a youth trying to get out of work. He was a grown-ass man who wanted a moment to relax before returning to enjoy the gathering.

A couple of moves adjusted the bales in one corner into a comfortable nest. Another quick grab nabbed him the blanket from near the ladder—the one they kept around for just such occasions.

He laid out the fabric to create a comfortable platform and crawled on top, rolling to his back to stare into the rafters as the peaceful sounds of a beautiful summer day drifted around him. At this distance, the voices in the background produced a constant hum, the occasional burst of bright childish laughter punctuating the air with joy.

Eyes closed, breathing slowing, he relaxed and let his mind wander.

It was a little annoying that images of the last time he'd been in the barn with Melody were the first to intrude. Hell, he had memories of her nearly everywhere on the ranch.

Now he had to find a way to make new ones. That was what he needed to put his energy toward.

A low creak sounded, and he rolled cautiously to one side, listening for clues of who'd invaded his territory. He wondered if the kids had escaped supervision, planning to make their own fun in the hayloft.

Instead of a laughing horde, though, a single set of footfalls crossed the floor below him, followed by a curious thump from the far corner of the loft. Steve lifted his head far enough to spot a calico cat mincing its way over the top of the bales. She stalked forward, a limp mouse hanging from her mouth.

The ladder creaked. Smooth, rhythmic—*someone climbing.* A pair of hands appeared followed by a lush mane of blonde hair as Melody turned her face toward him. Her pale-blue eyes shifted from side to side as she blinked hard and adjusted to the low light streaming in the small open window.

He waited until she was away from the ladder before saying something for fear of shocking her into falling. "In the far corner."

Melody jerked, a small gasp escaping before she focused on him. "Steve?"

"I didn't mean to surprise you," he apologized. "I didn't want you to think you were alone then get frightened when you spotted me."

She approached slowly, eyeing his nest in the bales. One brow rose, and he was sure she was making a judgment call about him hiding from all the work and people. Not that he could blame her—

"Taking a break," he offered. "The party will go on for a while."

To his surprise, instead of offering a critical comment, she moved closer, sitting beside him and letting out a long, slow sigh. "Me too. Allison invited me. This may sound stupid, but it's a little overwhelming out there. I swear there are more Colemans than I remember."

So he wasn't the only one who'd noticed. Steve chuckled, curling into a sitting position and draping his hands over his knees. "I think we borrowed a few extras. There really aren't *that* many of us."

She smiled before looking him in the eye. "Thanks again for your help the other day."

"Did Myrtle make it?"

She offered a slow, sad shake of her head. "She's gone."

"That's too bad. I'm sorry to hear of your loss."

His joke dragged a reluctant laugh from her lips. "As much as I'll miss her, I do have a new truck on order. It's supposed to be here by the end of the week."

"If you need to borrow a vehicle until then, let me know."

Melody stopped. Tilted her neck to one side and examined him closely. "That's generous of you."

Steve shrugged. "I figure you need a way to get around."

"I do, but Mathis gave me the vet truck to use."

"Like I said, just let me know."

Silence stretched awkwardly for a moment, and Steve scrambled to find the next thing to say.

He was rescued by a kitten, of all things.

"Oh, look." Melody held a hand toward him before pressing a finger over her lips.

Lips that Steve desperately wanted to kiss, but instead of following through on the primitive craving, he followed her pointed gesture toward the opposite corner, where a teeny furry body teetered on the edge of the hay bale.

"He's okay," Steve whispered.

"I saw the mama cat climbing up—it looked like she had a mouse with her. They must be nearly old enough to teach how to hunt."

Steve swung his feet to the floor, standing slowly and motioning toward the opposite corner. "Come on. Let's take a closer look."

She didn't hesitate, slipping beside him as they inched their way across the slab-board flooring. Steve reached the other side and got on top of the bales, crawling on his hands and knees with Melody at his side.

Talk about flashing back to his childhood—

But it was more than that. As they moved in what was now-companionable silence, Steve thought back to the days before Melody had broken up with him. There'd *always* been something not quite right in their relationship. Sure, he'd been pretty relaxed about things, and that was a large part of the problem. He simply hadn't noticed until all hell had broken loose.

But after some retrospect, even in their good moments, something had been missing.

He paused a short distance away from their target, resting on his heels and slowing his breathing to utter silence.

Melody slipped a hand around his arm and pulled gently to bring him closer. "Over here. You can see the nest she made," she whispered.

Damn if she didn't lean forward on a bale to peer into a spot that was impossible for him to see unless he moved right against her.

To hell with it. Steve reached over her body, pressing a hand to the hay bales on either side of her shoulders as he joined in admiring the litter of kittens curled around each other.

Two of them were awake, batting paws before falling over on wobbly legs. They rolled over their siblings who slept soundly in spite of being used as landing pads.

The mama cat reappeared with the most adventurous kitten held by the scruff as she returned it the nest. Typical barn cat, she ignored Steve and Melody as unimportant as she settled in to wash the face of her nearest baby.

But as fascinating as the kittens were, Steve was far more aware he wasn't just next to Melody, he was damn near covering her. His chest pressed to her back, her hip bumping his groin as she adjusted position.

He fought the devil of temptation and won *part* of the battle. He stayed in place, teasing himself with a taste of what he really longed for.

Between one breath and the next, she realized how

intimately positioned they were. Her body stiffened, her breathing grew shallower.

Steve shifted away as if trying to find a better angle to look at the cats. "I think that's the third batch for this mama. She's got it down pat," he whispered.

Only Melody wasn't checking the kittens anymore. She'd turned and sat, legs coiled beside her like a fancy mermaid statue, her weight resting on one hand as she stared at him.

Her expression was a whole lot different than what he'd seen a few days ago on the roadside, and a small burst of hope ignited.

He changed the topic before the urge to do something inappropriate struck. "You want to go find some food? I'll protect you from the masses if you protect me," he joked.

Melody got up on her knees. "Yeah, I suppose we should join the group. Allison will be wondering where I am."

They made their way back over the bales, prickly hay poking through the knees of his jeans and digging into his palms. He stepped onto the boards and reached back to help her. She caught his fingers with hers, willingly accepting the gentle tug he used to help her find her feet.

But then she didn't let go.

Steve glanced at their joined hands before lifting his gaze to meet hers. "Melody?"

She tilted her head to the side. "I'm...curious about something."

Then damn if she didn't free his fingers and instead plant both palms against the front of his shirt.

Lord, the temptation to wrap himself around her was strong. "Curious about what?"

"Kiss me." Her words were halfway between a command and a dare.

His jaw hung open for a hell of a lot longer than could be considered proper. "Excuse me?"

She lifted a brow, her expression growing sultry. "Don't tell me you've forgotten how to kiss?"

He didn't know the answer to that one. Well, he didn't know the *right* answer to that one. "Are you asking how many women I've kissed since you and I—?"

She pressed up on her toes, far enough to bring their mouths into contact, and suddenly it didn't matter what she was asking other than he was getting to do what he'd wanted to do since he'd seen her on the road days ago.

It was a soft caress at first, the faintest hint of mint on her lips growing as the kiss deepened. Maybe this wasn't part of the deal, but he couldn't resist. Steve curled his hands around her face so he could tilt her upward and taste her more fully. Careful to hold himself in check when what he really wanted was to take a deep, possessive approach that would make it clear that she'd asked for this kiss—but he was more than ready to take.

Cool down, animal.

Under his hands she moved her lips willingly against his. They'd had a lot of practice in the past, and not just at kissing. His body responded, eager to return to everything else they used to be good at, as well.

He shifted his hips to ease the pressure on his cock, focusing on her mouth and the exquisite sensation of her tongue slipping against his.

She leaned into him, body warm and soft against his growing hardness. A satisfied sound escaped her, sending a chill up his spine. Still he kept in control, paying attention to her clues so when she pulled back, he let her go even though retreat was the last thing he wanted.

There was a sparkle in her eyes and amusement in her expression. "Thanks."

And damn if she didn't turn and head for the ladder.

You're welcome? Any time? His tongue was stuck to the roof of his mouth as he struggled to find the words to say in response.

What the fuck just happened?

She disappeared before he'd come to any firm conclusions. But that was okay, because in a way, their short interlude was too damn amusing to get bent out of shape over.

It did answer one vital question, though. She was attracted to him—he was sure of it now. He was going to use that information to his benefit. And hers, because this was about both of them getting what they needed.

One step at a time.

It DIDN'T MATTER where she turned, there seemed to be something going on that involved laughter.

A lazy, post-dinner mood struck, and relaxing in lawn chairs in the sun while watching good-looking guys—Melody had no problem with her current agenda.

"Your eyes are the size of plates," her best friend teased. "Trust me, there isn't that much interesting to stare at out there."

"Speak for yourself." The pretty blonde who'd settled beside Melody said with a low hum of approval. Ashley bumped their shoulders, pointing toward where the guys had set up a horseshoe pit. "Why is it not the middle of summer and blazing hot? All we need is for them to strip off their shirts and we'd have the best view in town."

Melody wasn't about to argue. "Ice cream, watermelon, and muscular men tossing iron objects. The only thing that would make today better would be chocolate."

Out of nowhere, a chocolate bar appeared in her lap. She blinked in surprise as more laughter surrounded her. She glanced up to see Allison wink.

"Hidden stash in my purse," she confessed. "I'm trying to give it up, but it's about the only thing that doesn't make me nauseous, even in the morning."

Ashley stole the chocolate bar and unwrapped it, helpfully breaking it into three equal portions and distributing it among them. "Everything in moderation. Not as if you couldn't use the calories."

"I don't want to spend the next five months making a baby and the next five years getting back in shape," Allison complained.

"Don't worry too much," Melody said. "With how much running around you do in the restaurant, as well as everything you're helping with at the ranch, you'll be okay."

"Agreed." Ashley stared at her piece of chocolate for a moment before smiling. "It's like the best aerobic exercise in the world, living on the ranch." She popped the chunk in her mouth and hummed happily as she chewed.

Melody copied her, letting the rich morsel melt on her tongue. Dark chocolate slipped down her throat like heavenly pleasure, and she sighed, licking every last bit off her fingers.

"Don't look now, but I think you're being watched," Allison shared, tilting her head toward where the guys were playing.

Melody leaned back in her chair, looping her arm around the back of Ashley's as she examined the horseshoe pit.

Her friend was right. Something was going on. Something that involved an awful lot of ribbing in Steve's direction and loud bursts of masculine laughter.

On her right, Ashley leaned in closer. "Okay, tell me the scoop. I've only heard bits and pieces of the story. I know the first year I went out with Travis, you were seeing Steve on a casual basis. But then last year after we came back to town, there was this..."

"Incident?" If Ashley had to ask, then Steve hadn't told

stories while she'd been gone. Not that she'd expected him to, one way or the other, but it was kind of good to know he hadn't tried to blame her for anything.

Ashley twisted in her chair, lips curled into a brilliant smile. "Incident. I like that. Remind me to tell you sometime about the *incident* Travis, Cassidy and I had the day I came home from volunteering at the school to discover they were waiting for me to cook dinner."

The woman was so upfront about all three of them being involved. Melody wasn't about to pass judgment, especially since the trio seemed to be working hard to keep their relationship solid. No one else in the Coleman clan was vocal in disapproval either, which Melody liked.

Ashley had more energy than Melody did, though. One guy at a time was enough for her. Actually, one guy had been too much at one point, considering how much work Steve had been.

She could answer part of the question, though. "Yes. We had a bit of a misunderstanding. Also, I was going away for a year to complete upgrades on my training, and I decided a long-distance relationship wouldn't work very well."

To their right, Allison laughed softly. "You have a way with words."

"Thank you."

"Still, *someone* is very interested in you, no matter what broke you up last fall." Ashley gestured toward the guys before turning her attention back on Melody. She laid a hand on her knee and squeezed. "People change. I know I did, and so did Travis. We weren't right for each other back when you first met me. But the next time, it was like we'd grown up enough to be able to fit. Cassidy just made it better."

Allison added her agreement. "Gabe and I as well. I mean, we'd always gotten along, and I never dumped a pitcher of beer on his head, so it's not *quite* the same thing—"

"I will never live that down, will I?" Melody asked.

"It's in the annals of clan history. Steve will have it etched on his tombstone. *Doused in lager, all men should be so lucky.*" Ashley ducked back and laughed as Melody made a feint at her.

They visited for a little longer, but it was growing late, and Melody was ready to return to the quiet of her small home. She said goodbye to the girls, promised Allison she'd stop by soon, and headed toward her borrowed truck.

"Wait up. I want to talk to you." Steve turned from the guys to jog forward, waving her down.

Melody wondered what was going on as the rest of the bunch all grinned after him, masculine laughter and jousting continuing.

She slowed her step to allow him to catch up, then turned and marched at a brisk pace to where she'd parked at the end of the drive. "If the Colemans decided to leave Rocky in a rush, you'd decrease the population by fifty percent, unbalance the countryside, and tip us all into the Red Deer River."

"Good thing we're not planning on going anywhere then." He kept up with ease, those long legs of his eating up the distance in far fewer strides than she had to take. That detail wasn't something she was going to cry over—the man was bigger than her, stronger than her, but that didn't mean she didn't fit in just fine.

"I had a good time today," she said. "I'm glad Allison invited me."

"You're always welcome."

Silence.

They were closing in on the truck she'd borrowed from Mathis, and she didn't want to leave whatever was on his mind ignored. "Something you wanted to talk about?"

"Not quite sure how to say it."

"That's nothing new," she muttered.

"What's that supposed to mean?"

She shrugged. "Steve, you always knew when to crack a joke, but didn't tend to say much of anything any other time. Do you need to schedule me for a vet appointment, or—"

"I want to see you again," he blurted out.

Maybe if she'd never imagined hearing those words this would've been more awkward, but she'd had enough time to think it over. She'd prepared for every possibility when she'd decided to return to Rocky Mountain House, even this one.

Prepared, and planned to enjoy it.

She kept walking. "I don't know what you're talking about. I don't think we had an actual relationship, not one that I'm interested in rekindling."

"I get that. I told you I was a fool, but I've changed. I want a chance to prove it."

"Prove it?" A burst of laughter escaped before she could stop it. "Steve, when we were dating, half the time you didn't know what day it was. And I don't even know that I want to call it dating. More like *conveniently seeing each other when it worked out.* That part wasn't just your fault. I'll take some of the blame, because I was damn busy with my job."

"We were both busy, but that doesn't give me an excuse for being a shit. It also doesn't have anything to do with what I'm talking about right now."

Melody jerked to a halt so she could toss him her most disdainful expression. "What happened between us a year ago, and more? How does *that* have nothing to do with the fact you want to see me again? You're not making any sense."

His lips twitched upward as his gaze drifted over her, his attraction apparent. "Let's start with a clean slate. Hi, you must be the new vet in town. I'm Steve Coleman, and you're going to be seeing a lot of me."

Unbelievable. And yet...interesting. The old Steve would

have joked around, but never with that intense focus as if he was prepared to actually do something if she argued with him. "Well, it appears you've grown some balls since the last time we met, but I don't know that it's enough."

"Trust me, I've got the balls, for many things."

She shook her head, clicking her tongue as if in disbelief. "If that was some sly reference toward your sexual prowess? There's another place you're mistaken. I'll give you points for knowing where to find a woman's clit, and I had more than a few orgasms with you—thanks for them, by the way."

His grin broadened, and she was almost reluctant to deliver the killing blow.

"But, Steve? I'm afraid you're just too vanilla for me."

Melody spun on her heel and marched away, her own grin breaking free as he stood frozen on the spot behind her, sputtering in response. She kept walking, catching hold of her door and quickly crawling into the borrowed beast.

She got the door shut before he caught up with her, but there was no way she could ignore him. Steve stood inches from her closed door, his expression folded into a frown until she relented and rolled down her window.

He started in right away before she could speak, his utter shock apparent. "Too *vanilla* for you?"

Melody answered briskly. "I found out a few things about myself while I was away at school this year. So, I'm glad we're going to be friends, and I look forward to working with the Colemans now that I'm back, but that's pretty much all *us time* is going to be. Have a nice day."

She put the truck in drive and left him standing in the dirt, containing her laughter until she was on the main highway and headed for home.

This was where the Steve she'd known would saunter back to the party and forget about her. Oh, maybe he'd give a few moments' thought to challenging her comments, but then something would distract him, and the next time they met? It would be as if this conversation had never happened. He'd ask her out again, she'd turn him down.

Eventually he'd get bored and move on. It was sad, but inevitable.

Except...the flash of fire she'd seen in his eyes in her rearview mirror as she drove away wasn't familiar. Something fluttered in her belly, and she wondered if maybe she'd poked a little too hard.

4

*S*teve stared at the empty search engine in front of him. *Jeez.*

On a typical day he used his computer for work, like checking grain prices or the feedlot calendar. Occasionally he checked out some porn.

Tonight's task made him squirm in his seat.

He wasn't as ignorant as Melody seemed to think, but at the same time, no way did he want to misinterpret her comment.

There was also a part of him inside that was absolutely, fucking pissed she'd been experimenting with sex, especially anything beyond the norm, while she was away. It was bad enough to think of her fooling around with anyone else, let alone them having their hands all over her some way that he never had.

Even as he thought it, he knew the emotion was outrageous. He had no right to dictate what she'd done while she was gone, or who she'd done it with,

But damn if he didn't wish he *did* have the right.

He typed in the letters in deep reluctance. *Non-vanilla sex.*

The first screen popped up in answer to his search, and Steve felt his eyes rolling back in his head as the topics listed sounded filthier and filthier the farther down the page he went.

He was pretty sure she wasn't talking about some of the extreme shit out there. Knife play—

Christ.

That didn't seem her style. He jotted down a few notes as he went along, glancing away from the pictures without examining them too closely because even though some of it was interesting, the shots weren't of Melody.

If he had the go-ahead to do everything he'd ever wanted to without having to worry about pushing her too hard—? His face grew hot as his body reacted to the thought. His cock hardened, and he adjusted position uncomfortably.

No freaking way was he going to jack off, though. He wasn't sure he wanted to relieve the pressure, turned on by thoughts of Melody and yet equally turned on and disgusted by what he was seeing. Anything people wanted to do—he supposed that was their business, but fuck if it should be slapped up all over the Internet for everyone and their dog to see.

He wasn't sure where that opinion put him on the masculine scale.

Steve leaned back in his chair and stared at the computer screen without seeing anything as he focused on the past. The pictures scrolled by automatically on the website he'd clicked while he drifted in thought.

Melody had no idea how much he'd been holding back. Not because he wanted to tie her up and keep her in his bedroom—he had heard about that stuff. No, combining his laid-back lazy-ass attitude with everything else that had been wrong in their relationship simply meant that while he'd always made sure she'd had a good time, he'd made extra sure he'd been a gentleman. It was simpler. It was...less complicated.

He'd been all about less complicated.

They'd fooled around a few places other than a bed—he was sure of it. But it was true that most of the time when they'd had sex, they'd been at her place. He'd been living at the house with the guys, and there was no way he would have taken her back to the house and had someone toddle in and get raunchy around her.

Perhaps that had been a mistake—but then the thought of any of his friends or family seeing Melody naked just infuriated him.

Maybe that choice had been a blessing in disguise.

But after her snarky comment, he had some mileage to make up and no objections to it either. Although, from the photos on the screen, there were obviously a lot of things out there that floated people's boats but left Steve with a dirty taste in his mouth. He reached forward to click off the link that screamed "Way Too Far".

"Geez, Steve. Shut the damn screen off." The order snapped from behind him.

Steve slapped at the monitor as he pivoted his chair to discover Gabe Coleman giving him a very dirty look.

Shit. "Did you knock, asshole?"

"I didn't think I'd catch you masturbating in the middle of your damn living room, and no, I didn't knock, because you told me to come over, you shit."

Steve thought back, puzzled by his comment. "When did I say that?"

"When we were playing cards earlier." Gabe folded his arms over his chest and glared harder. "What do you want to talk about? Because you obviously have an agenda for the evening that I'm not needed for, and I'd far prefer to be home with Allison getting my rocks off with her."

Steve held back from making another glib comment. He had asked Gabe over—it had slipped his mind during the later distractions. "I want to get back together with Melody," he confessed, feeling a little like a scratched CD, skipping and repeating the same words over and over.

"Which completely explains why you're looking at money shots on your computer," Gabe deadpanned.

"I'm doing research," Steve insisted.

"*That's* what it's called." Gabe pretended to think about it for moment before pulling an exasperated face. "You know, if I tried that line on Allison, she'd take my balls and shove them up my ass. You don't have to explain to me—"

"Melody says I'm too vanilla," Steve confessed, regretting it the minute he finished speaking.

Only, out of all the Colemans who he could have admitted that to, Gabe was his safest bet.

His cousin's expression lost all mocking as he grabbed the chair next to Steve. "You're serious? I mean, about wanting to get together with Melody?"

Steve chose his words carefully. "You know what I was like when I was dating her before. Things were never bad between us, but they were never as good as I could've made them."

Gabe's lips twisted. "That kind of sums up most of us guys when we're not actively avoiding being assholes."

"Right, so when I fucked up and she left, I realized I had to change. And I did, I swear I did." Steve dragged a hand through his hair in frustration. "The trouble is, I spent the last year trying to become a man she could respect. Someone who puts energy into my work and the things I do for the community, but when I asked her to go out with me, that wasn't on her mind at all. She tossed back that I'm boring in the sack."

"But did she say no to dating you?"

Steve considered. "I kind of thought that's what telling me I'm too vanilla meant."

Gabe shrugged. "Sounds like an opportunity to me. Prove you can step up to the plate with some adventurous sex, and see she doesn't have any complaints. When you add that to everything else you've learned over the past year, you might find you've got what it takes."

"I'm not about to start taking a crop to her," Steve grumbled, waving a hand at the computer. "I mean, I've seen it. I looked at shit that made my head spin, and it's not my thing. What if it's what she wants? Because I don't think I can fake that, not even for her."

His cousin leaned forward, resting his elbows on his knees. A slight furrow appeared between his brows. "Do you think that's what Melody discovered in the last year? You think she's got some deep-seated dirty fantasies you can't answer?"

"Not the Melody I knew," Steve said, the confession burning as he made it, "but that's part of the problem. Maybe I didn't know her as well as I thought."

Thankfully Gabe shook his head. "From what I remember of you two, when you and Melody were getting along, you seemed to coast." Gabe offered a smile. "I think ladies like to know they've got more than your minimal attention. If you make exciting sex a part of your game plan, you should be fine.

"So I don't need to research all kinds of exotic sexual practices?"

"You could, but you should probably do that together." Gabe's smile stretched into a broad grin. "Sometimes it's fun to mix it up, but if I was going to give you any kind of advice, it would be let her know you're up for anything. That you can't keep your hands off her."

That was something Steve could get in line with. "I hate that I fucked up before."

"Hate more that you'll probably fuck up again, but the real test? Is what you do when you make a mistake." Gabe rose to his feet, brushing his hands on his thighs. "Besides, if Melody was into kinky shit, it's not as if she's going to find very many takers in this neck of the woods. You should make a list of the eligible date prospects for her. You know, just being helpful-like."

An evil, wonderful thought overtook Steve. "That's a good idea."

"Don't tell her I offered it," Gabe ordered. "Allison thinks a hell of a lot of Melody, and I don't want her upset because you've gone and screwed things up with her best friend. Because then I would have to come and beat you up, and that would take far too much energy."

"You would try to beat me up, you mean," Steve taunted.

They were past the days of scuffling like they had when they were preteens. When Gabe's fist moved in, Steve blocked it and turned their grasp into a warm handshake.

"Thanks," he said earnestly.

"No problem." Gabe adjusted his hat and headed for the door.

Steve shut down the computer and pulled out a pad of paper to start plotting. He had a date with Melody. One that she didn't know about yet.

MELODY INCHED OPEN the door to let him in. "I don't know what you think is so important."

Important enough he'd phoned to make sure she was home because he insisted on speaking to her in person. She braced herself for another invitation to resume dating.

Steve laid a hand on his chest as if insulted. "I can't believe you thought I would let your cry for help go unanswered."

Okay...

That was an unexpected twist. She thought back to what could possibly have been interpreted as a request for help and came up blank. "What is it you want to help me with?"

"Finding you someone non-vanilla, of course." Steve reached into his front pocket and pulled out an envelope, extending it toward her. A second before she could wrap her fingers around it he snatched it away. "Oh, wait, I forgot. I only jotted down notes. I'd better help you go through the list, or it won't make any sense."

He had his charming face on, and in spite of her better judgment, Melody couldn't help feel a flash of attraction.

And a whole lot of confusion. "*You're* going to find me a new boyfriend?"

"Well, you said you wouldn't go out with me, which makes me a friend. You've been gone for nearly a year, and it's only right that I extend the hand of friendship so you don't spend too much time searching through nuggets of fool's gold."

"Which is what a request for non-vanilla sex will produce if I date the locals?" Melody asked, fighting to keep her expression straight.

They'd settled into chairs kitty-corner to each other, and Steve reached across the table to lay his hand over hers. "There are a few fine men in our community you should examine in your quest for some hot, kinky, sexual experimentation."

The shudder that rolled through her was impossible to suppress. It wasn't one of anticipation. It was his choice of words.

Thinking about some of the local men who hung out at the Community Centre? Totally did nothing for her. Still, she was intrigued. How far was Steve willing to go with this façade because no way he was really trying to set her up with anyone.

Was he?

She cleared her throat and went for broke. "Let me have them. I'm all ears."

Steve smoothed the page on the table before him. She was surprised to see there were actual notes on the page. He hadn't simply written a few names—he had more to go along with them.

As he spoke she was drawn back to staring at his strong lips. "I thought you'd like this presented in the most logical way possible, so I've listed them according to age first off. Unless you have some specific requirements you want me to follow. You know, parameters and that sort of thing."

"Parameters?" Melody laughed "I draw the line at no one younger than twenty-one and no one older than forty."

Steve shook his head sadly. He brought out a pen and clicked it open. "That knocks one candidate off the list right then and there."

He drew a bold line through the first name on the page.

She leaned forward, curious to see who was listed. "You had someone older than forty you thought I should date?"

"Well, you said you wanted non-vanilla, and while people in these parts are pretty open about talking about their breeding routines for cattle and sheep, personal preferences in the bedroom only get talked about when someone ties one on a little too hard." Steve shrugged. "It took a bit of work to come up with these possibilities."

Melody somehow dragged her expression back to serious. She hoped. "I'm sorry for interrupting. You've obviously given this lots of thought. Please, go on."

Steve nodded briskly. "Now then, in terms of kink, if I hit something that is a hard no for you, I want you—"

She lifted a hand in the air and interrupted him. "Holy moly, Steve, I'm not looking for someone I have to call Master." *Hard no.* She knew what he meant because of some of her recent reading, but they weren't words she'd ever expected *him* to say. "Did you go down to the library and ask for the bright yellow copy of the *Dummies Guide to Kink?*"

For an instant his face flushed with embarrassment. Melody was enchanted. This was a side of Steve she'd rarely met, and his earnestness touched something inside her the right way.

"I just want you to be happy."

She looked into his blue-grey eyes, lost for a moment in the intensity of his gaze. As if she were the only thing that mattered at this moment. As if she were the only thing in the entire world. Her heart rate accelerated under his attention, and she caught herself hoping for things she really shouldn't hope for.

Then he broke eye contact and leaned back in his chair, paper held loosely in one hand. He began as if they hadn't nearly eye-fucked each other into sweaty comas. "Leon Treil is living out toward Drayton Valley. He's got a decent head on his shoulders." Steve stumbled for a moment before he continued. "And word is his last girlfriend left him because he insisted they dress up every time they had sex."

Melody couldn't stand it. "I'm going to grab some drinks, okay?" She twirled away before he could answer, opening the fridge to hide her smile. "Beer? Pop?"

"Coke, please." He cleared his throat. "This isn't making you uncomfortable is it?"

"Of course not!" she lied like an ace.

"I mean, I can go through it quicker if you have something else you need to do tonight."

She grabbed drinks, returning to the table once she'd regained control over the urge to giggle. She gave Steve her most innocent look. "No, this is fascinating. Please, go on."

"You want me to leave him on the list, or cross him off?"

Melody pretended to think as she opened her bottle of Coke and watched Steve do the same, his strong hands twisting the cap free before he lifted the bottle. She stared as his lips closed over the top, and he drank deeply, his throat moving in smooth, rhythmic pulses. He pulled the bottle away and licked his lips, and suddenly the room was unbearably hot all over again.

She blinked rapidly to remember what the question was.

"How about you tell me everybody you've got on the list, and I'll make a decision at the end."

Steve nodded. "All right, then, next up is Davis Grey."

"Davis? I heard he was dead."

Steve paused then shook his head. "Oh. You're thinking of Grampa Davis Grey—he passed away in the spring. Davis Junior is doing just fine, and Mark Orson down at the hardware store let it slip one time Junior goes through more udder cream than can be easily accounted for."

Udder cream. "What do you think he's up to?"

"Lubing something up," Steve said, not a speck of amusement on his face as if this were a simple conversation about shoeing a horse or tagging cows. "Protecting against chafing shows consideration and forethought."

They weren't sitting here discussing *udder cream*. She was dreaming the entire thing. "Kinky candidate number three?"

"Miles Tate."

"You've got to be kidding." Melody lifted her chin off the ground. "That's the pastor's son."

"Hey, you wanted a list, and he's over twenty-one, and that boy's freaky according to every rumour I've heard."

"No. Way."

"What people do in private is their own business—as long as they're not hurting anyone," Steve pointed out.

"I agree. I just meant that he's a baby," Melody insisted, before realizing all over the ridiculousness of the entire conversation. "You're telling me you think I should date one of these men."

Steve folded the paper, creasing the edge. Her gaze was drawn to his strong fingers and the memories of the pleasure she'd received at his hands.

"No, I think the best candidate for you isn't on this list." He shook the paper in the air before putting it back in his pocket.

Melody paused then went for it. "Who is it?"

Steve caught her fingers in his. "I know I apologized once, but I'll do it again, and dammit, I'll do it until it sinks in and you forgive me. I was a bastard. A thoughtless uncaring fool, but I've changed, and I think you and I together could be a good thing, Melody. I can be the man you need me to be."

The temptation was there.

So were the memories of the frustrations she'd experienced.

"Steve, you don't need to apologize anymore. Maybe you're right—you could probably step up to the plate and rock my world in all sorts of new ways. You're a smart man, and you're talented in the sack."

What she'd expected was to see him glow at the praise, but he didn't budge. All the compliments she was giving him, and he still looked as if she hadn't said the right thing yet.

She went on. "But I need a man not *just* in the bedroom. I need somebody who respects me all the time. While I'm at work, and while I'm at play." How much should she admit? Melody glanced up to find he was watching intently, and the confession spilled out. "I'm scared. Do I dare take another chance on you?"

Steve tilted his head in response. "And there's nothing I can *say* to prove that I've changed. You have to take a chance."

Melody stared at where the ceiling met the wall, small signs visible there of numerous paint jobs covering previous layers as each new occupant of the house came in and made the place their own.

She'd simply moved in because the house wasn't that important to her. What *was* important were people, and damn if the man in front of her didn't make her want to give him another chance.

His fingers tightened around hers, just enough that she lifted her gaze to meet his. "Melody, I respect the hell out of you.

You're good at what you do, and when you left last September, I kicked my own ass for being a shit and screwing up."

It was her turn to pause while she dealt with the images rushing her brain. The good memories mixed with the frustrations until there was no way she knew how to answer him.

And that was an answer in itself.

Melody turned her hand in his and returned the squeeze before withdrawing her fingers. "Steve, I need to think on it. I'm not gonna kick you out and say no, but I need more time."

That expression in his eyes changed. The hope she'd expected to see earlier when she'd complimented his sexual prowess, *now* that hope was there, and a flutter began deep inside her belly.

Steve eased his chair back and rose to his feet. "I have no objections to that. I want you to be sure." He flashed her that smile that always made her knees weak. "And trust me, sweetheart. I can make sure we aren't too vanilla this time around."

Somehow she believed he meant every word.

5

One blasted emergency after another filled his days, but in a way, Steve welcomed the distractions. He'd temporarily placed control back in Melody's hands—even though from her expression as they'd spoken the other night, he was pretty sure she'd come around to telling him yes.

This part sucked. The waiting. But no matter how much he itched to drive up to her door and demand she come to a decision, running off half-cocked was not the way to make anything lasting happen.

Damn if he didn't want to anyway.

To distract himself from his ever-growing impatience, Steve turned his attention to the things he could control. He fixed the tractor engines that had all decided to seize at the same time. He dealt with the animal shelters in the far pastures that had somehow overnight developed dangerous tilts. He and Trevor put in three backbreaking days hauling new timbers to replace rotting vertical posts, the grazing cattle glancing at them off and on as if they were an amusing dinner show.

In spite of his frustrations, as he examined the tasks he'd

completed, the change in his working habits and outlook stiffened his resolve. He would convince Melody they belonged together. He would show her that Rocky was a good place for them both.

And the *too vanilla* comment?

Not fucking likely...

The solitude of late-night chores had its place in knocking the edge off his bad attitude before, and he'd grown to appreciate the quiet moments to think.

He parked outside the barn, taking his time to pause at the edge of the field, one boot up on the bottom rung of the fence as he leaned on the top rail. His dog, Prince, roamed by his feet, the well-trained animal checking the new scents placed since the last time they'd walked this path.

The sun had already set behind the mountains, but the sky was filled with streaks of orange-lit clouds dotted with darker sections against the pale-blue summer sky. The same colour as Melody's eyes—and memories swept in like a gust of wind, rustling through his mind and stirring up desire.

Come hell or high water, by this weekend he'd find a way to get together with her.

The sound of crickets and the occasional dove cooing were all that broke the silence as he paced forward to complete his chores.

"Prince, stay."

The dog shuffled off to the side of the barn and found a place to wait.

Walking through the doors of the barn was like entering a chapel. The familiar peaceful setting gave him a chance to refocus and put aside his plans for a moment.

Only he wasn't alone. His father stood in the corner, back toward him. Both his hands were pressed to the worktable surface, his back swayed, head hanging low, as if he was barely keeping himself vertical.

Damn. "You okay?" Steve strode forward to join Randy at the bench.

His father jerked in surprise before looking away. "Of course."

Steve hadn't expected any other response. His dad could have both legs cut off and been bleeding out, and he still wouldn't admit anything was wrong.

Steve examined him closely. The older man's face looked pale, a sheen of sweat covering his brow. "Like hell you're okay."

His father tapped his fist against his chest, his face twisting into a grimace. "Just a little indigestion."

Oh, great, even better. Steve put a hand on his father's shoulder. "Is that not one of the signs of a heart attack?"

Randy turned away, leaning on the workbench. He spit to one side before folding his arms and looking disgruntled. "I'm fine—well, at least, I know I'm not having a heart attack. It's this damn heartburn, and yes, it's only heartburn—I got checked at the doctor last week when I went to town."

Steve eyed his father. The man's solid frame showed little sign of softening after years of heavy labour. Maybe he was thicker around the middle, his hair now shot with grey, but Randy seemed the same no-nonsense, get-it-done man who'd guided his family over the years without ever raising his voice.

It was hard to see him as something other than indestructible.

"How come this is the first time I've heard of this?" Steve asked.

Randy shrugged his broad shoulders. "Because it's nothing," he insisted before making another face. "Except I need to stop sneaking third helpings like your mother warned me."

"Ha."

His father lifted a finger in warning. "Don't you tell her that I'm under the weather tonight—she'd just give me hell and then refuse to serve bacon for a month."

"It is one of the four major food groups," Steve teased, moving into position to echo his father's body language as the man leaned on the workbench with his arms across his chest.

Steve stared into space, picking his words carefully. "Sucks to have to watch what you're eating, but it sucks more to feel like hell."

"God, sometimes it feels like something's trying to crawl out of my body," his father confessed.

Steve made a sympathetic noise. "You got anything to take for it?"

"Yeah." Disgust was clear in his voice. "Tastes like getting a mouthful on a windy day when we're spreading fertilizer."

Steve laughed. "Well, at least it's not some sugary sweet pink stuff that makes your tongue change colour."

"There is that," Randy agreed. He glanced up quickly. "Don't tell your mother," he warned again. "I swear she gets a kick out of making me take a dose."

It took a lot to keep from laughing. Instead, Steve spoke cautiously, trying to be nonchalant. "In the meantime, let me know if I need to take over any extra duties."

Randy made a rude noise before reluctantly nodding his head. "If I have to. I just hate to be slowing down."

"Don't think of it as slowing down." Steve stepped away, heading toward the nearby stall. He leaned both arms on the top rail, admiring the mare that turned toward him, her belly swollen with the foal that would be arriving in a few weeks. "There's always been too much to do everything by ourselves. That's why we hire help on the side."

His father sighed. "Too much to do to sit on my ass and loaf."

"It's not loafing to leave your least favourite tasks for us boys to deal with, however works best." He patted the mare's nose, stroking the white blaze on her forehead. Ignoring his father altogether as if he were not talking about making drastic changes in the man's life. "Figured that's part of the reason why you have sons. So you can get rid of the crap jobs and make us do them."

"You discovered my evil plan," Randy confessed. He closed the space between them to lay a hand on Steve's back. "You've grown up a lot in the last year."

The words thrilled him. Approval from this man meant the world to Steve. "This is where you're supposed to say 'and about damn time', isn't it?"

"You've never been a pain in my butt, so it's not as if you've become the most righteous son around. Just seems like there's something a little more serious about you." Randy patted him on the back. "I'm saying it looks good, that bit of responsibility."

His father walked away, closing the door behind him and leaving Steve to wonder how much of a change would really happen in terms of him lessening his load. His father could be very stubborn—one of the common traits found on most successful ranches.

Although...knowing his dad was trying to pull a fast one on his mom? Steve laughed. Heck, if Randy was stubborn, Kate was twice as bad, probably from having to deal with her silent, unmovable ox of a husband for over thirty-five years. Odds were Kate would figure out something was up by the morning, and Randy's little ploy to keep his rotten evening a secret would be over.

Steve wasn't a fortuneteller, but he was pretty sure another dose of the foul-tasting medicine was in his father's future.

He smiled as he grabbed a handful of oats for the horse, holding his hand steady to allow her to nibble the treat. As he finished his chores, his thoughts remained on his family. How much they were the same, how much they were different.

His mom was far more outgoing and boisterous than the rest of them, but that backbone of steel was undeniably there. Heck, they all had it in their own way. Trevor joked more often, lighthearted and devil-may-care like Kate. Steve before deciding to grow up had been somewhere in the middle of his folks, joking one minute, laid-back and quiet the next. And Lee—

His little brother was the quiet rock. Somehow he'd reached the ripe old age of twenty-three without anyone squashing his notion that he was smarter than most of them. Hell, maybe he was. Steve rarely won a debate when they did get into a disagreement.

And the most annoying part was Lee wasn't rude about it. Nope, he'd politely listen to them plan and organize, make a few suggestions, but never outright argue. If he didn't agree with whatever was decided in the end? He'd nod and then just damn well go do what he thought was right.

The winner in their family, though, had to be Steve's sister—the only one not working the ranch. Anna had fought for everything she'd gotten as an RCMP officer, finding respect in the community as a woman in a traditional male role.

Steve paused for a moment as he realized in some ways Melody had done the same thing. A lady veterinarian dealing with small animals wasn't unusual, but for the large-animal work, she should have lacked the strength. Yet before she'd gone back to school, she'd often been the one to come along and work at Mathis's side.

Suddenly a little more about Melody became clear.

He headed out of the barn to the corral, not wanting to lose this thought. Climbed up on one of the railings and watched the cattle in the distance silhouetted against the hazy red sky as Prince stood before him, tail wagging wildly.

Maybe he'd been going about this all wrong.

He'd changed—he was sure of that. But maybe Melody hadn't changed so much as simply continued to be herself. Someone he'd never bothered to get to know other than on the surface. He needed to come to understand the real her.

The thought excited him. This weekend, no matter what, he was going to catch up with Melody. Get an answer from her—and the only acceptable answer was yes, and then he'd make sure she knew he was able and willing to be there for her in a way that he'd never been before.

This time? He wasn't going to fuck it up.

~

TRAVIS WILLINGLY HELD the ancient horse's hoof for her, locking him in position as Melody finished the awkward chore of stitching a cut on the old-timer's leg.

"It's good to have you back," Travis noted, switching position and lowering the horse's leg as she put away her tools.

"It's good to be back." She gave the horse's rump a pat and sent him into the yard. "Been fun this week, going to familiar places and catching up with some of my old patients. Other than that little run-in with the fencing, looks as if Blaze is having a good retirement."

Travis passed over the flannel shirt she'd removed while working, too hot in the late-afternoon sunshine with all her layers. His grin flashed just as quickly as the previous year. He was the same handsome devil she remembered flirting with her before she'd left. Only there was something different to his attitude—a bit of reserve?

Contentment?

"The good thing about your patients is they can't taunt you about sticking the needle into the wrong part of their hindquarters."

"I'd never do anything like that," she protested. "That was Mathis who gave your dad an errant shot the one time."

"We'll never let him forget it."

That was the truth as well. Nothing that went wrong was

ever forgotten. She pulled her arms through the sleeves of her shirt and buttoned the front over her tank top. "Rumour says you've settled down."

His grin got wider. "This time rumour is right. Hey, that reminds me. Can you stop by the old barn for a minute before you leave? Ashley's gone and adopted a dog we rescued, and she's all worried about the beast getting treated right."

"No problem," Melody said as they made their way toward her borrowed truck. "Did you want to bring him into the clinic for a checkup?"

Travis shook his head. "We did that already, because Ashley is nothing if not determined. There's nothing wrong with the beast."

Only his tone of voice said differently. "What are you not telling me?"

He shrugged. "Convincing Ashley the dog belongs outside is taking more effort than I thought humanly possible."

"Stubborn?"

"You wouldn't believe it."

Melody laughed. "Oh, this I like. A woman who Travis Coleman calls stubborn? I seem to remember you standing in one spot and refusing to move for nearly an hour after your father gave you hell for fidgeting in the middle of a job."

His cocky grin faded, and damn if the man didn't look self-conscious. "How do you know about that?"

"Other than we live in a small town, and everything is open to discussion at every moment of our lives? I was there, don't you remember?"

Travis's face furled with concentration. "I could've sworn..."

"Trust me, this happens a lot," Melody said as he opened the door of the converted old barn behind their house. "As a vet, I find that quite often people forget that I'm around."

He gestured her forward. "Well, you are a lot older than me. I was far too shy to make a move on you."

"Someone's looking for a butt kicking," a feminine voice sang out from the top of the stairs. Melody glanced up to see Ashley leaning over the edge of the railing, glaring at Travis. "Number one, you're a lying bastard because the words 'I'm shy' just escaped your mouth. You've *never* been shy. You weren't shy on the day you were born. You probably hit on the nurses in the delivery room."

They reached the top of the stairs, and Travis went to wrap his arms around Ashley and give her a quick kiss, tweaking her nose as he stepped back. "That's my job. To bring sunshine and joy to people's lives."

"And secondly," Ashley continued as she made a face at him, "telling a woman they're a lot older than you is not the way to get ahead in the world. It's not a good way to continue breathing."

"Oh, I don't mind," Melody hurried to reassure her. "There's gotta be—what, three, maybe four years between us? And I've been in town at most for three and a half?"

Ashley's smile brightened as she did the math. "And you remember him pulling a hissy fit?" She glanced over at a far more sheepish Travis. "You ought to be ashamed of yourself. That means you were at least twenty-three, and acting like a jackass."

"He's twenty-six now, and still acting like a jackass," another voice joined in as Cassidy appeared at the top of the stairwell. He dipped his blond head in Melody's direction. "Good to see you. Thanks for looking after the horses."

Ashley rushed forward and caught hold of Melody's arm. "And now she's here to see my dog, right? So you two just go do something else."

She waved them off with her hand, tugging Melody toward the corner of the room.

"Ashley," Cassidy chided. "Did you sneak that dog upstairs again?"

There was no way for Ashley to hide her answer, not when a pair of sleepy eyes peered out of the box in the corner of the room, puppy whimpers clearly audible in the moment of condemning silence.

Melody knelt to press a hand over the golden retriever's tiny head. "What a pretty coat. What are you calling him?"

"Lucky."

She did a quick exam while pretending to pet the dog, but it was obvious the thing was small but healthy. "He seems little to have already been weaned."

"The mom didn't make it," Cassidy said quietly. "We found him at one of the outbuildings near the forestry reserve. Something must've attacked her and the litter, and this was the only one that survived."

"And that's why I need to take care of him," Ashley insisted.

Travis sighed. This was obviously not the first time they'd had this discussion. "Dogs don't belong in the house. Dogs belong outside."

"Why?" she asked.

"Because that's the way it is."

Ashley's brow rose. "That's not a good enough reason."

"But that's the way it's always been," Cassidy added.

She narrowed her gaze, taking in both of the men standing before her. Their arms folded over their chests, expressions stern. "Oh, of course. Because we all *know* that everything in the world stays exactly the same for good reason. Nobody in this family *ever* colours outside the lines, right?" she asked sarcastically.

Melody could see a point go up on the scoreboard for Ashley after that one.

The guys scrambled to try a different tack. "Dane stays

outside," Travis pointed out. "You don't seem to have a problem with *my* dog sleeping outside in all sorts of weather."

"He's a working dog. He needs to be outside to do his job. Lucky is a cuddle dog. He needs to be inside to do his."

Not that Melody wanted to get into the middle of what was the cutest domestic dilemma she'd seen in a long time, but she had to admit she felt for both sides. She did enough work with small animals to know that pets were part of family in ways that ranch dogs never were.

Ranch dogs were loved in different ways, for different reasons, but sometimes choices had to be made.

Melody thought she had the solution. "You're right, Ashley. There's no reason why Lucky can't live inside the house."

Cassidy and Travis both looked at her as if she'd just committed high treason even as Ashley lit up like a Christmas tree.

Melody continued quickly before one of the guys said something and ruined her plans. "If you're going to have him as a house pet, though, you'll need to have him *only* as a house pet. That means when he needs to be taken for a walk, you put him on a leash and make sure you keep him away from the farm animals *and* the other dogs."

Ashley's face folded into a frown. "But he'll be lonely. You mean that? He can't play with the other dogs?"

"He'll have you to play with," Melody said. "The trouble is, inside dogs get privileges that outside dogs don't—sleeping on beds, licking people. There are germs we don't want to carry from the ranch into the house, and the other way around. That's why we take off our boots and wash our hands a lot. I'm sure you understand."

Cassidy and Travis were both holding their breath.

The dog picked that moment to stand on his hind legs and paw at the edge of the box, tipping over sideways as he lost his balance. Melody helped him regain his feet, and the little thing licked her enthusiastically.

"He's too little to live outside," Ashley protested, but she wasn't as adamant this time.

Melody considered for a moment. "Not really. He's old enough to have been weaned, so what's most important now is finding him a safe place where he won't get hurt until he gets a little bigger."

"There's a spot in the barn where the dogs bed down," Cassidy offered. "I can take you there and you can help make a special nest for him."

Ashley wrinkled her nose. "You guys ganged up on me. That's not fair." She lifted her eyes to meet Melody's, winking briefly. "And you. Don't you have a soft spot for animals?"

"Definitely. But that means I want the best for them, and in the long run, Lucky will be happier outside."

They helped Ashley bundle up the little animal and carry it down the stairs to head outside. Melody was momentarily distracted as Ashley pulled pairs of brightly coloured rubber boots from the closet. She slipped her feet into a set with the pink flowers against a yellow background before handing a purple pair to Travis and a blue set to Cassidy.

Ashley stepped from the room for a moment, and Travis leaned in close to murmur, "Thank you. For a moment I thought you were about to throw us under the bus, especially when I remembered hearing you had a dog with you when you got back."

"Umm, you mean Lady?"

Cassidy grinned as he pulled on the boots Ashley had given him before taking the puppy from her hands. "Something furry and white with sharp teeth. I think that's what Steve said."

"You have a dog?" Ashley popped her head around the corner and directed a glare at Melody.

Travis folded his arms. "How the hell do you do that? You got bionic ears or something?"

"It doesn't make sense," Ashley protested, reaching for the puppy. "If you can have a house dog, then I—"

"I *don't* have a house dog," Melody informed her quickly. "I brought Lady for the nursing home. She was a companion animal at the local lodge near where I was doing my veterinary training in Saskatchewan, but the owner died. The dog is well-trained around seniors, so I brought her with me, and she's been adopted by the head of the long-term residency program."

Ashley made a face. "Fine. I guess we need to get this over with."

The entire way to the barn Melody could not keep her eyes off their boots. "Quite a fashion statement," she finally commented.

A rumbling noise of protest escaped Travis, while Cassidy only laughed.

Ashley twirled to walk backwards, grinning with evident self-satisfaction. "You like them?"

"They're much better than plain black rubber boots," Melody agreed. "I like bright-coloured things."

Ashley smirked. "They're fun, and there's the added bonus that every time Travis has to put his on, he pouts like a five-year-old."

"You're lucky that I wear them," he growled.

"You're the one who lost the bet," Cassidy pointed out. "You should know better than to bet with Ashley over something she really wants."

The grumbling and good-natured teasing continued as Melody accompanied them into the barn and saw the little puppy settled in place with a couple of the old-timers.

Ashley was happy, Travis and Cassidy were ecstatic—

Melody felt as if she'd done a good job. Something beyond just the letter of what she was hired for.

"You're coming to Traders Pub this Friday, aren't you?" Ashley demanded, slipping her arm around Melody's as they accompanied her back to her truck. "We're holding an engagement party for Anna Coleman and Mitch Thompson. We need more women to balance out the horde of Coleman men who'll be there."

A horde that would include Steve. Melody still felt his hands around her face at moments, the kiss shaking her to her toes for all that it had been gentle and sedate. She'd been thinking about his dating plans for the past week, slowly caving to the desire to tell him she would see him again.

"I don't want to crash a family party," she protested.

Travis grunted before lifting his hand to count off on his fingers. "You're friends with Allison, you know Hope, you know us, you know Steve *and* you dumped a pitcher of beer on him—that makes you as good as family."

She was really regretting having lost her temper that night so long ago.

"Please come," Ashley begged, bumping her hip gently into Melody's. "I promise everyone will behave. Unless you don't want to—"

"And then all bets are off," Cassidy teased. "Because if you don't want to behave, Ashley will be first in line to help you make mischief."

"We all have our talents." Ashley beamed as she nodded in agreement.

Melody was in her truck and headed home before it sank in. She was going to a party, one with Steve Coleman present. She had a feeling he would be waiting for her answer.

Fool that she was, it appeared Steve was going to get his second chance.

6

*F*rom the moment he heard she'd be attending the engagement party, Steve found himself dealing with the strangest sensation. Like he'd gotten a bellyful of butterflies or June bugs that were dancing in endless circles.

He was too old and too...well, *male*...to admit, even to himself, that he was nervous. He'd call it anticipation instead.

Tonight? Was the night.

Every time the door opened, though, his stomach took another nosedive. Not knowing when she'd arrive, or if work would call her away from the party at the last minute, sucked. Still, unless something went horridly wrong, this was it.

No more waiting.

The pub door opened, and his gaze jerked to attention, followed by disappointment as a couple of young women entered —neither of whom were Melody.

He eased back in his chair and let out a slow breath.

"You look as nervous as a virgin on prom night," Jesse teased.

Without a glance, Steve backhanded his cousin across the shoulder. Jesse just laughed harder, leaning his chair back on two legs. He crossed his hands behind his head as he glanced around the room, his cocky grin taking in the crowd filing into the pub for a good time Friday night.

A crowd that included pretty much all the Coleman family over the age of eighteen and under thirty-five. Steve's brothers were already there, as well as Gabe and Rafe—the Angel Colemans. Jesse's older brothers were gathered in a loose group near the bar, laughter rising from the Six Pack clan as Jesse's twin, Joel, clinked his beer bottle into his oldest brother's.

Huh. That was what seemed strange. Steve turned back to his cousin. "Isn't this about the time you usually take off?" he asked Jesse.

"What are you talking about?"

As if it weren't obvious to the rest of them. "Anytime there's a family event that your twin attends, you make yourself scarce. I'm surprised you're out tonight."

Jesse tipped his chair forward with a rush and reached for the pitcher of beer already waiting on the table. "Not true," he denied. "I don't try to avoid family. I wouldn't live with Rafe and Lee if I were."

"But you are avoiding *some* family. You and Joel are rarely in the same room together." Steve knew he should drop it, but the whole thing was getting ridiculous. "Whatever bee got up your butt about Joel and Vicki being together, I wish you'd get over it."

"Nothing to get over," Jesse insisted. "Just don't like to see my brother being played for a fool."

Steve gave up. He had other things to concentrate on tonight, and his cousin's failings with his twin were not front and center.

A cheer rose, fading to jeers as Mitch Thompson came through the door of the pub without Anna.

The Thompsons and Colemans and their friends had pretty much taken over the place that night. Steve glanced around, the beat of music on the opposite side of the wall explaining where everyone else was. Okay, so they had taken over *half* the pub. This side held the pool tables, dartboards, and long, low tables where people could sit and chat and make noise.

Gabe rose to his feet and slapped Mitch on the back, guiding him forward to one of the reserved seats of honour. Everyone poked in good-natured fun as he prepared to join the Coleman clan, but Mitch kept his cool, answering the teasing taunts with a smile and a wink.

Steve was still wrapping his head around the idea that his sister was not only engaged, but getting hitched to Mitch Thompson of all people. The heavily tattooed biker wore his attitude of *who gives a fuck* on his sleeve, and next to Anna, the straight-laced cop? They seemed a mismatched couple.

That's when it hit Steve again—Anna was as stubborn and as big of a risk-taker as the supposed bad-boy Mitch, just in her own way.

"Did she kick your ass to the curb already?" Trevor shouted.

Mitch waved a hand in the air, one finger higher than the rest. "She's getting your car hauled to the impound. I warned you to pay those fines."

Steve got up and wandered through the chaos, saying hello to people and exchanging brief greetings with those already neck-deep in other conversations. The entire time his gaze stayed locked on the door, waiting to add his cheers to Anna's arrival, and so he'd see the instant that Melody joined the crowd

Someone tugged his sleeve, and he glanced down to discover Allison grinning at him.

She tilted her head to the side. "This way. We need to talk to you."

He followed along willingly enough until he ended up at a table tucked toward the side of the room surrounded by Coleman women. He gauged the distance to the door, not because he was afraid of them but because—

Oh hell, there was no denying it. He *was* scared shitless, especially when they banded together.

Best not show any fear, though. "Ladies. Ready for the party?"

The undisputed ringleader of the Coleman gals leaned her elbows on the table and flashed him an evil grin. "So. What's this we hear about you being sweet on Melody again?" Jaxi asked.

He was going to kill Trevor. Or Gabe. They were the only ones he'd said anything to directly, other than Melody, and one of them had to have spilled the beans.

Steve offered Jaxi his most charming smile. "Do I need to get permission from the lot of you to say hello to a woman in the community?"

"Yes," Ashley stated without a moment's pause, and the rest of the table burst into laughter.

Jaxi motioned for them to settle down. "Of course not. You're a grown man. You can make your own damn mistakes. We just want to let you know that, all things considered, you're our cousin."

He waited for the other shoe to fall. "Why do I get the feeling that wasn't an entire sentence?"

"Smart man." Beth's soft voice held a note of amusement. "Maybe we should go easy on him."

"What she means to say," Allison offered, "is that while you're a Coleman, Melody's a part of our community in ways that go back real hard. So whatever you plan on doing, it had better inspire something more then pitchers of beer in the future."

Steve pinched the bridge of his nose. That damn mistake would haunt him forever. "Is that all?"

They murmured amongst themselves for a moment, excitement building as the door swung open and everyone scattered to greet Anna. Everyone, that is, except Jaxi who continued to look at him as if he were in a petri dish.

He lifted one hand in the air. "I solemnly swear I don't mean any trouble."

Jaxi kinked a brow. "Well, where's the fun in that? Maybe what the two of you need is a bit of trouble." She winked before heading to the front of the room and tugging Anna in for a hug.

Crazy family—but Steve couldn't stop grinning, and his happiness only grew as Melody finally joined them.

The neat ponytail she usually wore was missing, and her hair hung loose around her shoulders. She looked a whole lot younger like that, and for one brief moment the idea of making mischief with her set him worrying.

Then their gazes met across the room, and that fire flashed, and he remembered her challenge.

No way he was turning back. No way at all.

IT TOOK him forever to approach. So long, in fact, Melody thought maybe he'd decided to drop his idea of them getting back together. She would've been disappointed, and a little shocked, but at the same time it would've been good to know upfront before she put any more time and effort into him.

All he did for the first hour and a half of the party was give her a brisk nod hello, offer her a drink and then back off.

But no matter where she was in the room and no matter who she was talking with? His gaze burned her as if he were eating her up.

It was the most amazing thing. She moved around a lot, visiting with people and having a good time, but whenever she looked up, he was there. Staring at her—but not in a creepy way, more as if he'd found something so astonishing he didn't want her to slip out of view.

She had no idea if that's what he was actually thinking, but imagining it did her ego good.

The party had split into three groups an hour ago, after the initial toasts and teasing were over. Mitch had been thoroughly welcomed into their rosters and was holding his own decisively.

Trevor stood to one side, arms folded over his chest as he glared at Mitch who'd just scored another point in their ongoing insult volleys. "I don't know if I like this," Trevor complained to Anna. "Mitch has it way too safe, getting involved with you. It's not like we can threaten to do anything to him."

Mitch shook his head in mock sorrow. "I know. Sucks to have a cop in the family, doesn't it?"

A rumble of laughter carried over the group as the good-natured teasing continued, all of it complete with love and a sense of camaraderie in the extended clan.

This kind of crowd was something she'd never experienced within her birth family. Her, her mom—that was it for family growing up. But Allison had been right that first day when she talked about friends being family. There was nothing more exhilarating than being in the middle of the Coleman clan and watching them take care of their own.

And *their own* meant quite a variety of things. The atypical threesome of Ashley, Travis and Cassidy. The quieter couples like Daniel and Beth, and Gabe and her own Allison. Blake and Jaxi—heir apparent of the next generation.

Into all of this family she dared to tread. *Glutton for punishment* came to mind, and she laughed at herself.

A broad hand hooked over her hip, tugging her against a rock-hard body. "You look as if you're having a good time," Steve offered.

Melody debated protesting his familiarity, then decided

against it. Heck, she'd been waiting for this moment all night. Take what she wanted—and this was as good a time as any. Instead of pulling away, she subtly changed her position on the barstool. She leaned into his body and let out a long, happy sigh at how solid he was. "It's been a fun party."

"You haven't spent any time with me," he chastised.

"I've been right here all along," she pointed out.

"So you have." He leaned down, his chin brushing the top of her shoulder as his lips hovered near her ear. His warm breath caressed past her cheek, and she shivered, the involuntary move rubbing them together.

His grumble of approval sent another shock wave skimming.

"We need to talk," Steve said.

Melody bit her lip as she stared at the pool game in front of her, attempting to concentrate on the game while playing an entirely different one with Steve.

"We do?" she asked innocently. "That's funny. I thought we had a talk the other day, and we decided you were going to open the world's most boring ice-cream shop."

This time the noise he made didn't send a shiver over her, it made the hair on the back of her neck stand up.

"See, that's why I came over here private-like."

"Private?" She laughed. "We're in the middle of your relatives, plus another thirty to forty people. You call this private?"

"I could grab a mic and my guitar, put the question to music and ask you that way—if you'd prefer."

He would too. "You always were a showoff."

The hand on her hip was no longer still. He'd snuck his thumb between the edge of her jeans and shirt, and lifted the bottom corner of her T-shirt. With his fingers tucked into her front pocket, his thumb drifted over her belly, stroking back and forth, back and forth. Like a sensual pendulum ticking down the moments until she would spontaneously combust.

She twisted her head to one side, tilting back to speak toward his ear. "You have my attention."

"I've been waiting for your answer. I thought about offering you a dare. You know, setting up some sexual adventure to challenge your little vanilla comment, but that could lead to all kinds of problems. At least with this crowd."

His thumb dipped under the edge of her jeans, and her breath stuttered out as she enjoyed the rush of excitement spinning along her nerve endings.

"I thought about starting a drinking game," he continued. "Last man standing, that kind of thing. I know I could convince at least a half-dozen of my cousins to get involved, but you'd probably drink them under the table."

"I think I did that once," she admitted.

"Ha. Then I thought about playing pool, either with you or against you, but frankly, that's not the type of foreplay I'm looking for."

Oh dear. They were talking about foreplay already. Melody considered for an instant before nodding. "Go on."

"Tell me we're back together. Tell me I get a second shot at making you happy," he demanded.

Turn him down? Impossible. She pivoted far enough to look into his blue-grey eyes as she answered him. "Don't disappoint me, Steve."

His face lit up like magic. For an instant they sat there, grinning like fools at each other before the fire returned and Steve twisted her back toward the pool table.

At the same time, his hand slipped onto her belly, resting there briefly. Her T-shirt hid what his fingers were doing as he snuck into the front of her jeans. He'd picked the perfect place to do this—no one could see anything with the back of the counter directly in front of them. All it looked like was a serious conversation happening right there in the open, Steve at her back, whispering in her ear.

"You were pretty hasty the other day, sweetheart," he noted, changing the subject. "Making that smartass comment after the picnic and then running away before we could discuss it."

"We had an entire conversation about that comment at my place," she protested, fixing her gaze on the pool table. Focusing on the white ball gliding across the surface, connecting with its target and sending a half-dozen balls rolling in different directions. Ignoring the thread of fire inching over her skin as his touch stirred her senses. "And I didn't run away."

"Drove away. Same difference." He adjusted position, his muscular arm pressed to her side as he slipped her farther forward on the barstool. She went willingly enough, glancing to the side to make sure no one had noticed, but everyone was busy in their own little worlds.

"So, what are you going to do about it?" she taunted.

The change in position meant he had enough room to slide his hand all the way down, calloused fingers coming to rest on her mound. "I plan to do a lot, but first let us get this straight. I highly doubt I'm too vanilla for you."

She shrugged, partly to cover up that she wanted to rock into his hand so he would get to the good parts. "Going by what I remember. I didn't say you suck in the sack, just that I found I have a little more varied tastes than what we tended toward before."

She pressed her lips together to trap the hiss of pleasure he drew from her as he slipped a finger between her folds, rubbing back and forth over her clit.

"And that's why we need to start over. You and me, because some of what we had before was good, and some of it wasn't. But that's in the past, and what we've got now is a whole lot of time in front of us to work on making good new choices and avoiding stupid mistakes. You need to give me another chance."

Melody laughed, leaning her head back on his shoulder so she could speak into his ear. "You got your hand down the front of my pants in the middle of a bar. I think you're getting a teeny bit of a second chance, don't you?"

She stuck out her tongue and flicked his earlobe, quick enough that unless someone was watching closely, the move would be ignored.

The only one who knew what she'd done was Steve, and he growled in approval, his fingers continuing to tease her. "Then in light of your earlier comment, I'm going to set down a few rules."

Melody held back her amusement. "You think so?"

In response, he curled his hand around her and pressed a finger into her core. Deep inside for a moment before pulling back to apply hard pressure against her clit.

Her little gasp seemed all the approval he needed.

"I thought about you a lot when you were gone," he confessed, his words a rumble in her ear even as his hand worked her body. Heat from his chest scalded her, and she adjusted her hips to line them up in the exact right position, working to keep her breathing as calm as possible. "It took me a while, but I figured out how important you were. How special you were, and I'm determined to show you that. And I'm not going to hold back any longer."

She couldn't resist moaning with pleasure as he pushed in another finger, holding her pinned in place as he forced her body to respond. "You were holding back?"

"You called me lazy. Give that as an excuse, but the point is it's not happening anymore. I want you, and unless you tell me no right now, I'm going to take you any time, and anywhere I want."

His words should have infuriated her, or put up her back and made her instant response a decisive *no*, but she couldn't force out the syllable.

If he was serious, this was exactly what she was looking for. "You're talking about sex, right? You don't have some half-assed idea about trying to boss me around outside the bedroom?"

"Let's not confine it to any room, considering I've got my hand in your pants in the middle of a bar. But yes, this is about sex—at least the me-being-bossy part."

It was more than she'd hoped for. While he'd been a bastard before, he hadn't been a dangerous one. More like neglectful and thoughtless. "You got three months," she offered.

He withdrew his hand, circling her clit lightly with his fingers before pulling free. Steve adjusted his position until he stood beside her, an elbow on the countertop as he faced her. Then he lifted his hand to his mouth and licked his fingers clean.

Ohmigod.

"You kids are avoiding the party." Steve's little brother Lee appeared out of nowhere, and Melody blinked for a moment before smiling at the young man. "Come on, we're going to start some drinking game Ashley made up."

"We'll be there in a minute," Steve assured him before tilting his head to send his brother away.

Melody glanced at Steve, her body vibrating from his touch. "You saw him coming."

He placed his fingers under her chin, his thumb caressing her jawline as he stared into her eyes. "I'll take care of you, I promise. Whether that means giving your body what you need, or exploring all the things we haven't yet tried, you and me. I won't do anything that hurts you."

She was surprised how serious he sounded. "That's never been an issue. Trusting you that way."

"Three months," he agreed. His smile tightened. "And

Melody? I fully intend to prove you can trust me in other ways during that time."

The volume across the room was rising, and in spite of the buzz of anticipation in her body, Melody looked forward to more time with the others. "Let's talk about it later."

"When I take you home," he said, his expression hungry enough to make her shiver.

She wasn't sure what she'd expected would happen tonight, but hell, *yeah*, this was what she needed. She accepted his hand as she slipped off the barstool, wavering for a moment as she hurriedly tucked in her T-shirt. He didn't even try to hide his grin as he pressed a hand to her lower back and led her toward the game. Eyes lingered on them as they rejoined the group, knowing smiles breaking free.

By the time the evening was done, everyone in Rocky would know they were together again. Melody took a deep breath and hoped like hell that Steve really had changed.

7

---

*I*t was trite, it was stereotypical, but even as he celebrated that he and Melody were back in the game, only one thought filled his brain to the exclusion of everything else.

He and Melody were going to have sex, and he couldn't fucking wait.

They'd snuck away from the party, Melody leaving just before him. He pulled up outside her house and marched toward her door like his ass was on fire.

He glanced in the window, feet faltering to a stop as her silhouette moved past the thin drapes.

She pivoted, every curve clearly delineated against the background light, and he couldn't wait to put his hands on her. To touch every inch of her all over again.

He took the steps three at a time and didn't bother to knock.

Melody spun, her blonde hair flaring as she moved. She hadn't had time to do more than take off her shoes and coat, and he soaked in the sight.

"You got here quickly," she teased.

He stepped across the room and caught her in his arms, glancing around the room to decide where to take her.

"Am I a maiden about to swoon?" Melody asked, laughter in her voice.

He dropped her on the small island countertop in the kitchen area, pinning her in place with a hand on either side of her hips. "You can be any damn thing you want as long as it involves screaming my name and begging for more."

Damn if she didn't laugh. "You think that's likely?"

That's what they were about to make sure of, because he didn't want there to be any misunderstanding between them. "Sweetheart, let's get one thing clear. What we had before was good, but if you're able to handle all of me? It's going to get so much better you're gonna walk around with a permanent smile on your face. Everyone in town will think the reason you're tired at the end of the day is because you worked so hard, but you and I will know it's because I worked you over even harder."

He watched carefully as he spoke, and her response was better than anything he could have imagined. The flush on her cheeks grew rosier, and her breathing picked up. Her pulse fluttered visibly at her neckline.

He leaned in, licking the spot.

A tiny whimper escaped her, and he couldn't resist. He went back and nipped, then did it again when she caught hold of his shoulders and let her head fall to the side.

It'd been too damn long. He left the tender spot under her ear and went for her lips, soaking in every moan and gasp as she undulated against him, her breasts rubbing his chest. She arched upward and opened her legs, thighs spreading wide to accept his body against hers. He used the hand around her back to drag her hips forward so his hardness connected with the heat between her legs.

He thrust his other hand into her hair, closing his fingers and

81

tugging her head back so he could kiss her more easily. Licking her lips before slipping his tongue into her mouth to taste her. Feasting greedily until there was a roaring in his ears and a pulsing need everywhere in his body.

Her hands danced over his shoulders, her short-cut nails digging in as she dragged them over his muscles. Not enough. Her touch was only a hint of what he needed, so he broke them apart, grabbed hold of the bottom of her shirt and ripped the fabric over her head.

Her neon-yellow bra wasn't enough to distract him from his need to reclaim her lips. This time his hand on her back made contact with the warmth of her skin. He pressed her thighs farther apart, dragging her hips forward and rocking them together until she was squirming.

"Oh God, I need you inside me right now," Melody muttered, her hands diving between them as she attempted to undo his jeans.

He caught her wrists in one hand, holding her in place as he pulled back slightly. Gazing into her eyes and letting her see how much he wanted her as well. "Not yet. Not for a long time."

She frowned. "Here's a hint, Steve. Right now, I'm pretty much what you call a sure thing."

"You're not ready, and I haven't finished getting you there. We were interrupted back at the pub."

He lowered her until she lay flat on her back on the island countertop, chest moving rapidly with every breath. Her pale-blue eyes burned him with white-hot fire as she waited in anticipation for what came next.

"Now, where were we?" He leaned over, sliding a hand down her belly to open the button of her jeans and lower her zipper. "That's right. I was just about to get you off when my brother interrupted."

"That was rude," Melody agreed before qualifying her

statement. "It's very impolite to *ever* take a break in the middle of giving me an orgasm."

Steve grinned as he slipped his fingers through her folds and into her body. "Next time I won't stop."

Her eyes widened at his words, and Steve made a note of it, stroking in farther as her body wet his fingers. "Oh, you like that idea. Is that one of the things you played with while you were away?"

"Getting fingered in public?"

"Any kind of fooling around in public. You like the idea of getting caught, or the idea of being watched?"

She shivered, and he increased the tempo of his hand, slipping into her warmth then pulling back to tease her clit. Her underwear and jeans rubbed the back of his hand as he sped up, reading her body cues.

He leaned over, staring into her eyes as he continued to torment her. "It's been too damn long, Melody, and it's going to take days to do everything I want."

She lifted her feet to the countertop, knees spread wide as she rocked against him, the tension in her face increasing as he brought her closer to orgasm.

He kissed her, this time using his upper body to pin her in place as he continued to pump his fingers deep, dipping his tongue into her mouth at the same tempo.

The most amazing noises escaped as Melody wrapped her hands around his shoulders and tugged in an attempt to move him.

No frickin' way. He wasn't going anywhere.

He pulled back far enough his lips brushed hers as he spoke. "We have so many things to try that we've never done before. Everything you've ever imagined, everything I've ever dreamed of. I'm going to take you so far past your fantasies your feet don't touch the ground."

She whimpered, her breath puffing against his lips as she struggled for air. "Oh lordy. Oh, that's good."

Under his fingers her clit was a tight little ball, and he pressed down. Flicking his thumb back and forth rapidly until she cried out, her head tilting back as her body arched.

He moved away just far enough to watch as she came, her entire body bowing as he stroked her to climax. She shook, clutching his shoulders, her mouth tightened into a rosy pout, her eyes half-closed as she purred out her satisfaction.

He could watch her do that all day long. "Damn, that was sexy."

He slowed his touch, gentling the motion as aftershocks continued to rack her body.

"Nice." Melody sighed happily.

Nope. "Wrong word," Steve warned, shifting back into a position between her legs.

Melody leaned up on her elbows, confusion building. "What you talking about—?"

Then she didn't say anything else because he'd put his mouth between her legs and put his tongue in to play on her clit. Her thighs trembled under his hands, hips rocking as she moaned her approval.

He paused for a moment, glancing up to see a broad smile stretching her face. Steve hummed. "God, you taste so good."

He went back to work, lapping like a starving man. Melody thrust her fingers into his hair and held him in place, one gasp of pleasure after another escaping her lips until she was quivering.

Another burst of satisfaction rang out as she came, and the sound thrilled him even as his cock pressed harder against the confines of his jeans. It had been too long, and with every touch, Steve remembered a little more why he had enjoyed being with Melody so very much.

She lived life without holding back—he needed more of that.

But for now he would take this opportunity to prove they needed this new start.

Melody lay motionless with her eyes closed, body totally relaxed as she sprawled on the countertop. "Oh Lord, Steve, let me breathe."

He chuckled, slipping his arms under her. "You don't need to breathe, darling. I'll do it for you."

She draped her arms around his neck as he carried her toward the back of the house. Her smile? A whole lot of naughtiness. "You taking me to my bedroom to ravish me?"

"Sort of."

Only when he got there and placed her gently on the bed, he stepped back. She was naked from the waist down, her bright-coloured bra still covering breasts that he couldn't wait to see again.

He'd been given a challenge. Three months to rock her world, and he had every intention of starting that right now.

She shimmied up on her knees. "What are you doing way over there?"

Steve glanced around the room, eyeing the drawers and small table beside her bed. "Just getting my bearings."

He marched forward and tugged open the drawer beside her bed as she scrambled toward him.

"Steve, what are you—? Oh, no."

He'd guessed right. He pulled a fabric bag from the drawer and hefted it a few times. Under his fingers an assortment of cock-like objects rolled, and he laughed. "From the shape of things, you've got a few more toys than you used to have."

Her cheeks had gone bright red. "Variety is the spice of life."

Steve had no objection to adding a little spice to their sex. And no better time to start than right now.

~

STEVE HADN'T LIED. Something was different as he prowled up the bed to her side, his expression one of lustful intent. Sex had never been bad with him, but so far today had been extraordinary.

If he kept upping the ante like this, his threat would come true. She would have trouble walking, at least without a satisfied grin on her face that would far too clearly tell everyone what she'd been up to.

"You have a favourite?" he asked, the lumpy fabric bag in his hand making her smile even as shivers of anticipation rolled up her spine.

"All depends." The temptation to tease was too great to resist. She wiggled back to make room beside her and went to tug her toy bag from him.

"Reach in and take out what you need," he ordered.

Well, that little bit of bossiness earned him no mercy. Melody slipped up on her knees and thrust her hand in, going unerringly for the biggest vibrator in the collection. She pulled it out, keeping her face as neutral as possible as she laid it in his outspread palm.

She was impressed when he didn't flinch. One brow rose slowly, though, as he examined the plastic shaped like a thick, ten-inch cock, with a full curved head, veins on the exterior, and everything.

His lips curled into a full-out masculine grin. "Aww, you missed me."

Melody laughed. She couldn't help it. "Your ego is just fine."

He leaned in, caressing her cheek with his lips. "I'm going to make you feel good, and it's not going to be the toys, it's going to be *me*. My fingers. My tongue. My cock—no matter what else is touching you, I'm the one taking you there."

"Bring it," she whispered back, the dare all too clear.

He placed the bag on her side table, laying the vibrator on the mattress beside them. Then he placed her in his lap and proceeded to kiss her senseless as he stripped away her bra.

She liked kissing, and she especially liked kissing Steve. He didn't seem to think it was a part of the journey on the way to the fucking, or something to get past as quickly as possible. He made it an awesome part all on its own.

He caught hold of her lower lip and nipped, the slight sting making her gasp. The moment her lips opened, he slipped his tongue inside, this time teasing and retreating until she didn't know if she needed to lean into him to demand more, or take advantage of the brief moments when he'd let her breathe so she wouldn't pass out from a lack of oxygen.

She sat in his lap, the coarse fabric of his jeans and the soft cotton of his flannel shirt brushing her naked skin. Sensitizing every nerve to the point that when he finally took one hand away from where he'd been cupping her face, she stiffened in anticipation of where he would touch next.

He leaned their foreheads together, staring into her eyes. "You taste so good. Everywhere."

And still staring at her, he stroked the side of her neck, playing along her collarbone before he spread his fingers and lowered his hand to cup her breast. His fingers curled around to cradle her as he rubbed and teased, his thumb brushing her nipple. Intense concentration in his eyes as he got to know her all over.

He pressed her to the mattress, moving so he could take one nipple in his mouth, his tongue moving slowly at first and then with increased pressure. When he closed his lips and sucked, a shot of pure pleasure raced through her core.

Melody closed her eyes so she could soak in every sensation. So she could savour the wicked havoc his tongue and fingers were causing. He pinched and soothed, stroked and caressed. Every time he shifted on the mattress, his clothing brushed her naked skin, adding another layer of intimate sensation.

"I could do this all night," he rumbled. His lips teased the tip of one tingling nipple as her breathing grew more laboured.

He had his hand between her legs, talented fingers moving unerringly to her clit. He pressed the sensitive point just hard enough to make her hips lift in an attempt to follow when his hand vanished.

"Don't worry, sweetheart. I'll take care of you," he promised.

And even as his mouth made renewed contact with her breast, a low noise warned her what to expect.

A moment later the vibrator made contact, the cool, solid head bumping between her folds. Steve abandoned her breasts, but when she expected him to simply sit up, he surprised her. Instead, he adjusted position, headed down to where he was stroking the plastic cock against the entrance to her pussy.

For one moment he lifted his head. Cocky, masculine satisfaction scalded her as his gaze danced over her face. "If you've been playing with toys, you might appreciate a little extra attention."

She didn't bother asking what he meant—she'd find out soon enough.

And, *whoa Nelly*, she was right. Steve twirled the head of the vibrator against her pussy until it was wet with moisture before slipping it into her body. He'd set the vibrations to low, which was enough to tease, not nearly enough for her to reach a climax.

At least, not until he leaned over and put his tongue to her clit at the same time.

"Oh, hell *yes*," she encouraged him, slipping her fingers through his hair. She planted one foot on the bed, opening herself as much as possible as he leaned over her belly to lick her clit.

The thick head of the vibrator pressed partway into her body.

Just into the most sensitive part, especially when combined with his mouth doing wicked, wonderful things.

Melody was no longer comparing tonight to the sex they'd had before. She was far, *far* more interested in what was on the table now. Her whole world narrowed to pleasure, right here, right now.

When another orgasm hit, she let it roll through her entire body as her limbs shook and a long cry of satisfaction flowed from her lips.

Then the toy was gone, and Steve was gone, but only for a moment. Melody twisted her head to the side to watch in admiration. "I've never seen a man strip so fast," she teased.

She stopped talking because she needed her breath to enjoy the show as he ripped off his wife-beater to reveal a dangerously muscular torso, his golden skin contrasting beautifully with his dark hair. He had very little body hair, except for a thin trail of black leading into his jeans. Jeans that were rapidly unbuttoned, unzipped and discarded to the floor.

Melody leaned up on an elbow, her mouth watering as everything came into view. He had no need to feel inadequate to the toys of her collection, especially since his cock was Technicolor and warm to the touch.

The thick length rose from the dark curls at his groin, the smooth head fully engorged, a drop of moisture clinging to the slit. She wrapped her fingers around him, and he groaned, rocking into her grasp.

"I need to be inside you right fucking now," he growled as she rubbed her thumb over the top, spreading the moisture she'd found there.

He held out a condom, and she ripped it open, her fingers shaking with eagerness. "You have no idea how much I want this," she confessed.

"I think I have a faint idea," he drawled.

Even as the need to have him drive into her grew, she couldn't resist. She placed the condom on the head of his cock, then instead of rolling it down with her fingers, she put her mouth on him.

His shout of surprise was worth the delay in game.

"God, Melody. You fucking blow my mind." His voice trembled, and his fingers curled through her hair.

She couldn't answer with her mouth full of cock. She inched down a little farther on every rock until he was swearing a blue streak, and her lips had reached the coarse curls at his groin.

He didn't give her time to tease any longer. Her back hit the mattress seconds before he grasped her knees and pulled them apart. Opening her wide so when he put his cock to her and thrust forward, he was buried in her body in an instant.

The shock of the single motion tore her breath away, and she stayed motionless, attempting to adjust to the thick intrusion that simultaneously hit all her pleasure points and made her feel as if she were being gutted.

He caught her chin in his hand and stared intently into her eyes. "You good?"

Words would require air, and since she didn't have any available for extraneous things right now, she nodded.

Still staring at her, he pulled his hips back. So in control as every inch triggered more pleasure. When she expected him to drive forward, he surprised her. Small pulses only—in, then out, repeating the motion until she thought she would go crazy from want.

"I've missed this," Steve confessed. His dark eyes flashed as he braced himself above her body. His trim, muscular hips bumping her on every tantalizing stroke. "I've missed touching you. I've missed tasting your skin."

She licked her lips, trying to get some moisture into her suddenly dry mouth. Wondering what she needed to say.

He didn't give her a chance to respond, though, because his mouth was over hers and he was kissing her as he continued to move within her. Connections and pleasure, memories and new experiences blending together.

She wrapped her legs around him, pressing her heels into his tight buttocks. Her hands rested on his shoulders, and she took advantage of the opportunity to explore the contoured muscles within her reach as he rocked again and again.

Their lips separated, his head beside her ear as he increased the pace. Both of them gasped for air, panting along with each rapid thrust. The bed springs creaked with every motion, Melody using the leg lock she had on him to help slam them together as he drove in hard.

The pleasure building was rapidly headed for a peak, and she murmured his name. The angle was just right that he knocked her clit over and over, and even after coming earlier, there was no way to hold back the avalanche of sensation.

"Oh, Steve. *Yes—*"

She shouted as he put his teeth to her neck and bit, holding her in place as his cock undid her. She arched her back, trying to get him even farther into her body as her muscles clenched around him. He swore and froze, his groin tight to her as he gasped for air, her name on his lips, his hips jerking against her.

Breathing had never seemed so difficult before. Melody let the head-spin take her as pleasure rolled through her entire body. Steve rested on top of her, his weight a welcome trap. She could do nothing but enjoy the aftershocks and wonder if the tingling was ever going to end.

"That didn't suck," she confessed as soon as she could speak.

His laughter vibrated against her neck. "No. That didn't suck at all."

He nuzzled against her for a moment before rolling away to deal with the condom. Cold hit the instant he left.

A moment later he was back, curling around her and tucking her against his body. It was frightening how good the position felt.

She didn't want to analyze too much, not at this point. They had so much more than sex to figure out if this was going to be a better relationship than what they'd had before.

But...she had no objections to fantastic sex *while* they were figuring it out.

Still, she had to tease. "That wasn't anything extraordinarily kinky."

"You unhappy?" He slipped his hand off of her belly and up to her breast, fingers dancing over her skin. "Because I can start all over again if I need to."

She groaned. "I won't be able to walk tomorrow. Not too kinky was perfect for tonight. Everything's fine."

He rolled her to her back and loomed over her, licking his lips. Complete and utter lust in his eyes.

Oh damn. What had she said to set him off?

"Fine?" One brow rose as he stared down with a dangerous expression. "We can do much better than *fine*."

Oops. "Shit. No it's not fine, I didn't use that word. No, I didn't— Oh my *God*."

Steve laughed, relenting as he removed his hand from where he'd slipped it between her legs. "Okay. I'll give you a fifteen-minute break before we start over."

She wasn't sure if he was kidding or not.

Three months of this? That *would* be much better than fine.

8

"There's nothing wrong with your dog, Ian. He needs a little more time to recover between hunting trips, that's all." Melody patted the ancient mutt on its head. The animal thumped his enormous tail in response, his good-natured attitude visible in every massive inch.

"He's not suffering, is he?" Ian shook his head, his silvery grey hair pulled back in a ponytail and tucked under a worn but clean cap. The man couldn't be any taller than Melody's five-foot-five, but he was wiry and lean like all of the locals who lived off the land, toiling mostly by hand year after year. "Bear's been a good friend for a long time, and I know what it's like to feel the aches and pains of getting old."

"No, I don't think he's in too much pain. He's probably stiff in the morning, but by the time he's gone for a walk and sniffed around a little, he's a happy guy."

The old-timer nodded, obviously pleased with the news. "Good to know. He's one of my best friends."

Melody braced herself as she wrapped her arms around the

dog and lowered him to the ground. The animal immediately moved into position beside his master, no collar or lead needed. The two of them tottered out the door, connected by something a whole lot more than the line of a leash, and a shot of envy struck.

Someday she'd like to have that kind of connection with an animal as well. Now that she planned to settle down, and all her schooling was done, maybe it was time to consider finding a good four-legged workmate. Ideas flitted in her head as she cleaned her work area.

Thoughts of a working pet weren't the only thing distracting her. That morning Steve had still been in her bed, but he'd risen at dawn. She'd watched sleepily as he pulled on his clothes before leaning in to kiss her goodbye. "Chores," he whispered in explanation. "I'll call you later."

She'd pulled herself together enough to ease up on an elbow, enjoying how his gaze dropped over her in appreciation. "I have to work today too," she warned. "Nine to five for once."

Steve snuck back to kiss her one final time, the mattress sagging under his weight. "Then tonight we'll do something. Call me when you're free."

Because this was more than just sex—they were back in a relationship. The idea both amazed and terrified her. She hoped she knew what she was doing.

Melody restocked a supply cupboard to force herself to stop daydreaming, then answered a summons to Mathis's office.

Five minutes later she was staring across the desk at her boss in shock.

Beside her, Tom, the other main vet who'd been called in just for the meeting, was also motionless. If she'd been caught off-guard at Mathis's announcement, Tom had to be horrified.

Sure enough, his response was fairly typical of what she expected to hear over the next weeks.

"You're putting Melody in charge of the large-animal work? Seriously?"

Mathis glared at his employee. "Wasn't I speaking English a minute ago? It was pretty clear that's what I said."

"Yes, but that makes no sense," Tom protested. "I've been working here just as long as her. In fact longer because I didn't go gallivanting off for nearly a year—"

"A year in which Melody increased her training and her skills, to the point that she is the best person for the job," Mathis insisted, his gravelly tone deepening in displeasure as he glared at Tom. "This isn't some kind of military coup, man. I just want to go away for a damn vacation for the first time in twenty years. It's my business, and I'll thank you to let me pick the best person for the job."

Tom settled back silently in his chair, but Melody knew this was only the beginning.

"I'll be glad to help, Mathis," Melody offered.

She refused to add anything to placate Tom's wounded ego. It wasn't a case of him being given a shitty deal, only that he thought he should have what Melody had been offered. The responsibilities he'd been put in charge of were just as important to the livelihood of the clinic.

Mathis, on the other hand, knew all too well what was going on. He folded his arms over his chest and frowned.

"Tom, this isn't some kind of judgment on your skills. You're excellent with the small-animal work, and I need you here in the clinic to keep that side of things going smoothly while I'm gone. Let Melody go tromp through the fields and deal with the weather, and you can enjoy an extra hour in bed in the morning and avoid most of the middle-of-the-night emergency calls."

Tom nodded, but the waves of frustration and displeasure rolling off of him were easy to sense.

Melody changed the topic. "Where are you going for your vacation?"

"Somewhere exotic and completely devoid of all animal life?" Tom grudgingly played along even though his tone made it clear he wasn't happy.

"You know it. Heading south. Camping and hiking in a bunch of the national parks. Plus, I've got tickets to Vegas, and I'm going to every single one of them fancy shows that I can." Mathis offered them a wink, working hard to distill the tension filling the room. "It's good to get the old ticker going a little harder, and at my age looking at pretty girls is the only thing I'm capable of."

"Go on with you," Melody taunted. "You still know what to do with them if you catch one."

Mathis laughed, and they moved into discussing the specifics of his time away, but the end result was clear. Her boss was taking a well-deserved vacation of six weeks, and he'd left Melody in charge.

Her world continued to whirl as she wandered into her residence, and picked up the phone to touch base with Allison over the shocking change of situation.

"That's wonderful!" Allison cheered before pausing for long enough to get Melody's curiosity up. "I bet Tom didn't like it, did he?"

Ha. "Went over like a sack of angry cats. *Wet* angry cats."

Allison sighed, the sound echoing over the line. "Welcome to the hell of facing the old boys' club."

"I've been dealing with it for years," Melody reminded her.

Only, she'd dealt with it, and put up with it, and fought against it while in a subservient role. Mathis hadn't ever let things go too far. Allison was right, and if Tom's attitude was any indication, it wasn't going to be easy.

She refused to panic. "I'm not the only large-animal vet in the area, so if anyone really objects to working with me while Mathis is away, they can call Baker's Clinic in Drayton Valley. And I can get Tom to help me, if I need to."

"You won't need his help."

"I hope not. I mean, technically I'm more advanced than him, and I'm stronger than him considering his age and attitude." Heck, she bet Tom would have had troubles lifting Bear onto the examining table. "But I'm still a woman. You know that makes some of the local ranchers assume they can smack me on the ass and send me into the house to help prep lunch when I'm done vaccinating a herd."

"Kick a few of them in the nuts," Allison suggested evilly.

Melody was already anticipating having to do that. "I'm just going to need to grow bigger ones than any of them," she said firmly.

"Good for you." Allison paused. "And I'll say it again, congratulations. I think you'll do a fabulous job, and if there's anything you need, you let me know."

"Sure. Because the most intimidating thing on the face of the earth to most of these ranchers is a pregnant woman," Melody drawled.

"Pregnant woman in tears," Allison offered before getting serious. "I'm kidding. You've got the skills—focus on that. The macho attitudes will be a pain in the ass, but there's not much they can say when you do your job right. Plus, I'm not beyond helping get their heads on straight if they need it. You know I worked in the industry for a lot of years. I think I still scare a lot of them—they run when they see me coming."

Allison had done organic inspections on ranches and farms throughout Alberta. "Oh, that's right. They loved you as well, didn't they? Having to deal with a woman approving or refusing to stamp their paperwork."

"You get a tough skin," Allison admitted. "But in the meantime, we need to celebrate. When do you officially start?"

"Mathis leaves on Monday."

"Then there's no time to waste. Barbecue at our place tonight —bring a date if you want."

Oh, right. There was something else she needed to share. "We're going out again," she confessed. "Me and Steve."

Allison's musical laugh echoed over the line. "Tell me something new, honey. You might think you were being sneaky, leaving Traders at different times, but you two could barely keep your hands off each other before you left. I figured out where you were headed in such an all-fired hurry. Especially when Steve took off without threatening Mitch with death or dismemberment like a true Coleman brother should at a typical engagement party."

"You're a nut," Melody complained.

"Hey, you're the one going out with him again. Although, if he messes up this time? He'll have the wrath of the Coleman women to deal with."

She didn't try to hide her amusement. "That's worse than the wrath of God, I hear."

"God is more forgiving," Allison agreed.

CRAWLING out of Melody's warm bed that morning had balanced the line between heaven and hell. He couldn't believe he'd actually spent the night. He couldn't believe he had to leave without doing it all over again.

All through his morning chores, images of what they'd done entertained him—picturing her naked, remembering the sounds she made as she moved under him.

The way she was so alive and willing to rock his world.

He was walking around the ranch with an enormous grin, and he didn't mind one bit. In fact, he whistled as he exited the barn, Prince picking up on his good mood as the dog pranced along at his side. Steve smiled at his antics as he made his way to the tractor to meet his father and get to work loading bales.

Only it wasn't his father waiting by the tractor.

His mother was decked out from head to toe in sturdy work clothes, one of Randy's old baseball caps on her head. It wasn't unusual for his mom to give a hand around the ranch—everyone put in time and labour when it was necessary, but her without dad wasn't typical.

"You driving today?" he asked, glancing around cautiously, but there was no one hiding behind the tractor.

Kate flashed him a grin. "Think you can keep up with your mother?"

"Yes, ma'am." He eyed the two machines. This was a task that he and his father had a definite routine they followed. Same with him and Trevor, and him and Lee. Whenever two people worked together for a long time, they'd develop their preferences. "You okay driving the truck?"

"Yup. And don't worry, hopefully it's just for a couple of days." She smacked a pair of heavy work gloves against her thigh to clean them off before pulling them on her much smaller hands. "Your dad's got a new medication, and it's not agreeing with him. Doctor said things should settle down within the week, though."

Steve nodded. "Just give me a shout if you need a break."

"I'll be fine," his mom insisted.

It added a twist to his morning. For the first hour he went slower than usual until he was sure Kate had things under control. It was far more about him watching out for her than his mom actually slowing the task down, and once he realized that, they got the job done as efficiently as usual.

Lunch was an entirely different situation.

They stopped at the house to grab some food. There was no sign of his father, although his brothers were there, Lee slapping together sandwiches while Trevor stirred something at the stove.

Their mom glanced around in confusion as she pulled off the dusty baseball cap and wiped her hair off her forehead. "Where's Randy?"

Trevor and Lee glanced at each other, looking a little too amused. Lee turned back. "I might've suggested something for lunch that didn't sit too well. I think he's lying down for a while."

Kate sighed, shaking her head in exasperation. "You boys are evil. You know he's not feeling well. Why would you pick this time to taunt him?"

"Heck, this is the best time." Trevor chuckled as he scooped soup into bowls and brought them to the table. "Just think, we're getting even for that time you had food poisoning, Mom, and he asked if you were going to come help butcher the chickens."

His mom grabbed drinks from the fridge before joining her sons. "I still say you're terrible."

"But you love us, right?" Trevor teased.

She eased back in her chair, stretching her back with a grimace as she offered him a wink. "I know where you get your terrible sense of humour from, so I can hardly blame you."

Even with lunch being a hurried affair so they could get back into the fields, Steve felt a rising sense of satisfaction. It was strange not having his father present, but working with his family was right. They knew what had to be done and usually agreed about how to do it, and that made a world of difference. He trusted them to have his back and to work hard to achieve their goals.

And now you can have Melody as well that little voice inside his head pronounced.

It was far too early to be making long-term plans, but at the same time, that *was* where he was headed. It was one thing to insist he'd changed. If he didn't have a long-term reason for changing? Just having sex with the woman, well, that wasn't enough.

"We'll be done baling well before I thought we would," Trevor commented.

"It's because we left that one section as grazing land. Letting it lie fallow for the year changes the amount of work," Steve said.

"It also changes how much hay we'll put up." Trevor made a face. "I'm trying to get hold of the owner of the next spread. I know the Rylers' rent out the house, but I didn't hear from anyone who's in charge of the fields."

It was a good point. "If you can find out, we could cut them this year. We could use the extra, or sell it if we don't need it for our stock."

Lee spoke up. "Whiskey Creek clan are looking for extra hay if we have any to spare. I was talking with Lisa the other day, and she mentioned it."

His mom nodded. "I was talking with the rest of the ladies, and it sounds as if Mike and Marion will need extra as well."

It was strange having this kind of discussion without his father in the middle of it, and Steve felt uneasy. "Let's make a note to talk about it with Dad when he's feeling better."

"Don't put it off too long," his mom prodded, rising from the table and brushing her hands together. "He trusts you. You boys think we've got the time and the energy to deal with extra fields, I'm willing to help if Randy's not feeling up to it."

Changes.

Steve thought about it the entire afternoon as he bounced around in the truck, following after his mother who had insisted she wanted her turn driving the baler. He wasn't the only one who'd changed over the past years, and while he had new goals to set with Melody, his family was changing as well.

It was both exciting and uncomfortable, and he wasn't sure

from one moment to the next, which he felt more. Luckily, anticipation overrode them both as he focused on the end of his day and getting together with Melody.

His grin was back in full force.

9

*I*t was as if he couldn't get enough of touching her, and Melody wasn't about to complain.

From the moment he picked her up after work, he'd been nothing but agreeable. Running back into the house to grab the salad she'd forgotten without a word of complaint. Tucking her in at his side, his arm around her as they headed down the back roads to Gabe and Allison's house.

"How long did Mathis say he'd be gone?"

"Six weeks at least, but he didn't seem very firm in his return date," she shared. "And even if that makes things more difficult for us, I'm glad to know he's not going to rush. The man deserves every minute of his getaway."

"I agree." Steve went quiet for a moment, his hand on her shoulder rubbing gently. "I don't think I've ever heard of him going on a holiday before."

"Don't think he ever has. It's not as if there's a good season to take off and leave people in the lurch."

"He didn't take a holiday until now because he didn't have

you." Steve pressed his lips to the top of her head, but his words warmed her more than his touch.

She'd already gotten some of her concerns out while talking with Allison, and she didn't want to dwell on it. Still, Steve was as good a person to ask as any. "You don't have any trouble with me being your main contact for the summer?"

He made a rude noise. "Of course not. Never had issues with any of the work you've done when Mathis brought you out. Why should you do a lesser job just because he's not there?"

A little of her tension faded at his words. "Thank you for that."

It was hard, though, to put aside the rest of her worries and concentrate on enjoying the evening.

Steve pulled into the yard and parked beside Gabe's newer vehicle. Melody offered her hand to Steve, and he pulled her out the driver side door, sliding her down his body until her feet hit the ground.

They paused, her head tilted back to stare up at him as the physical attraction between them flared. He cupped her face, running his thumb over her cheek as his eyes burned brighter. "Barbecue, and then I'll take you parking."

She laughed and tugged him toward the house.

The aroma of rich tomato sauce hit the instant they opened the door. "Now I know we're in the right place. Forget about hiding your silverware, I've come for your ribs," Steve called out.

Gabe caught his hand in a friendly clasp and shook it. "You can have the spoons and forks. There's no way you're taking Allison's cooking out of here without a fight."

Melody left Steve's side after giving a final squeeze to his fingers, crossing the floor to her friend and offering Allison a hug. A small black cat with white paws slipped around the corner, rubbing against Steve's shins as it purred a welcome, but Melody wasn't too distracted to notice the slight swell of her friend's belly pressed between them.

"Looks as if someone's going to need maternity clothes soon," Melody teased.

She wasn't sure who looked happier at her comment—Allison or Gabe. "I've already been given enough things to get me through the first while."

"Let me guess. Jaxi?" When Allison confirmed it, Steve shook his head. "That woman runs ninety percent of Rocky Mountain House, doesn't she?"

Gabe wrapped his fingers around Allison's arm and led her to a chair, settling her into it with a smile. "Don't exaggerate."

Melody thought it through, but from what she knew the young woman got tangled up in almost everything that happened in the community. "You sure?"

Gabe's grin broke free. "Jaxi's one hundred percent in charge, but she's nice enough to offer the illusion other people occasionally get a say in the matter."

Steve tilted his head toward a pile of ribs on the side counter. "Do I need to help you burn things?"

The men were out the door and headed to the barbecue in no time flat, leaving Melody and Allison grinning good-naturedly at each other.

Allison rested her elbows on the table as she examined Melody. "So?"

It wasn't the easiest question to answer. She took a moment to scoop up Puss in Boots and stroke his head, the small creature rumbling with pleasure at the attention. "So... Am I excited about my new job? How do I like my new truck? Did we break any bed springs last night?"

"You didn't," Allison gasped before schooling her features. "And I was totally talking about your truck."

"Sure you were..." Melody prepared to give an update on her

and Steve, but the guys wandered back in before she could say anything. Maybe it was backlash from her nervous energy, but a spirit of mischief struck as she looked Allison straight in the eye. "Seems to have as good of a payload as I remember. And there's definitely some power under the hood."

Her friend caught the dirty innuendo, and her smile widened.

The guys joined them at the table, Gabe's interest high. "So you're enjoying the new ride?"

Allison made a noise somewhere between a laugh and a whimper, turning it into a cough before offering Gabe a watery smile. "Sorry. Something in my throat."

Melody considered carefully before answering. "So far, so good. I'm still figuring out how hard it can go, but it seems to be living up to the promises."

Another small sound escaped her friend, and Melody had to bite the inside of her cheek to stop from joining in.

"You know the best way to break her in is to just go for it," Steve advised. "None of that keeping it steady or riding under the limit. Take it right up to the max. That's the only way you'll know if it's got everything you need. Pound those pistons a little."

Allison rose to her feet and headed for the counter, the tortured grin on her face just about setting Melody off.

"Sounds like a good idea," she agreed, fighting to get the words out without her voice trembling with laughter.

He caught her fingers in his, the cat abandoned them for the floor, and talk turned to some of the organic changes being made to the Angel Coleman ranch, much to Melody's relief.

She didn't want to have to explain why she'd never again be able to hear the word *piston* without wanting to laugh.

It was good being around friends, and as the meal progressed, the sense of familiarity Melody enjoyed so much returned. Something was very different as well, though, as not a moment passed without Steve following up on her. Checking to be sure she had enough to eat and drink, offering Allison help.

After the meal was over, the guys took over the dishes and left her and her friend sitting in lawn chairs by the fire pit with the promise of marshmallows to come.

Steve pressed a kiss to her cheek "You still like those sticky sweet things, don't you?"

"My one and only vice," Melody confessed.

He dipped his head lower, his mouth by her ear. "I don't know about that. I think you have plenty of other vices for us to explore..."

If a small moan escaped her, it couldn't be helped. She watched his fine ass in his faded Levis until he vanished behind the door, rejoining Gabe in the house.

Allison let out a sound like a balloon losing its air. "Holy *cow*. If you two keep this up, I'll need you to leave immediately after your first marshmallow so I can jump my husband."

Melody didn't bother to hide her smile. "I have no idea what you're talking about."

"Look, I'm pregnant. And I do know what causes that." Allison leaned forward. "I'm serious. You said you were going out again. Does that mean you plan to do anything other than light the bed sheets on fire? Because that one you're clearly accomplishing."

"I hope so." Melody squatted by the fire pit to arrange the kindling. "It's only been twenty-four hours. Don't start putting me in a white dress yet."

"Not unless it's made of fire-retardant material."

Ha. She picked up the lighter from beside the fire pit and applied the flame to the kindling she'd prepared. Ignoring Allison as she gathered her thoughts.

It couldn't all be about sex.

She sat back as a flicker took hold of the wood shavings.

Awkward thing to ask, but it was in her head... She glanced around first to make sure they were alone, then went for it. "Do you think it was too soon to hop into bed with him?"

Allison never hesitated. "I don't know what broke you up other than it wasn't anything horrific, so—no. I don't think it's too soon."

Melody settled back in her chair. "It's not creepy, or slutty, or something?"

"Melody Langley." Her friend glared at her. "Don't you start shaming yourself for having a good time with Steve. So what if you've got other things to figure out. A little physical satisfaction is not something to be ashamed of."

"I know, but it can't be everything."

"And it's not. You said it yourself—you just started going out again, so this is like the honeymoon stage. And frankly?" Allison waggled her brows as she gestured toward the house. "You two already had carnal knowledge of each other. I think it would've been a little much to expect to keep your hands off each other while you figure out the rest of your relationship."

A burst of laughter escaped Melody. "Carnal knowledge?"

Her friend reached beside her and pulled up a plastic bag full of marshmallows. "Are you really going to taunt me for my choice of words when I'm the keeper of the treats?"

Melody straightened quickly, pretending to be worried. "No, ma'am. Yes, ma'am. Right away, ma'am."

They grinned at each other, and Allison handed over the bag without any further teasing.

"Good decision," Melody praised her. "I was about to go Rambo on your butt to get these."

"Steve, your woman is threatening mine," Gabe complained as the guys rejoined them, adjusting chairs and settling in close.

Steve rested his arm over the back of her chair, taking control of the marshmallow stick with his other hand. "I'm sure Allison did something to deserve it."

"Hey, how come I'm in the middle of this?" Allison protested.

Gabe rested his hand on her knee. "You're an Angel Coleman, now, too. You know this. We *always* end up in the middle."

~

STEVE WATCHED his cousin tease Allison for another couple minutes—watched closer than usual to be honest even as he enjoyed having Melody's fingers linked through his.

Changes meant being more observant, and in this case, knowing that Allison and Melody were each other's closest friends, he figured they could end up spending a fair amount of time with the other couple.

They hadn't before, not during what Steve had taken to think of as his Asshole Years. Back then Steve had occasionally brought Melody out to family gatherings, but more often the times they'd been together had been few and far between. Convenience rather than companionship.

It was a time he didn't want to dwell on, but he had to consider it if he was going to learn his lesson and not screw up again.

The sound of an engine interrupted their conversation, Gabe and Steve going to their feet to check who was buzzing over the nearest hill on a quad.

"It's Rafe," Allison commented without looking away from the fire.

Gabe disagreed. "He's out of town tonight."

"You want to bet? I get a foot-rub if I'm right." She poked the fire with a stick as she flashed him a smile. "Insider knowledge here, Angel Boy, just warning you."

"What about the truck coming in from the south?" Melody asked, raising a finger to point at the dust trail marking its approach.

"Matt." Allison lifted her chin. "Your cousin called earlier to see if it was okay for him and Hope to stop by."

"So much for our quiet evening," Gabe grumbled.

Steve knew the complaining was a fake—his cousin always had the energy to help out, and he never turned away a person in need. Thank God, because Steve had received more than his own share of pep talks from the man.

Rafe was greeted enthusiastically by his older brother, and extra chairs were brought out for the others. Melody gestured for Allison to stay put, and she and Hope disappeared into the house, returning with drinks for everyone. Conversations grew noisier, and the laughter just got louder.

Steve found himself sitting next to Allison as she stared past the fire to where her husband was talking quietly with Rafe. He studied her expression, but she didn't seem upset that her house had a revolving door on it. "Do you ever get any peace and quiet around here?"

She turned her gentle smile his direction, and warmth washed over him like the glow of the fire.

"It's a part of who Gabe is. I don't want that to change."

On his right, Melody's fingers around his arm remained a small reminder of the new promise they had made to move forward together, even as she laughed out loud at something Matt had said.

He wasn't sure what he was trying to ask, but he said it anyway in the hopes Allison could figure it out. "And you never want to put up the *No Trespassing* sign and lock the door?"

Allison's eyes flashed with amusement. "Good question. There are times, yes, I wish the world would go away. That the things we have to deal with would just stop, because frankly? Our troubles, Gabe's and mine, aren't usually as hard as the ones we get handed to deal with."

"But you don't hide."

"Nope." Allison tilted her head toward Melody for a moment before leaning closer. "Hiding doesn't work to deal with most things. And with Melody—you can't hide away or keep your entire relationship in the bedroom. No matter how fun that part is."

His cheeks were heating up. *For fuck's sake*—what had the girls talked about while they were setting up the dinner date?

"Ummm—"

She took pity on him, or maybe it was because the conversations behind them were getting too loud to ignore, but Allison hurried to finish. "She needs family. Always has, always will. And hey, that's one thing you have in spades." Allison knocked his arm with her fist. "Don't try to lock that part away from her. It didn't work last time, so don't be selfish. Share what you got."

"Yeah, share that bag of marshmallows," Matt demanded, overhearing the last part of the discussion. "Greedy. Didn't your mama teach you any manners?"

Melody caught the bag in mid-air, pulling it to herself and dragging out a fistful before passing it on to Matt. "There you go. Your share."

Matt stared into the bag in mock disgust. He pulled out what was left, opening his palm to reveal...not much. "Three? You left me three?"

His wife snatched one from his hand and popped it in her mouth, licking her fingers innocently. "Two. You counted wrong."

Matt growled and curled his arms around her, kissing her soundly as everyone laughed.

Being there felt good. It felt right, and the heat of Melody's hand in his as they finally made their farewell and headed for the truck—that felt even better.

They were partway home, sitting in a companionable silence, when she sighed, resting her head on his shoulder. "That was nice."

"Good. I had fun too. And congrats on your promotion."

"Oh, God, you had to remind me."

"You've got nothing to worry about." Steve slowed for the corner before heading down a narrow gravel road. "You're going to do an amazing job. You're good at what you do."

She tilted her head back, and their eyes met for a second before he focused on the road.

That's when she clued in he'd turned off the highway. "Umm, Steve?"

"Yeah?"

She scooted upright, edging forward to stare out the front window as they topped the crest of the hill and he turned toward the bluffs. "Where are we going?"

He took a quick glance over the open room at the top of the lookout, planning carefully for maximum distance between them and the next vehicle. "Parking."

She laughed lightly. "You're kidding me."

Steve turned off the truck and locked the brakes before reaching for her seat belt. The instant she was free he scooped her up and arranged her over his lap, knees on either side of his hips. "I told you we were going to do this up right, and we're gonna. Now—shut up and kiss me."

Melody draped her arms around his neck, adjusting her position until she nestled tighter to his rapidly expanding cock. "You're bossy tonight."

"Every night." He put his fingers to her shirt buttons and undid the top three. Just far enough that her bra showed, and the faint light from the dash made her bared skin glow. "There. Perfect."

"Not going to strip me down and have your way with me?" she teased.

"Nope." She may have pushed his buttons with the vanilla comment, but he refused to give in to the urge to keep upping the ante. "First base only."

"Really." The total disbelief in her tone went well with the flirty expression in her eyes.

He wrapped his fingers around the back of her neck and moved her toward him, close enough that their lips brushed as he spoke. "Really."

Her eyes sparkled. "Then why is my shirt open?"

"Because I like the view." He traced her lips with his tongue, exploring as he held her in place, the back of her head cradled in the palm of his hand. "Melody—the next time we have sex, do we need condoms?"

Her voice trembled as she answered with a question of her own. "You been with anyone since last fall?"

"Nope. You? During your time at school?"

It took a while for her to admit it. "...no."

He knew it. Inside his ego gave a fist pump that her little *I experimented while at school* had been for effect. "Good."

She opened her mouth and he snuck inside. Tasting her delicately but without hesitation. Her breath fluttered past his cheek, a warm rush that along with the kiss sent heat racing over his nerve endings.

Melody wasn't protesting anymore, threading her fingers through his hair as she got into what they were doing. Even as he kept the kisses soft, it was clear she was getting just as turned on as him, moving in slow undulations against him as their breathing picked up.

It took some doing, but he pulled them apart, kissing her jaw and cheek. Nuzzling against her neck with his lips. "I'm headed to Red Deer tomorrow. You want to come?"

She purred as if he'd petted her. Stumbling for words as if she was surprised at the question. "Oh. Oh, I can't. I'm booked to supervise at the 4-H rodeo."

"Damn. Okay—next time then." He drew her earlobe into his mouth and bit down, and a shiver rocked her. "Next time we go parking you can bring the new truck."

The noise escaping her was somewhere between a sigh and a gasp as he focused attention on the tender spot at the base of her neck. "Sure. New truck." She shuddered. "*Dammit*, Steve. Only first base? I want your mouth on my breasts."

"I want that too. And my mouth on your pussy. And my cock buried deep inside you while you come around me, squeezing me tight and getting me wet." The whimper that escaped her didn't help. He wanted it so much he was ready to burst out of his jeans and stab her onto his length right this instant. *Control.* "But that wouldn't be following the rules for tonight."

She swayed above him, lips curled into a pout as her blue eyes caught his. "Who the hell set up rules saying you should drive me crazy with lust?"

"Just prolonging the anticipation," he murmured, sneaking in for another quick kiss. "And I'd totally leave you hot and bothered, but I've seen your toy collection. I bet if I dropped you at home right now you'd have the batteries roaring on high within three minutes."

"Thirty seconds," she gasped, clutching his shoulders. Her breath escaped in short puffs, chest moving rapidly. "Ten, maybe. You don't want that, do you?"

He caught her by the hips and slid her higher, rubbing the seam of her jeans over his impossibly hard length. "Hell, no. So, let's do this instead."

It took a couple tugs to get her lined up right. He was going to lose his mind, along with his load, but the escalating moans escaping her lips told him they were paying enough attention to her clit to make her come.

Steve tightened his grip for a second and locked her in place. Melody used his name like a rather nasty curse, and he laughed, catching hold of her chin. "No, sweetheart. First base is all I'm giving you."

"Bastard—"

"Doesn't mean you can't take your pleasure," he interrupted. "Do it. Get yourself off on me while I watch."

Those perfect lips of hers formed an O of surprise for a second before her tongue darted out, and she licked them.

"That was...*dirty*," she moaned.

"Do it," he ordered, his voice just above a growl. "Now."

The slight hesitation that followed was her adjusting position, rising on her knees and leaning over him. Her lush breasts swayed as she rocked, her hair swinging around her shoulders as she held on tight and rubbed her clit over his cock. Slowly at first, her teeth sinking into her lower lip as she found the right alignment. Lashes fluttering as she stared into his eyes and the pleasure built.

His cock swelled harder and hotter, and not being inside her was fucking killing him. But watching arousal streak over her face, a flush rise to her chest—the way she could barely keep her head vertical as she sped up, grinding harder now—amazing to witness.

"That's it, sweetheart. Get yourself all heated up. Feel how hard you got me? My cock is like a fucking rock, and that's because of you." His mouth was going dry, he was breathing so hard, but the passion in her eyes urged him on. "I bet you're tingling everywhere—like there are a million sparks about to explode into a flash fire racing through your veins. Your pussy's jealous because your clit is pounding so hard."

She came, shuddering over him. He caught her chin and stared into her eyes, and *that* was what sent him over. The pure bliss washing over her face, satisfaction in every bit of her expression was too much to resist. His cock jerked in the confines of his jeans, her hot pussy separated from him by too many layers, but hell, *yeah.*

They'd as good as fucked their brains out.

He pulled her mouth to his and kissed her while they fought to regain their breath. Open mouths, sucking for air. The faint lights of the truck interior blurred against the foggy windows.

Melody cupped his face as she pulled away, smile settling into place as she glanced around and laughed softly. "We steamed up the windows."

"You're hot stuff, sweetheart. Next time, your truck, right?"

She crawled off him and curled up on the bench at his side, waiting as he rolled down the windows and turned the fan on high to clear them. "Next time, second base or farther. Promise me?"

Steve raised a hand in the air and solemnly swore, "Next time, I will not neglect your breasts."

Another laugh escaped. "You're a goof."

"You're the one who just rode me like a pogo stick." He winked, then put his arms around her waist and tucked her in tight for the ride home.

Three months of this? Rocking her world while he proved he'd changed?

Not a sacrifice at all.

10

Of course, after weeks of nothing but sunshine, on Monday the skies were overcast and grey. It seemed appropriate somehow. Worry hovered like a carrion bird, ready to see what the day would bring—feast or famine.

Melody shoved aside her misgivings and tried to focus on the good parts of her position as she parked her new truck at the side of the road and headed into the café.

She was in charge. That deserved a celebratory breakfast before heading into her day.

She waved to the girls behind the counter and settled on one of the barstools as a familiar waitress stepped forward, coffee carafe in hand.

"Want a hit?" Stacey asked.

"Plus the breakfast special, please."

She added a little cream to her coffee and took the first sip, hot liquid rolling down like molten satisfaction. Only then did she look around to check who else was in the café.

In the far corner of the room, local farmers had pulled

together two of the square tables, surfaces now littered with coffee cups and plates.

She grinned. Just like hobbits. That was probably their third breakfast—but she would never tease them in public because she knew how hard and how long most of them had already worked.

Sean Dalton was in the group, which solved one of her most current problems. She rose from the counter and headed to the table, nodding at people who acknowledged her.

Masculine laughter broke off as she paused beside the joint tables.

The group of men glanced up at her, some smiles fading, a couple a touch too familiar for her liking. Still, she gave them all the benefit of a doubt, offering greetings to everyone before focusing on Sean.

"I'm headed your way to do some inoculations later this morning."

His smile froze between one heartbeat and the next. "Why isn't Mathis coming out?"

"I thought you'd heard. He's taking time off, so I'll be your contact for the next while." She tilted her head toward Justin Williams. "You're on the list for later this week. Depending on how things go at Sean's, I'll give you a call to let you know when I'll be out."

He didn't seem nearly as concerned as Sean. "Just let me know."

"What's Tom doing?" Sean demanded.

Melody worked to keep her polite face firmly in place. "He's taking care of things at the clinic. Anyway, I see my breakfast is ready. I'll let you finish your coffee in peace." She made direct eye contact with Sean. "Call and let me know where you want me to join you. Or leave me a voicemail, because the notes don't say where you want the job done."

"I'll get my lead hand to call," Sean answered briskly then

ignored her, which was fine because her plate of food was being laid on the counter, and nothing was worse than eating cold eggs.

So. It had begun.

She tried to enjoy her breakfast, but the meal sat heavy. She was pulling open her truck door when her phone rang. A familiar tone. A guitar riff that made her smile, especially remembering their explosive adventure two nights earlier.

It had been far more pleasurable for how unexpected it was.

"Steve. How are you doing this fine day?" she teased, crawling in the cab and switching the phone to hands-free so she could hit the road.

"I want to see you," he started with no preamble.

"That won't be for a few hours. I have a date with a herd." Her fingers crossed involuntarily that everything would go well. "I'd love to see you tonight. I don't know what time I'll be done, though."

"Hell, I know what it's like," he reassured her. "Sweetheart, it isn't as if I haven't dealt with your schedule before, or you with my last-minute cancellations. Neither of us is working a nine-to-five office job."

No, but that didn't mean she had any intention of being delegated to the back burner like in their previous dating lives. She was enjoying the attention he'd been paying her.

Although...they didn't have to spend every waking moment together. She didn't expect him to hold her hand and fawn over her.

"I should be able to see you this evening. If it works, you want to try for dinner?" After poking animals with sharp objects and having them object, she would enjoy not having to cook. "My treat."

He growled, the sound raising goose bumps on her skin. "Now, don't you start that. I can afford to buy you a burger."

The highway flew by as she talked with him, finding out what his plans were for the day. She turned down a side road that was a shortcut to her first job of the day, thankful for the new wheels underneath her. "I'm loving this new truck," she mentioned to Steve.

He hummed in approval. "I look forward to taking her for a drive."

She opened her mouth to answer him, stopped by his low chuckle of amusement coming over the phone line. "Grow up," she teased.

"I can't help it," he insisted. "There are so many things I want to talk to you about. So many things I want to *do* with you."

A heavy pulse of heat struck between her legs, and she smiled that he could have such an effect on her so quickly. "You've got a damn dirty mind, that's all I can say."

"I think you like my dirty mind. And my dirty talk, and everything else about me that's dirty."

"Not true. I'm not going near you after you've been cleaning stalls."

He full-out laughed, and the sound was contagious. Melody caught a glimpse of herself in the rearview mirror, an ear-to-ear grin stretching her cheeks wide.

Past the mirror, a decrepit horse shelter caught her eye. Weathered grey boards were tucked against the mixed spruce forest. She remembered seeing the building before, but what was new were the horses wandering in the small yard outside the shelter.

"Hey, Steve. Who owns the land just off of 532?"

He paused for a moment before answering. "Dalton. He bought during the last spring auction after Jensen passed away."

Melody slowed her truck and pulled to the side of the gravel road even though there wasn't another vehicle anywhere in sight. "Did he buy animals as well?"

"I didn't think there were any animals left. Jensen sold off most of his stock years ago, and his kids sold the rest when he moved into the Seniors' Home."

But there were horses on the land. Scrawny ones, the most swayed-back beasts she'd ever seen. She needed to take a closer look before she said anything, though. "Thanks for the info. I need to get rolling."

"Call me anytime," he offered. "I like talking to you."

"Yeah, it is rather fine, isn't it?"

The sound of his rumbling amusement echoed in her ear as she hung up, a pleased sensation rolling over her at his quick response.

She caught another glimpse of the horses, and her amusement faded. She checked her watch, but there wasn't time to take a look before getting to the first scheduled appointment, so she put it on her mental agenda for when she was free.

Walking into the first barn of the day always gave her a thrill. It didn't matter whose land she was on, not really. The animals and what she knew about their habits and behaviours made her step with confidence into the middle of the action, whether she was at a mom-and-pop hobby farm or a billion-dollar-ranching operation.

The first few jobs passed quickly as she fell into a routine, taking every back road possible to cut time off her trips.

She hadn't lied to Steve. The truck was amazing, and she wasn't worried at all about it dying. Not like Myrtle, rest its soul.

Melody checked the battery on her phone, wondering if she'd missed a call from Sean while she was out of range of the lone cell-phone tower in the area. It was possible, and when she called him back and got no answer, she was even more convinced there'd been a communication breakdown.

But the time was closing in when she needed to get to his land for the long, sweaty task of inoculating the herd, and she wasn't sure where she needed to be. Time to check in at the office.

"Rocky Mountain Animal Care, Callie speaking. How can I help you?"

The line was barely intact, and Melody rushed to get information before she lost contact altogether. "Hey, Callie, it's Melody. You see a note from Sean Dalton saying where to meet him?"

The front-desk receptionist at the clinic hummed. "I don't see anything in the logbook, and there's nothing that's come in since I arrived."

"Drat." Melody checked her watch again. "Can you call—?"

The line crackled one last time as the connection between them severed.

She thought a few choice words, then took a shot and headed for the main homestead, hoping along the way she'd pass a field or outbuilding with a batch of vehicles surrounding it. Something that would give her a clue to tell her where to go.

Her detecting skills sucked, yielding not a single hint along the way. What was worse was when she pulled into his yard, it obviously wasn't the right spot. There were trucks gathered, parked to the side, but the herd of cows that were supposed to be in the yard waiting for their turn to be prodded—they simply weren't there.

Melody made her way to the ranch house, cursing under her breath at the delay. She knocked loudly, peeking through the window for a sign of life.

Emily Dalton came forward, wiping her hands on a towel, a frown creasing her forehead, dark hair pulled back in a neat ponytail. "Can I help you?"

"I don't know if you remember me, but I'm Melody Langley, one of the local vets. I'm here to do your inoculations, but I didn't get word where to go."

The woman's mouth hung open for a second before she slammed it shut, her frown increasing. She shook her head and turned on the spot, headed into the house. "Come with me, I'll get a hold of Sean on the walkie-talkie."

"Thanks."

Melody took off her boots and paced farther into the neat farmhouse, the smell of home cooking filling the air.

"Well, she's here now," Emily announced into the microphone in the corner of the room, glancing toward Melody with concern as a voice rumbled back, barely recognizable as words. "I don't know why she's here. You have everything ready for her?"

Sean's response was another buzz Melody couldn't understand, but it set Emily nodding before she hung up and turned with a sigh.

"They're waiting for you down at the White Pine barn."

It wasn't Emily's fault. Melody held in the rest of her frustration as she headed toward the door. "That's the one I reach off Simpson Road, right?"

"That's the long way around," Emily muttered, pulling off her apron and slipping on a pair of boots. "Come on, follow me and I'll get you there in no time."

Still took them nearly twenty minutes, which was a lot less time than it would have if Melody had taken the only other route she knew. Emily drove confidently through side fields, popping out of the truck to steal through gates Melody would never have known to use.

She waved at Emily in thanks as she parked beside the barn, grabbing her equipment and heading in to the corrals behind the barn at a near run.

The cattle had been there for a while—that much was obvious from the mess in the yard.

Sean looked daggers at her as he folded his arms over his

chest. "You've wasted over an hour of my time, and my men's time."

"I could have been here on time if you'd left word where you would be," Melody pointed out as politely as possible. "I mentioned that to you this morning."

"I called. Left a message at the clinic." He turned his back on her, jamming his hat farther on his head as if he were fighting to control his temper.

Melody suddenly wasn't sure what to do. Had she missed the update? Dammit. Until she found out who had screwed up at the office all she could do was move forward. "Let's get started then."

She kept her head high in spite of the rocky start, but from the expressions on the hands waiting to help, Sean wasn't the only one holding back from giving her hell.

It was going to be a long afternoon.

STEVE SPENT MORE time checking his watch that afternoon than he had in a long time. By the time his phone finally rang, he was done for the day and eager to get together with Melody. He'd done some thinking about their evening, and his plans for the night included more than just rocking her socks.

Although, that was on the agenda.

Only she didn't have good news for him.

"I have to cancel." She let out a long groan as if stretching sore back muscles. Steve recognized the sound—he'd been there often enough himself. "I'm so far behind I can't see the finish line. I need to finish this round of shots at the Daltons', plus I just got a message from the clinic that I have to head over and check the last animal I did surgery on—Tom insists it's my work, and he doesn't want to interfere."

First day Mathis was gone, and Tom was already being a dick, but Melody probably didn't need anyone pointing that out. "I don't mind waiting," Steve said.

"I have no idea what time I'll be done. Let's call it quits for the night and get together later this week."

The urge to deny her request was so strong he nearly bit his tongue in two, but instead he pulled in his hard-earned smarts and listened. At least for now.

"Take care of yourself," he ordered, not sure what else he could do.

"I always do."

Frustration swept him. *He* wanted to be taking care of her.

He'd barely hung up when the phone rang again.

"I'm looking for trouble, and I know you're the man to help me find her." The familiar voice of his cousin Jesse.

This could be a good distraction from the fucked-up change of plans. Maybe. "I don't know if I want any of your brand of trouble," Steve warned.

"Wimp."

"Jackass."

"Fuckhead"

"Stupid."

Jesse snickered. "We could do this all night. Or you could get your ass over here so I can show you what I've got."

"What? You're actually at home? I thought you'd decided to turn into a hobo and live out of your truck."

"Screw you." Only the words were said without any heat. It appeared the enthusiastic smartass version of Jesse was back—the guy everyone enjoyed spending time with. "Come on, Steve, I can't keep this under wraps for much longer."

His curiosity shot skyward. Steve turned his truck reluctantly away from Melody and down the back roads.

On the low porch outside the rental house, Jesse, Trevor and Lee were gathered in a tight knot, their broad backs blocking the view of whatever the hell had Jesse in an uproar. He ordered Prince to stay, his dog settling back on its haunches by the truck, peering toward the house with interest.

Steve made his way forward, jerking to a stop at a low growl that rang out as the first step creaked under his foot.

Instantly, Jesse spoke, employing the low, singsong tone used everywhere to soothe a cranky animal. "It's okay, Charlie. That's Steve, and he's okay. No, wait. He's a bit of an ass at times, but he's *mostly* okay."

Trevor and Lee chuckled as Steve pushed himself between their shoulders to check out the center of attention. On the ground before them lay a sleek German shepherd with four large pups nestled against her nursing.

"Seriously?" Steve didn't know if he should laugh or smack Jesse one. "You called me over because you want to show me a dog?"

His cousin squatted and ran a hand over the bitch's head. "Isn't she a beauty?"

Steve glanced at Trevor and didn't bother to hide his amusement. "She's gorgeous. So, where did you meet your new girlfriend?"

Jesse multitasked wonderfully, continuing to pet the dog while he gave Steve the bird. "Consider it my good deed for the day. I'm thinking about keeping one of the pups. If any of the rest of you want one, the bitch is supposed to be a prize-winning tender."

"And you know this? How?"

His cousin stiffened before shrugging and answering noncommittally. "Oh, something I heard."

"Does she have papers?" Trevor asked.

Jesse shook his head. "If she did, I don't have them, and I'm the one in charge of her now."

There was something his cousin wasn't saying, but Steve

wasn't sure he wanted to know much more. "Just tell me no one's going to come after you for having stolen their *prize-winning* dog."

"I am shocked and dismayed at your lack of trust," Jesse muttered, sniffing the air before flashing a grin. "Well, no, I'm not. But since I'm a bigger man than you, I'll put your mind at ease. I won her in a bet."

"Gambling?" Trevor caught hold of the pup that was now exploring by their boots, picking up the little thing and looking him in the eye. "I don't know you're much of a bargaining chip, tiger, but I suppose you might be worth a buck or two."

Inside the house, the phone rang, and Lee shook his head. "I'd better answer that. It's Mom, Aunt Dana or Auntie Marion. Our moms are the only people who call the landline."

As he vanished inside, Trevor passed the pup in his hands to Steve. "Which reminds me—I left my phone charger here the other day when I had supper with the guys."

"Do you ever eat at your own house?" Steve demanded.

"Not if I can help it." Trevor pushed through the door with his back, his grin lighting his face. "I like to eat. I don't like to cook."

"Bad thing to confess," Steve shouted after his brother. "We'll find a way to make you pay for that."

"I'm shaking in my boots," Trevor called.

Steve turned back to Jesse with a chuckle, the small animal in his arms wiggling in an attempt to rejoin his family until he replaced the pup next to his mom.

She thumped her tail a couple of times, knocking against the wood of the deck. "She's pretty good-natured," he commented. "And I have to admit the pups are damn cute, all feet and big wide eyes."

"They're old enough to wean. So let me know if you want one." Jesse rose to standing, his mischievous grin suddenly gone solemn. "Don't let this get around. The truth is the guys I was playing cards with weren't going to keep them, so I made a big show of wanting to try my hand at training." He made a face. "I don't know what came over me. They're just some dogs."

"Award-winning dogs. Don't forget that part," Steve reminded him. Maybe rescuing the pups didn't make a lot of sense, but it was a generous thing to do, and Steve had no problem encouraging Jesse in that direction.

His cousin had been running hot and cold a lot over the past year. The entertaining and good-natured man was still there, somewhere underneath the cocky, almost impossible arrogance that could show up at times. Steve enjoyed Jesse's company when he wasn't being an ass.

Probably a little like himself, before and after his makeover. Before, selfish asshole. After? Decent human being who looked out for others instead of just himself.

Even as he thought it, another idea struck. "Hey, what are your plans for the bitch?" he asked.

Jesse paused. "It's funny. She's already well trained, and I could use her on the ranch once the puppies are claimed, but..."

It was his turn to scoop up one of the litter, stroking between the ears of the black ball of fur as his eyes got a far-off look to them. Steve shuffled his feet away from the pup that'd crawled over and started chewing on his boots.

"I wasn't kidding around when I said I want to train a pup. My last dog passed away two years ago, and he was kind of my dog and Joel's." Mention of his twin brought a momentary grimace to his face before he pasted on a smile and presented it to Steve. "You interested in the female?"

"Not me. I already got Prince, and there are a couple other dogs on the ranch, but I'm wondering..." He wasn't sure if he should mention the idea to Jesse first, or check with Melody. "I've got a friend who might like her. Can you give me a few days to find out?"

"Not a problem with me. I have to find homes for the rest of the pups, first," Jesse said. "The dog population at the Six Pack ranch is going up rapidly."

It was kind of amusing. "You know these things happen in cycles. Always seems as if we have a lot of dogs around then suddenly the place is empty, and we all start looking for new animals."

They moved the pups and the bitch farther under the eaves, Jesse bringing out a blanket for the box. The pups curled up around their mom. Steve took an extra minute to check her over, but as far as he could tell she seemed sound.

"Hey, Steve. We're going to go grab some burgers in town." Trevor called over his shoulder as he and Lee shot out the front door and went for their trucks. "Maybe hit Traders for a while and shoot some pool. You want to come?"

He was torn, but only for a moment. Over the past half hour he'd figured out exactly where he wanted to be. "You go on without me."

Trevor waved a hand and didn't bother to look back. Jesse took off as well, and Steve headed home for long enough to grab a bag and shove a few things into it, just on the off chance his idea was successful.

The lights were still off at Melody's house, so he drove on past and picked up food at the grocery store. Some of that premade dinner stuff that was far better than anything out of a box.

Then with the bags sitting on the small table outside her door, Steve pulled his guitar from the crew cab and found himself a comfortable spot on the porch to wait for her to come home.

He didn't play as much as he used to. He didn't have dreams

of making it big and heading out to commercial success. He didn't want to play in Nashville—he just enjoyed playing.

And frankly, even that was difficult at times with the wear and tear ranching placed on a man's body. Hands and fingers got rough from the cold, and sometimes in the middle of winter it was impossible for him to play anything, his fingers like thick slabs of unresponsive meat. Trevor teased him for it, but Steve used cream and took care of his hands best he could.

The reward was moments like this, when his brain was rambling too hard to settle in one direction. Better than any drug, a bit of time at the strings, and a kind of blissful calm settled over him.

He picked songs he loved as the sky grew bright, the sun just starting to set behind the mountains. Reflections of brilliant bronze and gold highlighting against the wisps of cloud strung over the sky.

Music calmed him. Soothed his soul.

He was downright mellow by the time a set of lights bounced toward him as Melody's truck approached.

She swung down from the cab, shutting the door firmly before heading his direction. As she drew closer, he put the guitar aside so he could focus on her.

She'd probably worn coveralls for most of the day, so her jeans and T-shirt were mostly clean. But there was dirt on her face and in her blonde hair, her hands scrubbed but with traces of dirt under her nails as she came to a stop in front of him, her expression bemused.

"I thought I told you not to bother coming over."

Steve rose to his feet. Even with shit on her boots and God knows what in her hair, he still thought she was the most beautiful woman he'd ever seen. "I brought supper."

"Oh, God, thank you," she breathed, opening the door with

one hand and offering a tired smile as she gestured him forward. "I was going to have a shower and pass out."

"Sounds like a great plan," Steve teased. "We'll just add a little food to your list."

He placed his guitar to one side before dropping the bags on the countertop. "Go have your shower," he encouraged her. "I'll get things ready."

She hesitated.

"Go," he commanded.

Melody hesitated. "How come you're in my house bossing me around?"

"Because you didn't come over to my house so I could boss you around there. And it's more private here than bossing you around down on Main Street."

She groaned. "Lord, I'm so tired, I'm not going to attempt to figure that one out."

"If you hadn't argued in the first place, you'd already be under the shower," Steve pointed out. He let his gaze drop over her. "Or are you looking for some assistance? I can get you naked damn fast if you want."

She held up a hand in protest. "I can't even think of flirting with you right now."

She certainly wasn't going and doing what she needed to do, either. Steve scooped her up and headed to the bathroom, ignoring her laughter and mock attempts at beating her fists against his chest. "I'm just getting you into the shower," he protested.

Her smile widened as he lowered her to the floor and helped her find her balance, her fingers brushing his chest as she stared at his eyes, passion there in spite of the exhaustion.

"Maybe I should come in with you," he offered. "Help scrub your back. Stop you from falling over, that kind of thing."

Both their stomachs picked that moment to rumble, and she burst out laughing.

"I won't be long, honest." Melody didn't wait until he'd left the room before peeling her T-shirt over her head.

Steve resisted the temptation to join her. He'd barely made it to the hallway when the water turned on, her sigh of exhaustion drifting after him.

Warming up the food in her kitchen was a strange sensation. They'd been together for nearly two years before she'd left. The number of times he'd made a meal for her—he was sure it had happened, but somehow this felt different. More intimate.

Heck, he'd even considered carefully when he bought the food. Not picking his favourites, but trying to remember what would put a smile on her face.

As if there were a giant calendar on the wall, and every day another block was marked off with a bold black X—he only had so much time. Which meant the rest of the evening had to be uniquely Melody-aimed and making-Melody-happy focused.

Changing had taken a lot of work over the past ten months. Proving it would take even more.

11

*M*elody stood in the center of the shower, hoping the water would wash away the cares and worries that had built over the past twelve hours. She was exhausted and furious—not a great combination. Right now she was ready to claw somebody's eyes out, but that wouldn't be a very professional way to react.

The entire crew working Daltons' had been pissed. Most of them were too polite to say much, but she'd heard it. Grumbles and under-the-breath comments she couldn't defend herself from. And of course, having the timing on one job messed up meant the other couple appointments she'd hoped to work into her afternoon schedule also fell through, leaving those ranchers wondering what the heck she was doing.

Back at the office, no one could confirm or deny Sean's claim —the answering machine had already been erased, and if he'd left a voicemail they'd missed, it was gone.

She tilted her face back and let the water beat down on her in punishment. Even the warmth didn't help, though. Her shoulders were rock tight, her fists curling automatically into fists. She had

133

to let the tension go because there was no way to change how the day had gone.

A distraction would have helped. After about two minutes, she expected Steve to make an appearance. His dark-haired head would pop around the door so he could leer at her...

Was it happiness she felt when he listened to her request and didn't show up, or disappointment?

By the time she cranked off the water and wrapped herself in a towel, she was ready to eat an entire cow all by herself. When she opened the door and the scent of cooking wafted in, her mouth watered so hard she nearly choked on it.

"What are you doing and why does my house smell so good?" she called, stepping toward the kitchen. She poked her head around the corner to take in the table set with plates and utensils.

He'd pulled on her frilly apron, and the bright white and yellow flowers tugged an instant laugh from her lips.

Steve glanced up as he placed a casserole dish on the table and pulled off her yellow oven mitts, all the time smiling unselfconsciously. "Hurry and get dressed," he said, waving his fingers. "Or I'll start without you. And I'm hungry enough to eat everything by myself."

Melody shot to her bedroom and jerked on a pair of pajamas, tucking her hair into a ponytail holder so she could race back to the kitchen before he made good on his threat.

He pulled out a chair for her, then they both spent more time scooping food onto their plates and shoveling it in their mouths than being polite to each other. It wasn't until the elastic on her waistband needed to be rearranged that she came up for air.

She glanced across the table to find Steve eyeing her, a satisfied smile stretching his lips.

Oops. "And that was my imitation of 'Melody makes a pig of herself'. Did I get it right?"

Steve waggled his fork. "Trust me, I'm glad there's no security camera in this room recording, because I swear I finished two bites ahead of you. That was a long, tough day."

Melody pulled a face, drawn back to the many things that had gone... Well, not everything had gone wrong, but so much had gone worse than it should have, at least in her estimation.

His comment caught her attention. "Are we really going to talk about what happened during our days like a regular couple?" she teased.

Some of Steve's smile softened. Not that he lost it, but more like he was attempting to be both solemn and reassuring. "You gave me three months, and if you're serious about that deadline, I need to make sure you know I'm serious about you."

Well, now. Melody sat back in her chair and drank the juice he'd poured as she pondered his words. This wasn't the man who'd been thoughtless and uncaring not that long ago.

She liked what she was seeing, and he needed to know. "Do you plan on being this sweet all the time?"

He sat forward and caught her hand in his, playing with her fingers. "Yes. Except, of course, when you don't want me to be sweet."

The wild brow waggle he offered made her giggle.

"Oh, God, don't set me off. I'm tired enough to be giddy."

"Was it that much of a change being in charge? You usually enjoy your work, even when you're busy."

Melody paused, not wanting to go telling tales, but then... It had been her challenge to Steve in the first place regarding their relationship. If she weren't willing to open up and be real about more than what she wanted during sex, they might as well call this entire thing off right now.

She had to trust him with some things to find out if she could trust him a whole lot more.

She pulled her fingers from his and leaned back in her chair, folding her arms as she thought about the best way to word it.

"We had a mix-up in communication at the clinic today, and the result was an utter nightmare. I kept everyone waiting with a herd for over an hour."

That was all the explanation Steve needed. "Lovely. Had a few acres of shit to manoeuver through, did you?"

"I got everything done in the end, but playing catch-up all day is not what I want. That's not the impression I want to make on people, especially since I had a good reputation before I left last fall."

"You have a good reputation now," he assured her.

"Thanks, but today still sucked."

"I hear you."

That was enough dwelling on what made her crazy. It was time to move on. Melody turned and asked brightly. "And you? What was earth-shattering and unique about your day?"

He got such a serious look she wondered if something terrible had happened, but it appeared he was only choosing his words. "You know when I rescued you at the side of the road?"

"You didn't rescue me."

"Did too."

Melody smiled. "Dreamer."

Steve moved his chair around so he could be next to her, catching hold of her hand again as if he were put out she'd escaped him earlier. "I was surprised you had Lady in the truck. It made much more sense when I found out she was going to the Seniors' Home."

Interesting. "Why?"

His shoulders eased in a shrug. "She didn't seem like the kind of dog you'd talked about wanting. I know you have to be careful since you're always visiting different places, but in case you're interested, looks like Jesse found a well-trained German shepherd today."

"Found?"

He hurried to reassure her. "More like acquired, and I didn't get a chance to put her through her paces or anything, but Jesse swears she's supposed to be a quality animal."

Melody was unsure where this was going. "Does he need me to come over and check her out?"

Steve gave a reluctant smile. "I'm doing this badly. What I meant to say is the dog is fine, the litter she had recently is fine, but Jesse's looking for a new owner for the female. If you're interested, she might be a good match for you."

Melody waited, because it seemed he still had something to say.

He rose to his feet and tugged her toward the living room. "It's not comfortable at the table," he complained. "You're too far away."

Melody laughed. "I was all of five inches from you."

Steve made it clear that five inches was definitely too far as he settled on the couch and caught hold of her waist, tugging so she lost her balance and tumbled into his lap.

Instinctively she grasped him around the neck, her new position not at all unwelcome. "Well, now. Hi there."

Steve bumped their noses together, but to her surprise, went right back into their previous conversation. "I know with you starting up the extra job hours, you won't have time to train a pup. But if you're interested in a good, quality dog, getting one that's more grown would mean you don't have to wait as long. And any training you need to do is easier in the summer, anyway."

He was surprising her left and right tonight. "You've given this some thought, haven't you?"

The most adorable grin shone back at her. "I think it shows more because I was such a blasted fool before. Any time I do something halfway civil, you make a comment about it."

Melody stroked her hand over his cheek, his five o'clock

shadow growing thicker as the day faded into evening. "I hope you don't mind. I like pointing out when you're not being a jackass far more than when you are being one."

And then because it seemed the right thing to do, she slipped her hands behind his neck and tugged him toward her, pressing their mouths together for a sweet, tender kiss.

～

THIS WASN'T why he had come, but hell if he would turn down a chance at Melody's lips.

It felt so right to have her in his arms. The flaming-hot sex they'd shared was wonderful, but he wanted it all. He wanted to experience more with her. Ease her frustrations, share her joys. Every thing that made her so amazing.

He focused on her in his arms, her smooth curves covered by a thin layer of soft cotton, hips resting in his lap, her chest pressed to his as she hummed in approval at his kiss.

She'd wanted things hard and wild the other day, but now wasn't about that kind of excitement. Instead he nibbled on her lips, teasing his tongue along the surface before biting gently. Soothing the nip with another kiss, and another.

Her fingers played in the hair at the back of his neck, and he let his hands roam over her curves, feeling the strength in her arms and the power in her petite torso. The softness of her skin and whatever she'd used in her hair sent his senses reeling—a damn fine aphrodisiac under any circumstances.

He wrapped his fingers around her ponytail and tugged, separating their lips so he could speak against her. "Tell me what you want. Tell me what you *need*."

Melody rested their foreheads together. "Play for me."

Another one of those inescapable chuckles burst free.

"Anything you want in this world—as dirty as you want me to get —and you choose guitar music?"

Her eyes lit up. "I know your playing caused some trouble between us before, like when you'd get lost in your music and forget the time. But I do like listening to you. I've always wished I could play, and you've got talent."

Talent hadn't been enough—not for what was really important. He shifted them apart. "Okay, if that's your request." He eyed the clock as he got to his feet to fetch his guitar. "Are you ready to hit the sack?"

Melody nodded. "Let me brush my teeth and crawl into bed?"

She went one way, he went the other.

Another first—tucking her into bed without fooling around. Steve grabbed his guitar while he waited for her. As strange as it seemed, it was right. Melody was half-asleep on her feet by the time she crawled onto the mattress next to him, dropping the light quilt over herself and resting her head on the pillows he'd fluffed up.

"Any requests?"

She covered a yawn. "No, just something laid-back."

Steve let his fingers drift over the strings as she settled in, her beautiful eyes staring upward as she listened.

He played and sang one of her favourites, and followed it with another until her eyes closed and her breathing settled.

And then he played one more without singing the words because he couldn't bear to leave the room, stroking the guitar gently and trying to let a bit of what he hoped for come out in the song.

When he came to the end, quiet wrapped around them like warmth. Her breathing even in the stillness, the faint moonlight shining down to turn her into a pagan goddess. He went to stand, but her hand dropped on his thigh and held him back. Her lips curled into a smile, her eyes open just a crack.

"Put your guitar down," she whispered.

He laid it aside and stretched out on the mattress, letting her caress his face and shoulders, all tension long since escaped from her body.

"Being serenaded is better than a four-hour bubble bath," she said with a satisfied sigh. "I'm so relaxed."

"Good, although if this were a bubble bath, you'd be naked. I would have enjoyed that."

"If I'm naked, you're naked."

"Hmm." He shook his head. "That doesn't sound familiar."

"It's a new rule. From now on, you need to be naked when you play guitar for me," she teased.

"Like that's going to happen."

"I'll go first," she offered.

The edge of the quilt rolled down, and she tugged at her shirt. Steve willingly helped her strip it over her head, pushing aside her hands when she reached for his buckle. "You're nearly asleep."

"I'm all wide awake now," she insisted. "Steve Coleman, you are one fine man."

He pressed his lips to her temple, easing back beside her as he stroked the hair off her face. "I see you need to be tucked in the rest of the way."

She looked confused for a moment, but her secretive smile remained as he stroked a hand down her body, not lingering anywhere, but enjoying a brief contact with her breast, sliding over her waist, and the swell of her hip. Then he slipped his hand over her pussy and held her. Her lashes fluttered and her breathing hitched before settling.

He moved slowly, wanting her to stay relaxed, easing her like a skittish animal. By the time he slipped his hand underneath her pajama bottoms and slid his fingers through her folds, she damn near purred.

Tiny strokes, back and forth, playing with her clit until the pulse visible at the base of her throat throbbed. Still he didn't change what he was doing. Just gave to her carefully. Tenderly.

Her breathing picked up, a low gasp of pleasure escaping as she twitched against him, turning her head to the side and pressing her face into his chest. Under his hand her hips jerked, moving into his touch as she clutched him.

Absolutely mesmerizing. He was hard and aching, but so damn willing to shove aside his need because he needed this even more. Making her day a hell of a lot better than it had been a few hours earlier? This sensation in his gut, the one that made him feel a million miles tall—

That was what had been missing in their relationship before. And now that he'd experienced it? He never wanted it to stop.

Melody kissed him back when he lifted her chin with a finger, falling asleep between one breath and the next. Her eyes stayed closed, a smile on her lips, and then she was out, solid as a rock. Unmoving as he crawled off the bed and rearranged the covers over her.

He cleaned up quietly then headed home, leaving a note on the table for her to call him when she could. His cock might be aching, and his bed damn lonely, but it had been worth it.

12

The week rushed past faster than Melody expected. After the hellish start, work turned around and offered her moments of pure joy. Melody savoured every one of them, from the contented look on an animal's face after she'd helped ease their pain, to the grudging acknowledgment of a job well-done from a few of the old-timers who'd reluctantly called her out.

What she hadn't managed was more time with Steve, which was par for the course with everything that had been going on, but still made her pause.

He'd gone out of his way to be there for her after her disastrous Monday, but she was too damn tired at the end of most days to get together.

Tonight she swore it would be different, or sooner if possible. One of the best parts of her job was her work often brought her in contact with her friends during the course of the day.

The next couple tasks on her list were on Coleman land. She slipped from her truck, grinning a welcome as Allison came out of the house to greet her, a loose T-shirt hanging over her jeans.

"You're a couple months early if you're looking for fresh mutton."

"And here I thought I'd need to convince you they weren't pets," Melody teased. She glanced around the yard for a moment, admiring the changes. She had been here only a few days earlier, but then she'd been focused on the social gathering that evening, and on Steve, and not really paying attention to the land. "You guys are doing a great job."

"We are," Allison agreed before she shook a finger at Melody. "But don't distract me. I'm mad at you. I know I can't go out drinking right now, but I want to see more of you."

"It's been less than a week since the barbecue," Melody protested.

"That's no excuse."

So instead of heading straight toward the barn where she saw Gabe, she changed direction and went and hugged her friend close. "I'm not avoiding you on purpose," she said. "I'm just excited and overwhelmed at the same time, keeping up with everything while Mathis is gone."

No need to explain in any more detail. Allison gestured to where Gabe was waiting. "Come on, I'll walk up with you."

All around them the land had turned the vivid green of summer, and there were contented-looking sheep scattered over the nearest hillside. "Looks as if your diversification plans are going well."

"We've got cattle on the far fields, and while transitioning the herd is still moving slowly, the sheep are fully certified," Allison reported. "This portion of the Coleman ranch is closer than ever to organic status."

There were more healthy-looking sheep waiting behind the corral fencing as they approached, and Melody smiled as she extended a hand to Gabe. "Those animals don't need a vet. You're going to put me out of a job," she protested.

"You know it." He winked. "You want to head inside and check the new breeders we purchased? I'll be in in a minute."

It was cooler in the barn, and a lot darker, and for a moment she stopped, Allison at her side, as they blinked hard to get their eyes to adjust.

Soft masculine laughter drifted over. "You look like owls," someone teased.

She twisted to the side and discovered Gabe's younger brother standing with a rake in hand, blond hair tucked under a cap and a hesitant smile on his lips.

"*Whooooo*," she said mischievously.

Rafe's smile bloomed, and his face transformed. High cheekbones and square cut jaw revealed a shadow of the handsome man he'd be once he put on a few more years. Now he was good looking, with a few cuts and scrapes adding to his appeal.

All of them had that Coleman cast to their features. Melody smiled back as she considered the differences between the youngest in the clan and Steve.

"Good to see you again, Rafael."

He offered a quick nod then turned away, striding toward the darker recesses of the barn. She bit back her amusement. There was something she'd never expected. A shy Coleman?

Allison stepped close enough to whisper, "I think he's got a crush on you. He was watching you most of the barbeque when Steve wasn't looking."

Oh dear. "Well, that's...sweet."

No way she would let the boy know how hilarious she found this idea. Not because Rafael wasn't attractive, but because she simply didn't need any more trouble on her plate, and having more than one Coleman vying for her hand would be trouble with a capital T.

She went to work, Allison chatting for a short while before

taking off to go help her siblings at the family restaurant they co-owned. That left Melody with the Angel Coleman boys, which was fine by her. They worked slowly but efficiently through the animals, taking a quick break at the house for lunch.

Melody got back to the barn before the boys did, headed into the pens to finish the last of her tasks.

She'd been working for about thirty minutes, enjoying the calm of the barn. The only noises the shuffling of the sheep's feet and their low bleats. So when a gruff voice startled her from her intense concentration, she just about jumped out of her skin.

"What the hell are you doing in there?"

She gripped the sheep under her hands solidly to stop it from escaping after being spooked by his loud question. Melody glanced up to find Ben Coleman glaring at her.

"Afternoon. I'm here on a vet visit," she reminded him. "Your son contacted me."

If anything that made him glare harder. "Bullshit."

Wow. She might have had issues the other day with Dalton, but this was beyond the typical response. Melody rose to her feet, brushing her hands on her jeans as she made her way cautiously toward the gate and left the pen. She extended a hand in the hopes of turning around his attitude. "We've met before. Last year I was out when Mathis was checking—"

"Where's he?" Ben interrupted.

Melody fixed her smile in place, reciting the now familiar words. "Mathis is on vacation. I'm filling in for him, and—"

A stream of curses interrupted her, low and vehement, and far more in-her-face rude than any of the previous ranchers had been. Melody stumbled backwards as Ben crowded forward.

"Dad."

Rafael stepped between them, the young man casually leaning the rake in his hand toward his father to halt his progress.

Ben jerked to a stop. He blinked, then twirled on his heel and stomped from the barn.

Melody stared at his retreating back, and the broad shoulders of the young man standing before her, and wondered what the heck had just happened.

"Are you okay?" she asked.

Rafe twisted on the spot, an unreadable expression on his face. "Of course." He cleared his throat then motioned back toward the pen she'd left. "Are you done with them?"

So they were going to pretend nothing strange had happened. Fine. Melody knew the rules. "I'm done everything here, unless you have other animals I need to check somewhere else on the ranch."

Rafael shook his head. "Just whatever Gabe contacted you about."

They were silent as he walked her back to the truck, because there wasn't really anything she could discuss with him.

All she knew for sure was walking off the Angel Coleman land and onto the Moonshine section was like moving from a very solemn event to a daycare.

Trevor and Lee greeted her with loud whoops as they waved from the backs of their horses, headed for the rails to dismount and tie up the animals. Dogs barked as they raced underfoot, and the herd of horses shuffled excitedly behind the railing as they were funneled toward the barn.

She raised a hand to wave back when a lariat dropped over her shoulders and tightened around her torso.

"Looks like I caught myself the nicest filly in the batch," Steve teased as he pulled her toward him and planted a lusty kiss on her lips before setting her free.

"Bad boy," Melody warned, glancing around to see if anyone had noticed his public display of affection.

Steve stepped in closer. He lifted her chin with his fingers. "Are you trying to hide?"

She hesitated. "Not really. I mean, I just want to be as professional as possible."

His I'm-sexy-and-I-know-it grin was firmly back in place. "Who says it's not professional to lay one on me?"

Trevor paced by and caught wind of their conversation. "Is Melody passing out kisses? Because, hell yeah, I'm in the lineup for that."

Steve ducked past her and lunged at his brother, laughter rising from both of them as she rotated on the spot to watch their hijinks. Steve's dog, Prince, sauntered over to greet her, and Melody bent to brush a hand over his ears.

"It doesn't matter how old they get, I doubt they'll ever grow up." Kate Coleman stood beside her, her long hair pulled back into a serviceable braid as she smiled at Melody. "Good to see you again."

This woman was one of the reasons Melody had been extra pissed off at Steve a year ago. Breaking up with him made it awkward to stay in touch with anyone in his family, and Kate made her long for all sorts of family-like things she tried not to dwell on. "It's good to see you too."

Kate watched her boys for a moment before shaking her head and motioning toward the yard. "Let them catch up with us. I'll show you where we need to go."

Melody searched the area as they walked side by side toward the horses. "Where's Mr. Coleman?"

There was a beat before Kate answered. "He's not feeling well, so he's traded some chores with me."

Made sense to Melody. "Then let's get to it."

With the three boys and Kate chipping in, her job was over in no time. When they were finished, Lee and Trevor took off on their horses, headed for another part of the ranch and the rest of their work.

Kate planted her hands on her hips and stared directly at Melody. "Now, you stop by again before we call you out to do your vet thing. You know you can join us anytime."

The welcome made her feel warm inside, and Melody smiled. "Thank you."

Kate headed back to the house, and Melody was ready to hit her truck when Steve caught her by the hand. "I need you to look at something for me."

Melody glanced around, positive she had finished checking the herd. "Do you have more in another sector?"

Steve didn't answer, just pulled her along. "Come on, I'll show you."

She went with him willingly, around the side of the barn to where his truck and a horse trailer waited. He helped her into the driver side and she slid into the middle seat, checking her watch to make sure she didn't get too far behind schedule. No way did she want another repeat of her hellish Monday. "I've got thirty minutes tops, otherwise I need to phone the clinic and let them know I'll be late."

"You won't be late," he promised.

They rattled down a short side road but instead of turning toward the highway, Steve took them along a back trail that led through the trees into a clearing at the side of wide-open ranch land. Nothing lay before them but miles of low rolling hills. To the west, the Rocky Mountains rose above to the sky, the craggy peaks decorated with a tiny dusting of white in the highest cracks and crannies. The tree line broke off to expose granite greys and flashes of white quartz.

It was an amazing view, and she was glad it was something she got to see every day of her life.

She was still staring in admiration when Steve parked the truck and jerked open the door.

Melody followed him out, but couldn't see any signs of an animal that needed attention. "Do you want me to be a veterinarian to the squirrels?" she teased.

He whirled, catching her under the hips and pulling her against his body so he could kiss her fiercely. Her back pressed against the cold metal of the horse trailer as his overheated body met hers.

"You're driving me crazy," he confessed when he finally let her breathe. "I've been aching to touch you since the weekend. I need to be inside you."

Melody didn't have the words to protest, especially not when he put his lips to her neck and sucked. A flash of heat went from his mouth through her entire system, and she clutched his shoulders.

She was in motion again, this time her feet on the ground as his hands scrambled at her belt buckle. "I want you right now," he demanded.

The clock was ticking, but his hands were doing incredible things even as Melody tried to make the right decision. "Oh, God. Here? You're not serious, Steve, right out in the open—?"

He shoved her jeans down to her ankles. He stripped off his shirt, dropping it on top of the wheel guard of the trailer while she stood, pants around her ankles, admiring the broad bands of muscles on his torso.

Then she was on top of his shirt, her knees spread wide as he pulled her forward to his eager mouth. Her ankles were trapped together by her pants, but Steve didn't seem to care.

Melody shoved her hands into his hair to catch her balance, but there was no catching her breath as he ate greedily. His tongue danced over her clit until she was gasping, the sound loud in contrast to the wind in the trees behind them. Everything that had to be done that day vanished as her world closed on this time, this place.

This man—

The one sending her reeling toward an orgasm. Melody smiled and took the ride.

~

IT WAS as if everything he'd ever kept hidden inside could no longer be contained. Steve relished being able to touch and taste. The last hour had been a challenge. He'd wanted nothing more than to crowd her against a wall and take her right there.

He stripped away her pants, lifting her knees in the air until she was wide open to his touch. With her death grip on his hair, neither of them was moving too far apart, but now he slowed, teasing the tip of his tongue over her clit and listening as her muted curses rose in volume.

"Jeez, Melody. So fucking delicious. Come on my tongue. I'll fuck you hard once you've come."

He slipped her feet onto his shoulders, admiring the perfect positioning that allowed him to lick along one side of her folds and down the other. Thrusting his tongue as deep as possible. He paused to wet his fingers, getting them slippery so when he placed the tips to her sex and pushed in, a happy groan escaped her. In the brief moment he watched her face, all he saw was pleasure.

Then he was busy with his mouth on her pussy, lapping and licking and driving her wild as she squirmed under his touch. With two fingers buried deep in her body, he pumped slowly, focusing on the sensitive spot of her clit with his lips until her fingers tightened, pulling his hair as her body clamped down on his fingers, her moan of pleasure floating toward the trees.

A second later he was on his feet, his jeans unzipped and

cock in hand. He didn't bother with any of the niceties other than lining up and pushing deep. Hot-white pleasure surrounded him as her pussy squeezed the daylights out of his cock.

"Oh my word," Melody whispered. "You feel twice as big as usual."

He couldn't stop his grin from widening. "Way to stroke my ego, sweetheart."

Then he caught her around the waist and lifted her in the air, moving away from the wheel well so he could push her back against the metal trailer and thrust up hard.

A gasp escaped her, air brushing past his ear as she caught her hands around his shoulders and clung on tight. Her ankles were locked at the small of his back as she used her legs to help him drive in deep.

"Look at us. Look where we are," Steve demanded, one hand catching her chin and lifting until their eyes met. He held her there so he could stare into endless pale-blue pools as he drove his hips forward. "You wanted our sex lives to get more exciting, and for me to give you new experiences. How's this?"

No need to wait for an answer, because he already knew she liked it. Oh hell, yeah, she liked it a lot.

At least that's what her nails digging into his shoulders told him. And the small noises that escaped her lips in an endless stream. Nothing sophisticated, nothing planned. Just raw pleasure and straight-out fucking, and it was very good.

"*Yes*," Melody cried, her nails leaving furrows in his skin in spite of the awkward angle.

He switched position enough to support her on one hand while he slipped his other between them, rubbing his fingers over her clit as he increased the pace.

The wind picked up in the trees creating a rushing sound, almost like applause as stars floated in front of his eyes. He was seconds away from coming, but damn if he would lose control before she found release.

He placed his lips near her ear. "Let go when you're ready," he coaxed. "And get ready, because I'm going to fuck the daylights out of you. The next place you stop, you're going to have to take your time getting out of the truck. Not only because I fucked you silly, but because my come is gonna slip from you, and you'll feel it, and you're going to remember this moment. And *this* one. *Me*, inside of *you*, and us both *losing* our fucking *minds*."

Steve emphasized every other word with a thrust of his hips. Low feral noises escaped her on every breath until he was out of time and he was one pulse away from...

"Oh, yes, that's... *Yesssss*."

Melody's forehead hit his chest as she shuddered against the trailer. Steve drove forward once more, pinning her to the wall like some twisted sexual tableau, his cock jerking hard as his seed shot into her. They stayed there, locked in position, pleasure drifting around them like an intoxicating mist. He couldn't see, his head was spinning so hard, and it was only the fact that his knees were locked that kept him from plunging to the ground.

She gasped for air. "Sweet Jesus, what have you done to me?"

Steve let a chuckle escape as he rotated them, his legs giving out as he collapsed onto the makeshift seat of the wheel well. "I'll tell you as soon as I can think. I don't have any blood north of my waistline right now."

Melody wiggled her legs to a more comfortable position, still speared on his cock. She looked up at him, absolute delight on her face. "That was a surprise."

"A nice surprise?"

Her cheeks flushed brighter. "Damn you for talking about your come leaking down my legs. I'm going to die of embarrassment if that happens."

"That would make it tough to keep dating if one of us bit it during or after sex." He leaned in closer and offered her a satisfied smile. "I'll stop short of that. I'll only make you pass out with pleasure, deal?"

Satisfaction was written all over her as he lifted her and they found their clothing.

She drove off with five minutes remaining on her thirty-minute window, Steve grinning like a fool as he watched her go.

13

She barely made it through the door of the clinic before Tom shoved paperwork under her nose.

"Are you trying to put us out of business?" he demanded.

Her jaw ached from clenching every time she was around the man. She got it, she really did. Tom was pissed off, and she seemed to be the cause of his disappointment.

That made her his first target. But when she added in everything else she had to deal with, her patience with his childish behaviour was rapidly fading, and it had only been a week since Mathis took off.

She pulled it together, brushing past him and speaking as politely as possible. "Let me change my shoes, and I'll look at whatever is causing the trouble."

Tom whirled on his heel and stalked back into the office.

Callie appeared in the doorway between the front waiting room where they greeted small-animal patients and the back of the clinic. Her gaze met Melody's, and she wrinkled her nose in sympathy. "He's been in a foul mood all morning," she warned.

Melody didn't give a shit. Mathis had put her in charge, and while she'd do what was possible to keep staff morale high, she wasn't catering to Tom's whims to keep him happy.

She put on a pair of runners and grabbed a coffee before heading into the office. "What's up?

Tom glared harder. "What the hell were you pumping into the cattle the other day? Gold?"

He shoved the clipboard across the desk so hard it slammed into her legs, and she had to scramble to catch it. A quick glance showed it was the invoice sheet she'd authorized Callie to put together for Sean Dalton. "What's the problem? Did you find a mistake in the math?"

"You know damn well the computer program does all of the calculating," he snapped. "It's the initial cost of the inoculation." His eyes narrowed in suspicion. "If I find out you've been padding the bills and pocketing the money..."

Oh, hell no. Melody was not putting up with that baloney. "Don't start with me. If that's a straight-up accusation, you go right ahead, but I will not stand for—"

Tom tapped the bill as he interrupted. "The last time I did inoculations, they were a good sixty cents cheaper per animal."

"They probably were, because you used last year's methods. There's been an update, and we can provide three things at the same time." She spun the clipboard around and pushed it back toward him, drawing a finger along the fine line that showed the contents of the shots.

"And that's just as effective?" Tom grumbled for a moment, settling back in his chair, most of his bluster fading away. "I suppose it is. You learn that this last year at school?"

"Partly. Plus I got some advanced papers from one of my profs and I've been in contact with the company producing the drugs." She didn't want to be nice, especially after he'd been a complete jackass, but she was in charge, and Mathis would expect her to try to get along. "I can send you the article if you want to read it."

All she got was a grunt.

For Mathis. She pointed at the columns in the ledger. "It does look more expensive than last year, I agree."

"There's no way any of these ranchers want to spend more money, especially when you start adding it up per head."

Tom was back to complaining, and Melody wasn't sure she could keep smiling for much longer. Trying to explain anything to a person who didn't want to listen in the first place was tough enough. Add in that she suspected he had limited mathematical skills...

Still, she tried.

"It does add up, but in the long run it's cheaper because they don't have to get us out as many times and pay our visitation fee. It's just the initial cost that seems high. And you're right, it could be a shock the first time, which is why we need to make sure before we go out that the information is there."

"But Sean Dalton didn't know ahead of time, did he?"

He would have, in a perfect world, but of course with everything else that had gone wrong that day, Melody had completely forgotten to point out she was using a new method along with all the benefits. "We send a note along with the bill. Explain this means one less visit from us over the year. You know with these ranchers it's the bottom line that counts."

Tom made another noise before pulling out some other paperwork and ignoring her altogether, and that seemed to be the end of the conversation. Fine by Melody, because she didn't want to talk to him anymore either.

She stepped to the front desk to grab the roster for the afternoon.

"Melody," someone exclaimed, the summons accompanied by a gentle woof.

Lady was too well trained to lurch at Melody, but her tail wagged rapidly as she sat at attention at the feet of Susan Paule, head administrator of the Rocky Mountain Seniors' Home.

"Oh, hey. Good to see you both." Melody walked around the desk, squatting to pet Lady. "How's she been doing?"

She checked the dog quickly as Susan hurried to assure her. "Wonderfully. I brought her in for her booster shots like you mentioned I should after we got her registered."

Right. She'd forgotten it would be this soon. Melody brushed a hand over Lady's furry body. "She looks happy."

"I think she is. And she fits in beautifully at the home. Thank you so much for bringing her to us—the residents love her." Susan rose to her feet along with Melody, leaning around to speak to Callie at the front desk. "Is it okay if Melody does Lady's checkup?"

"Oh, I'm sorry, I don't have time," Melody protested. "I just stopped at the clinic for a minute to grab some materials, and I need to get back out into the field."

Susan smiled. "Well, anytime you want to come for a visit, you're always welcome."

A small hand caught hold of Melody's wrist and tugged. She looked down into dark brown eyes of one of the younger residents of Rocky Mountain House. She scrambled to remember his name.

His chin quivered. "You're not going to look at Hopper?"

She glanced into the waiting-room area where his three smaller siblings were lined up in chairs, each with a rabbit in their lap. For the first time that day, her smile was genuine. "What a lovely-looking family of bunnies. But no, I won't be checking them today because I have some cows that asked me to visit them first. Dr. Tom will take care of you and your pets."

The little guy made a face then nodded and went back to his seat.

The warning alarm she'd set on her watch went off, counting down to her next appointment. Melody gave the kids and Susan a final wave, grabbed the information needed for the afternoon from Callie, and headed back to prepare the medications she needed to take with her.

She ignored Tom who stood in the open door of the office, staring into the lobby, his expression unreadable.

Grumpy bastard. Hopefully he wasn't planning on being an ass the entire time Mathis was out of town.

Fortunately for her, one of her afternoon stops was back at the Moonshine Coleman ranch. She followed the directions she'd been given that led her to a small outbuilding with a neat fence enclosure. Steve moved toward her, his grey T-shirt encasing muscles that simply wouldn't quit, and she found herself heating up just watching him saunter closer. She hurried out the door so she didn't miss a moment of admiring the way his biceps bulged the fabric of his sleeves, his thigh muscles tight to the faded jeans wrapped around his legs.

Every inch mouthwatering delicious. Nope, she'd never had an issue with the packaging, and the treatment she'd gotten over the past week and a bit had been a heck of a lot more mature than she remembered.

As he drew closer, her gaze drifted up and met his eyes. Dark and intoxicating. So addictive she couldn't look away.

He wrapped his arms around her and lifted her off the ground as if she weighed nothing, kissing her firmly before breaking it off and offering a steamy grin. "Hey, lady. You want to come for a ride with me?"

One of his exaggerated leers followed, and she laughed. "I don't see any horses," she teased.

"Now if that's not an invitation to start singing 'Save A Horse', I don't know what is."

He'd already started humming the tune as she pushed on his

shoulders to get him to release her. "You're a bad boy. No singing or riding right now. And you need to put me down."

He lowered her, backing up only a few inches instead of a few feet like she'd hoped. "Sweetheart, you keep that complaining up, and I'll think you're shy or something."

"It's not that," Melody insisted, glancing around to see if any of his brothers were about to pop out of the woodwork. "I told you before, it's not professional for you to be kissing and hugging me in public."

Steve paused as if thinking it through then shook his head. "Nope. I can't wrap my brain around that one. You'll have to explain it a little more thoroughly."

She rolled her eyes. "Look, you never offered to kiss Mathis when he showed up to take care of your animals."

He laughed. "No, but that's because I don't swing that way. If he were ten years younger and I had a thing for guys, maybe. He's not a bad fellow overall, but that has nothing to do with me giving you a kiss when I see you."

"It has everything to do with you not kissing me when you see me," she insisted.

"Now let me take a hard think on this." Steve narrowed his eyes and counted off on his fingers. "Considering the people I know and respect the most, seems when my mom and dad meet it doesn't matter what they've been doing or how long they've been apart, I always see him give her a peck. Same goes for my Uncle Mike and Aunt Marion. And I won't tell you what shenanigans go on any time Travis meets up with one of his partners."

"But that's different. They're not datin—" Melody slammed her lips together as his expression changed from joking to far more serious.

"Ah, you're making some smartass comment about the fact they've been together for a long time, and we haven't." He gave her a stern glare. "In fact, when it comes down to it, you and I have been together longer then Travis has with his partners."

Melody shifted uncomfortably from side to side. "Okay, maybe it's just me, but I feel as if public displays of affection are something I should avoid. I'm having enough trouble since Mathis left convincing people I'm competent at my job, I don't need to have them focusing on the horrid, terrible fact that I'm a —*gasp*—woman."

One brow rose as Steve started at her toes and examined every inch of her, lingering on her breasts long enough to make her want to squirm. No matter how much she tried to avoid it, the obvious pleasure on his face sent tingles racing through her.

He finally looked her in the eye again, a happy grin breaking free. "They'd have to be blind and stupid to not be aware that you're a woman. I don't think me giving you a kiss is going to change that."

"Doesn't mean I want to rub it in their faces."

He caved slightly. "What about a compromise?"

Her lips twisted. "If you're about to suggest kisses with no tongue, I don't think that's a big enough compromise."

"How about for every orgasm I give you, you owe me one kiss in public."

Damn, he got her attention with that one. The temptation to accept was there, but mostly because he was too charming in this mood to resist. Still, she clung to common sense. "Steve, this isn't a good idea."

"You don't like orgasms? Strange. I could have thought differently, what with all the screaming *yes, yes, yes* that was going on the last time we fooled around."

True on that one. Melody caught hold of the front of his shirt, twisting her hands in the fabric and tugging hard. He willingly bent until their eyes were on the same level.

"Hell if I can say no to you," Melody complained. She stuck

her finger in his face. "But you started this rash plan, and I'm holding you to it. One kiss for every orgasm, no more, and we start counting now."

"That seems unfair," Steve teased. "I don't even get credit for one kiss after last week?"

Melody let go of his shirt and smoothed the fabric, enjoying running her hands over his body far too much. "Well, I suppose I'll give you credit for *one* kiss."

Steve cupped her chin in his hand and tilted her head back, moving in close. Anticipation rose, but instead of pressing their lips together, he brushed his thumb over her lower lip. "One kiss on file, it is. I'll be sure to redeem it as soon as I'm ready."

Her sheer disappointment must have shown, but at the same time, it was fun to not be able to guess what was coming next. It added something to their relationship, and it made her warm inside.

That's when it struck—this was about her contributions as well. So far, Steve had been incredible. In fact he'd been the one who'd gone out of his way to deal with her schedule and issues.

If this was going to work, *really* work, she needed to give as well. Maybe Steve needed a little knocking off balance. A little giving to...

"Where's my patient?" she asked as ideas raced through her brain.

He tilted his head toward the small lean-to. "In the corral."

~

It didn't take long for Melody to finish her work, and Steve was about to escort her back to her truck when she paused, stretching her arms above her head.

Irresistible temptation. He took a slow perusal from top to bottom all over again, thrilled he was allowed to not only admire from a distance, but had the privilege of getting up close and personal as well. His life was damn fine these days—as long as she was feeling the same way about him.

Only the expression she turned on him didn't make for an easy answer. Something in her eyes made him pause. "What's up, sweetheart?"

Melody took a look around, head tilted to one side. "Where's the rest of the family?"

"Back at the ranch house or the barns, and Lee is in the southwest fields." He offered her a grin. "Technically, I can kiss you without it costing me anything. We're definitely not in public."

She hummed. "I had something else in mind."

"Why does that sound dirty? Or am I being hopeful?"

"Oh, you're being hopeful, but sometimes even optimists get Christmas in July." She caught him by the hand and pulled him toward the lean-to, directing him until he was leaning against the rough wooden boards.

"Now who's being bossy?" he asked, smirking at her determined expression, his body reacting in interest at the sexual innuendo. If she wanted to do something raunchy, he was all for it.

Melody pressed one palm against his chest as if she were locking him in place. "Tell me now if you don't want me to have my wicked way with you."

"First, I'm not stupid, and second I'm not a liar." He wasn't quite sure what was going on, but hell if he wanted her to stop. "I'm at your mercy."

Famous last words. Whatever had lit a fire under her, Melody was red-hot and willing to burn.

"You don't mind if I do a little exploring, do you?" Her hands were on his T-shirt, lifting it upward to expose his abdomen and chest. Another happy sound escaped her as she traced her fingers over his stomach muscles. "You are so gorgeous."

She leaned forward and slid her tongue along the ridges of his abdomen, and his body was alert and reacting. His cock had gone hard, crowding the front of his jeans as he willed her hands lower to set him free.

He could've wished for the moon. Instead of giving him breathing room, she stole his mind for the next ten minutes, kissing her way up his torso, sliding her fingers over his nipples before licking and using her teeth.

Her hands and nails moved constantly, teasing and scratching and making him mad with desire until he had to grit his teeth and press his palms to the wooden wall behind him. It was the only way to keep from catching hold of her and changing her agenda to one that matched the speed he'd like to go. Hard. Fast.

Right fucking *now*.

She paused, tilting her head back to gaze at him, mischief dancing in her eyes. "You doing okay?" she asked.

"Just peachy," he lied, his hips pulsing forward involuntarily as her hands grazed his belly.

"That's good." One hundred percent trouble in her attitude. "Because I'd hate to have you suffering. You've been so kind and generous taking care of me, I thought maybe I should return the favour."

He shouldn't have let images of her lips wrapped around his cock leap to mind. It only made the waiting more unbearable.

"You want to be in charge?" he double-checked, just on the off chance he'd misunderstood her.

She dashed his hopes. "Oh, I'm totally in charge."

This time. Only this time, and thank God that meant she was finally undoing his buckle and zipper, pulling his cock free and wrapping her fingers around the shaft as she squeezed expertly.

"Please tell me you intend to get me off."

If she wanted him to beg, at this point he had no objections. He'd get revenge for it later, but right now his vision blurred as she moved her hand with enough pressure to set him trembling.

"I'll get you off," she promised.

And before he could ask any more questions, she lowered herself to the ground, sliding to her knees between his legs as she tugged his jeans and boxers to his thighs. His erection snapped upright, its hard length hitting his belly. When he looked down, his cock rose as the lone barrier between them.

A drop of fluid already clung to the head, and she leaned forward, her tongue darting out to lap it up. The movement was kitten soft and irresistibly sexy. He wanted to close his eyes to enjoy every sensation more fully. He needed to keep his eyes open to admire every move she made as she explored.

Melody tilted her head back and smiled seductively as she licked her lips, and a shiver of lust tore through him.

"Take me in your mouth," he demanded, threading his fingers through her hair and bringing her closer.

"Hmm, in time." She lapped at the head of his cock, tormenting him with the promise of more. She licked along the underside of his cock, the heat of her mouth burning him, slick moisture coating him and drawing his balls tight to his body. Melody soaked him enthusiastically before adjusting her stance.

She tugged at his hips, and he followed her command, standing away from the wall. Scalding heat covered him as Melody engulfed his cock, her fingers digging into his ass cheeks as she controlled the speed, the depth. The girth of his erection stretching her lips as she pressed her nose closer to his groin.

She drew back slowly, applying wicked suction, and he throbbed in the best way possible. Maybe throbbed a tad too much.

"Hell, *yeah*. So frickin' good." Steve tightened his thigh and ass muscles in an attempt to fight the urgent need to thrust. She worked him over as if this blowjob was the best thing in her entire world, and nothing was going to distract her from her task.

Everything about her turned him on. Everything she did drove him to the breaking point. His body was screaming for him to catch her up off her knees and find a flat surface to lay her on.

She slid down his length, taking him all the way to the back of her throat, and in spite of her barely having touched him, Steve couldn't hold back any longer.

"Fuck." He caught her head in his hands and pried her off his cock, snatched her up and stomped all of four feet to the rail fence surrounding the corral. "Hold the top rail and stand on the bottom one," he ordered.

She followed his instructions as he undid her pants, jerking them past her knees. "Steve, I was going to—"

He caught her hips and jerked them backward, putting his cock to her pussy. "Yes?"

Melody answered by pressing against him, clinging to the top rail as she offered him paradise.

He had just enough presence of mind to slip his fingers through her folds to make sure she was wet. "Did it turn you on, sweetheart? Doing wicked things to me right out in the open air?"

"You talking or fucking?" Melody rocked her hips back and he rocked forward, his length sinking in deep. Sweet, hot pressure surrounded him.

This wasn't helping with his control issue.

He reached around her and put his hand to her clit in an attempt to catch her up.

"You're going too fast," she teased.

One hand clutching her hip, Steve pulled back, fingers shaking as he fought the urge to fuck her like a mad man. His cock was covered in her moisture, and seeing the way they connected, seeing his shaft disappear into her didn't help one bit.

He must have made a strangled sound or something that

indicated his troubles. Didn't matter that he was trying to keep it together, Melody seemed determined to ruin his plans.

She pushed back, speeding up the motion between them enough to send him careening toward the cliff. "It's okay, just do it. Don't wait for me, I'm having a blast."

Even without her permission, he couldn't have stopped. His cock jerked, and he covered her, pressing as deep as possible, eliminating the air space between them as his head spun and he fought to keep his balance. Body spinning with pleasure as he lost himself in her heat. Emptying until he had nothing left to give.

He ended up with his hands on either side of hers, death-gripping the railing to stay vertical.

"I'm a shit," he confessed when he could speak. "You didn't come."

Melody laughed as she untangled them, twisting to face him. Both of them had their pants around their knees and the rest of their clothes disheveled. The look on her face?

Priceless.

"I wasn't looking for an orgasm. I planned to finish you with my mouth."

Impossibly, his cock twitched at the thought. "*Fuck*, Melody."

She tugged her clothes back into position. "Just remember, that's one kiss in public you can't have."

He lifted her to the top railing and perched her there as he stepped between her knees and let his satisfaction show. "Thank you."

Her grin dazzled him. "You're welcome. And you can make it up to me later."

"Hell, yes. More than once," he promised.

"I like the sound of that."

So did he, and as they grinned at each other, something clicked. Something right was happening, and he hoped like hell it wasn't only him feeling it.

14

wo days later Steve got to be amazed by another view of Melody.

She was dwarfed by the men working to bring the cows into position, and the animals moving in protest against being corralled for their pregnancy check, yet she didn't seem the least bit intimidated.

Preg-checking was one of the ranch tasks Steve tended not to think about too much, other than from an organizational aspect. Testing the cows to see if they'd been caught made sense, but it was a horridly messy and yet boring job.

Plus physically demanding. Mathis had always done the testing before, and he'd end up knackered by the time they were finished. Some of the hands were already making bets on the sly regarding how many tests Melody could complete before she ran out of steam.

Still, they had a lineup of cows waiting and in position at the rail—the first of them, at least. Steve had his clipboard in hand ready to record her announcement based on the size of the fetus she found during the test. The results would let them put the cows out in different fields and know approximately when the calves would start to drop. And any cows that hadn't been caught the first time, there was still opportunity to breed them this year.

Melody stood to one side of the yard chatting with his cousins who had come to help. Matt Coleman and Cassidy grinned at something she'd said as she adjusted the long protective coat covering her torso and pulled on a rubber glove that went up to her shoulder.

She was going to need it.

Even though this was a part of ranch life, and vet life, Steve wished he could protect her. Wished he could save her from the exhaustion that would set in after an hour's time, or sooner. Save her from the filth and the sheer boredom of repetition. No matter how much he admired her, he joined the others in wondering how long she'd last when pitted against the strength of the cows.

Unwilling cows, he mentally added, as the first one she approached shuffled its feet, as if knowing what was about to happen.

No hesitation. The task was unpleasant, but Melody simply did it. She lifted the cow's tail to the side with one hand and slipped her other hand into the animal, a look of determination on her face.

Steve saw it. The moment she located the cow's cervix below her hand.

"Three," Melody announced, withdrawing her arm cautiously to avoid creating a disaster.

Steve made a note matching the tag number on the cow's ear before glancing up, expecting it to take a moment for Melody to move down the line.

She was already in place, already shouting the next number, and he had to still grab the tag information from the next cow. He hustled to catch up, scrawling the numbers as carefully as possible as Melody moved at an impossibly quick rate.

Once she'd finished the first dozen tests, no one was smirking or laughing anymore—the men were fighting to keep up. Rushing to get the rest of the cows in place to keep from making her wait. The only thing that saved them from looking like a bunch of useless slackers were the times when Melody had to pull a stool over to reach into an exceptionally tall cow.

Steve was sweating before long. "Slow down, you're going too fast," he croaked, glancing at her, his jaw tight from holding in multiple curses.

She tossed him a sympathetic grin. "Gee, I thought that was my line, Steve."

He was so busy scribbling down the next tag number that what she said took a minute to register. The amused chuckles from his cousins and brother were what finally clued him in.

A loud snort escaped Trevor, and Steve snapped his head up to glare at his brother, hoping to scare him into silence. The only thing that happened was the clipboard slipped from his fingers and he had to crawl under the nearest cow to retrieve it, awkwardly scrambling until he was back in position.

By that time, everyone was waiting for *him*.

Trevor cackled. "Still trying to set the pace, are you, big bro? And here we put you in charge of the paperwork because we thought you'd like having something to hang on to."

"It's not the size of your equipment, it's knowing how to use it," Melody commented dryly, which only set up another round of howls.

He eyed her carefully over the next hour, but other than giving back as good as she got from the boys, she never wavered. By the time lunch break rolled around, Steve was impressed—hell, he was *beyond* impressed.

He had to admit her manner with the crew was perfect. Preg-testing was a dirty task, and there were always a few coarse jokes bandied about. If they hadn't acknowledged that, or tried to avoid it for Melody's sake, it would have been more awkward than the good-natured ribbing going on.

So he joined in the taunting but made sure it never went too far. Directing the jokes back to himself whenever he felt the dirt talk was getting out of hand.

Melody Langley was one remarkable woman, and he looked forward to telling, and showing her, that he thought so.

The fact he planned they'd be naked while they had the discussion? A win on both sides.

~

SHE KNEW there'd be hell to pay for her teasing, but she was more than willing to foot the bill.

The whole time they'd worked together, she'd felt that edge of attraction. The moments their shoulders had brushed, excitement raced through her body like she'd bumped into an electric fence. The lure between them created a sense of anticipation and arousal that lasted long after she'd finished the final test.

Even with the hormone high she got hanging around Steve, though, she would have been exhausted if it weren't for the other amazing thing.

The congratulatory slaps on her shoulders from the team she'd spent the day with were an incredible contrast to the disapproving attitudes she'd faced at other jobs over the past days. What a difference it made to be celebrated for her skills instead of looked at with suspicion.

She was tired and filthy, and felt so alive the adrenaline rushing her system could power her through dancing for hours.

It wasn't just the crew. She'd also been pleased with Steve's work ethic—last year when she came out to the Colemans to help

Mathis do this same job, she remembered Steve wandering off at one point and never returning.

Not today. And even though they'd started the day by joking at his expense, he'd stayed on top of what needed to happen next. He'd kept the guys rolling, twice noticing she needed a stretch break before she'd said anything, and then he'd called a stop for the entire crew rather than making it about her and *her delicate constitution* like at other ranches.

She wasn't sure a simple *thank you* would be enough.

Steve walked her to her truck. "I'll admit it. What you just did was amazing. I've seen grown men twice your size reduced to tears while testing that many cows. Hell, I've seen a vet get his arm broken when the cow decided to fight back in the middle of a test."

"Trust me, I've heard the tales, maybe worse ones than you." Melody made a face. "They like to tell us horror stories during vet training, like some morbid *I can top that* game. And I know it takes strength, but maybe it helps that I'm not as big as the average vet."

Steve frowned in confusion.

She caught his hand in hers, pressing them palm-to-palm to showcase the size difference. "Tell me honestly. If you were getting your prostate checked, whose finger do you want shoved up your ass?"

He shuddered. "And on that note, can I take you out for dinner?"

Melody worked to hide her amusement. "Not getting into another discussion of taking it up the ass?"

"I think we talked about that enough today to last us for a long, long time, don't you?" But his eyes were laughing at her. "Dinner?"

"After I shower and disinfect myself? Sure."

He opened her truck door and waited until she'd crawled

inside and settled. "I'll pick you up in an hour. You okay with casual?"

"Perfect."

An hour was just long enough for her to scrub her skin until she was tingling, pull on clean jeans and a shirt, and sit on the front steps waiting for him while she brushed her hair. A moment to breathe and forget the worries and work of the week.

He pulled up, and she was at the passenger side in a flash, jerking to a stop when she tried to open it, but instead of swinging open, the lock clicked down. Steve put the truck in park and came around, grinning as he opened the door and helped her in.

"Such a gentleman," she teased. "Locking me out."

"You're so independent, it's difficult to do all the polite things without having to manage you at the same time."

Melody laughed. "Yes, I can see where I take a fair bit of managing."

He had her door shut and was back behind the wheel in seconds, pulling her into the middle seat next to him and heading them down the road. He linked fingers with hers, giving her one of his sexy smiles that made everything tingle more than her Buf-Puf in the shower. "I told you casual. You okay with *really* casual?"

"Of course." She fought to keep a yawn from breaking free, but it was no use. She covered her mouth and ignored his teasing laugh. "I'm not doing too much more before crashing."

"That's what I figured, so I picked up what we need for a picnic. We can sit back, relax and just spend some time together."

Perfect. "Not trying to impress anyone else today," she said.

Melody laid her head on his shoulder as he drove toward the bluffs, the tall grass in the fields around them swaying in the gentle breeze.

He'd gone to town and bought her favourite things. Half an

hour later she leaned back in the camping chair Steve had brought, her hunger more than sated.

She glanced up to find him watching her closely. "I did it again, didn't I?"

"Did what?"

"Ignored everything but the food."

Steve waved a hand toward the limited remains on the plates in front of them. "Unless you ate it all when I wasn't looking, I was involved in the carnage as well."

True. Melody folded her hands in her lap, curious for more information. "Things went well today at the ranch. Or at least, I thought they did."

The expression on his face was unmistakable. Pride followed hard by guilt. "You did a great job, and I have to apologize for ever thinking it was going to be too big of a task for you."

Melody paused. "I never once suspected you were worried I couldn't do my job."

"Oh, hell no. Don't get me wrong—I have zero doubts about your skills as a vet." He ran a finger down her arm, slowly and intimately. "You're strong, and today you proved it."

His honesty still sat a little uneasy. "I try not to take on more than I can handle. I know I'm not the size of you. Even someone my size like Ian Mailer is potentially stronger than me because he's a man, but there's *always* a way for me to do my job."

"Damn right," he agreed.

She thought back over the day. "Trevor and Lee were helping, and a bunch of your cousins, but your dad wasn't around. Is he still not feeling well?"

Steve made a face. "No, and while he insists it's nothing serious, he hasn't been able to do nearly as much as he wants to."

"That's got to be driving him mad." Nothing worse than a rancher being tied down, especially when he'd know what chores were being left undone.

"I don't know who's going crazier, him or my mom," Steve confessed. "Kate is out helping every chance she gets, but in the meantime Randy isn't feeling well enough to take over her tasks. It's turned into a giant juggling act."

Melody would've offered a hand, but she had too many balls in the air herself. "Does he need to go for extra testing?"

"He's waiting for some results, but you know that takes time. In the meanwhile, we just have to do our best to keep up."

Steve rearranged his chair so they were side by side looking over the meadow. Cattle grazed below them, red-tailed hawks rode the air currents far above their heads.

When he lifted her hand and linked their fingers together, she smiled. "It's nice to have a quiet time to talk."

Steve paused for long enough she leaned forward to look into his face to see what was wrong. His lips were twisted up on one side as he returned her gaze with a sheepish expression. "I was such a bloody idiot last year."

Well, now. "What brought that on?"

His shoulders lifted. "It's not the big things that point out what was wrong with us before. Not really. It's the little moments when you say something that should be so inconsequential, and it hits like a dagger because I should've known better."

"It's done. Stop beating yourself up over it."

"How often did we take time to sit and talk?" he insisted. "How often did I come over and give you a hand when you were tired from a hard day's work?"

"As often as I came over to your place," she admitted. "Not very often."

"That was different." Steve shook his head. "I didn't want you stopping by and being surrounded by the guys. Besides, the place was a wreck most of the time."

Her point was still valid though. "I'm just saying it wasn't *only* your responsibility to make our relationship something more than casual sex and party partners."

It took a long time before he nodded. "I hated it when you left, especially because you left pissed off at me. For good reason."

They'd never really talked about that day. She'd been so angry, and then one thing had led to another.

Melody adjusted her chair so she could hold his hand and look him in the eye. "I was disappointed, I'll admit that."

"Disappointment and full-out furious look a lot alike, then," he teased.

"You forgot me, Steve. You left me stranded at the Calgary airport four hours away from my vehicle and all my stuff, simply because you weren't paying attention."

"It was terrible."

She leaned forward and slid her palm against his cheek, cupping his face so he had nowhere to look but straight at her. "Yes, I was furious, which is why when I finally made it back to Rocky Mountain House you got assaulted by a pitcher of beer. But back to our earlier comment, even that wasn't *just* your fault."

"Right, it was your fault for asking me to pick you up in the first place," he drawled.

"Actually, yes." His eyes registered his shock, and she hurried on to complete her thought. "Steve, we were never a couple. We were two people who got along in the bedroom, and occasionally hung out, but there was nothing else to us. No sense of protectiveness or companionship, or anything that would make it important for either of us to go out of our way for the other. It wasn't that the potential wasn't there, but nether of us chose to make it more than what we had."

He pressed his hand over hers, dark eyes burning. "Tell me you feel something different this time, because I sure the hell do. I want what's best for you, and I want you to be happy."

It was good to be able to answer him honestly. "That's why I was hesitant when you first asked me out—I didn't want a repeat of what we used to be, which was not much. But I think we're doing better. I feel like there's a connection between us."

Pure relief lit his eyes. "Sweetheart, that's the best news I've heard in a long time. And I'm going to keep working to make sure you feel that way two months from now."

"I'll do the same," she promised.

He leaned forward and kissed her, tender and sweet. Her heart skipped a beat, and something inside seemed to crack open a tiny bit. Maybe she'd been holding back. Worried this was going to end the same way as before?

Not anymore. He'd done enough to prove that *some* things were different.

"Hey, did you want to meet up with the dog I found you?" Steve asked when they were walking back to his truck, hand in hand.

A shiver of excitement hit. "You think she's ready?"

He nodded. "The pups have all been adopted. I had Jesse bring Charlie over to our ranch, and she's been hanging out with Prince and the other dogs. She's definitely got some moves, so if you've got time this weekend, let's set it up."

She waited until he'd put the lawn chairs into the back of his truck before wrapping her arms around his neck and letting him lift her in the air for a hug. "I'm excited. I really hope this works out."

"Me too," Steve agreed.

New dog, new relationship.

New tomorrow.

15

Steve's truck pulled into the driveway, and Melody found her heart fluttering. She jiggled on her feet with both anticipation and concern, which was kind of crazy when she considered it.

She was getting a dog. Holy moly, and *oh my goodness*.

She also didn't know who she was more excited about seeing —the dog or Steve.

Steve's dog Prince hopped out of the back of the truck and made a beeline for her. She squatted to greet him, her gaze lingering on the truck to take in the two men striding toward her. Every move Steve made seemed to threaten the existence of his black T-shirt, and Melody smiled as she gave Prince a final pat on the head and stood to continue to admire the view.

Solid arms and broad shoulders, with trim hips filling his *faded in all the right spots* jeans. On every step the toes of his cowboy boots poked out, and he adjusted his hat as he sauntered forward.

Man, did she ever love living in cowboy country.

It was only after she'd ogled him for a while that she took a quick peek to discover Trevor was the other man rapidly approaching. The two of them stopped a few feet away as Prince ran in excited circles around the three points of their triangle.

"Good to see you again." Trevor offered a wink.

Melody tore her gaze away from Steve's bewitching eyes, nodding politely at his younger brother. "Good to see you, as well." She glanced around in confusion. "But I don't see Charlie, only Prince."

"We didn't bring her." Steve held a hand out. "We've been working with her at our ranch, and she's familiar with the location and the animals. I thought maybe you'd like to run her through her paces there for the first time."

"Good idea." Melody patted her pockets to see if she had everything she wanted. "You should've called. I could've driven over to your place."

"We were in town anyway," Trevor admitted. "Picking you up works better than trying to coordinate where to meet."

"And don't fuss about anything else. Come on." Steve caught her fingers in his and pulled her to the driver side of the truck, whistling for Prince who obediently came away from where he was sniffing fence posts.

The dog raced forward like a banshee until he was within jumping range, crouched momentarily then sprang into the truck box without pausing. He moved to the front of the box and vanished.

Melody glanced over the edge, curious to see what he was doing. She was surprised to discover Steve had a dog bed in the corner, and had trained Prince to stay.

Interesting.

"There's a sight I don't see very often in this community." She reached her hand over and gave Prince a quick pat. He pressed his head against her hand, his tail thumping, but he didn't get up.

"He's not riding in the cab with us," Steve explained, "but I've never liked seeing dogs bouncing all over the place."

"You baby him," Trevor teased. "Everyone else lets their dogs ride as they will."

Melody had seen it often enough, and most of the time it was fine. "This is a lot safer, though."

"I don't like the distraction. There's no reason why he can't lie down and take it easy for the trip. He gets to run around every other hour of his day."

Steve helped her into the cab, and Melody slid to the middle, boxed in on both sides by one hundred percent Coleman male in their prime.

It wasn't a bad place to be.

She glanced over her shoulder to see Prince lying contentedly on the thick mat, the animal curled up as they headed to Moonshine land. "I like that. I'll have to see if I can train Charlie to do the same thing."

Steve lifted his hand off the wheel and laid it on her thigh. He didn't say anything else, but he didn't have to because Trevor started a travelogue, pointing out all sorts of things outside the window.

This was a good thing, as well as a great distraction. Melody knew bits about the area, but missed the history. "Hey, do me a favour," she begged. "Point out some of the old landmarks."

Trevor paused, twisting in his seat to give her a confused look. "Old landmarks?"

"You don't know how frustrating it is when people give me directions. Even after having lived here for a couple of years, I often have no idea what they're talking about."

Steve chuckled. "I know what you mean. People tell you to 'turn right where Pearson's barn used to be'?"

"Exactly." Melody glanced out the window at an old shed

and snapped up a finger. "See that? I got heckled the other day for not knowing the locals call it the Crestview Castle."

This time Trevor laughed out loud. "Hell. That's a tale I haven't heard in a while."

"You know the story?"

"That place has been there on the edge of Winston Crest's land forever. Anytime he went out drinking, his wife, who didn't approve of hard liquor, would lock the house doors and refuse to let him in, and he'd end up sleeping in the shed for the night."

"Only she was nice about it," Steve cut in. "She had the soul of an angel, just hated liquor with a vengeance. She didn't want him to be uncomfortable, so she hauled an old rocking chair under the overhang. And she didn't want him to catch cold, so she bought him an extra pair of slippers and robe on sale one time and kept them in the shed. In the morning after he'd tied one on, everyone driving by would see Winston sleeping in the rocking chair, all done up in regal purple."

Melody found herself smiling. "How come nobody's ever written a history of the area?"

Steve thought for a moment before answering. "Probably because it doesn't feel like history to us. It just is."

She caught hold of Steve's fingers with hers, squeezing tighter the closer to the Moonshine ranch they got.

He flipped his hand over, linking their fingers together, and while Trevor continued to ramble, Melody sat and enjoyed their company. Protected and surrounded for a short period of time by a couple of gentle giants.

But by the time they'd reached the ranch, her butterflies had returned.

"I'll go get her from the barn," Trevor offered, sauntering on ahead.

Melody was held back, Steve's hand firm but gentle on her arm to keep her in place as he turned her toward him. He tucked his fingers under her chin and lifted her face to his as he leaned down and pressed a kiss on her lips.

She let herself enjoy the moment. Running her hands from his wrists up his arms until she was holding onto his broad shoulders. Just a momentary interlude in the middle of the excitement, and it was amazing how pleasurable she found it.

She was the one who stepped back, breaking contact between them but offering him a smile. "I guess I forgot to say hello to you properly before, didn't I?"

"That was part of my master plan. Right now there's no one around, so it's not considered a kiss in public," he teased. "I'm still good to lay one on you whenever I want."

Prince let out a bark, and she turned her focus toward the new dog joining them, shuffling around their feet.

"Oh, she's a beauty." Melody offered her hand to the shepherd who sniffed her before turning her attention back to Prince and other more important dog-type duties.

Steve motioned toward the side of the yard. "Trevor said he'd get some of the calves ready if you want to see her in action."

Melody nodded. "Let me say hello first."

She dug her hand in her pocket for one of the ever-present treats she carried. Prince paced forward eagerly—he already knew the routine. Melody offered him a treat, patted him on the head and got another biscuit ready, this time extending it to Charlie. "Hello, girl. I hear you're looking for a new job."

Charlie took the treat then nudged forward as Melody scratched behind her ears. It was comfortable, and it was right, and a few minutes later when Charlie bumped her head into Melody's leg for attention, it felt like the start of a beautiful friendship.

For the next hour they put the dogs through their paces. Trevor and Steve ordered their dogs to round up the calves or herd them into the side corral. Melody observed how Charlie reacted, both while she was waiting, and when she was allowed to join in the work.

"She's been here for a week, and we've had no incidents." Steve smiled as the dogs danced around each other for a moment before coming sharply to heel when Melody called them. "Damn if Jesse didn't do something right. Charlie might be a better-trained dog than Prince."

Another rush of joy hit as Melody smoothed her hand over the dog's head, happiness rising. "I think Charlie's going to work out well," she agreed.

~

HE'D CAUGHT himself staring far too often, but there was no way to resist. The expression of sheer delight Melody wore was enough to make the strangest sensation rise in his gut.

It wasn't nervousness, so he couldn't call them butterflies. But there most definitely was something going on as she got to know Charlie.

Trevor took off ahead of them, but Steve laid a hand on her shoulder. "Stay for supper," he offered.

Melody glanced toward the ranch house. "Here? With your parents?"

"I mentioned you were going to be around, and Mom insisted you should join us."

"Okay. I didn't have any other plans, and I like your folks."

He tucked an arm around her and led her toward the back door. "Of course you like them. I've trained them to be fabulous parents."

"All your doing. Are you sure about that?"

Steve jerked to a stop and grinned guiltily at his mother. "The only bad habit I haven't been able to break them of yet is eavesdropping."

Kate tilted her head to the house. "Get in there and wash up. Your father's in the living room, and Anna called to say she and Mitch will be here in ten minutes."

"I'll just take Melody—"

"Run along, little boy," his mother ordered, flicking her fingers at him. "I'll take care of her."

It wasn't as if he were afraid his mother would do something to ruin his chances with Melody, but at the same time Steve hurried to the boys' bathroom, as his mom called it, and washed up as rapidly as he could.

"Bringing her for supper with the folks already. It's that serious?"

Steve glanced in the mirror to discover his sister, Anna, standing behind him, her long dark hair loose around her shoulders, the hint of a flame tattooed on her shoulder peeking out from under her tank top.

His sister, the straight-laced cop who was head over heels in love with the last guy he'd expected her to fall for. But then over the past month, he'd never seen her happier.

Maybe they all had someone special who'd bring out the best in them.

But now he had to head this one off before it went out of control and made things tougher. "It's nothing like that. I mean, yes, I want this to be serious, but having dinner with Mom and Dad is just dinner—I don't want Melody to feel rushed or anything."

Her expression remained serious "You know people are talking?"

Steve paused. "About me and Melody?"

"They're talking mostly about her, and a little about you."

He turned to face his sister, leaning a hip against the counter. "You're not making any sense."

She hesitated then spoke clearly. "Mitch hears a lot of gossip down at the shop and out on the street. Some of the old-timers aren't happy with her work."

"Well, that's bullshit on their part. I've seen her in action. She's been working for us and the other Coleman ranches without any complaints."

A slim finger pointed in his direction. "That's the biggest talk. How maybe you aren't the best judge of whether her work is any good or not, since you two are involved."

Steve grabbed the towel off the rack, drying his face and hands as he prepared to go back upstairs and join the family. "And if all they have time to do is sit around and gossip, then I don't know that I give a shit about any of those old men's opinions. Melody knows her job, and she's good in the sack, and she's a ton of fun to be around, period. Those are three separate things, and if they're not smart enough to see that, fuck them."

His sister's smile bloomed. "Good. You're not an idiot anymore."

"Nope," he agreed, before grinning back. "Did you bring that bad-ass fiancé of yours along tonight, or do we get to eat dinner without having to fight him for it?"

Anna backed down the hall, her smile taunting him. "He's here, so don't let your guard down. I hear we're having meatloaf, and he'll do anything for third helpings."

Steve shook his head at people's foolishness. So what if he and Melody were going out? They weren't hurting anyone, and that was the plain truth. He paused at the top of the stairs, mesmerized by the sunlight shining in the window catching a loose strand of her hair and turning it into molten gold.

She'd pulled a stool beside the La-Z-Boy his father had settled in, a ball of wool held in front of her. Yarn draped across to his father.

Randy was explaining his situation. "Until we figure out

what's wrong, I'm stuck looking for things I can do that don't mess everyone else up."

"I'm sorry you're still not feeling well," Melody said. "But it's good to see you're keeping busy."

Steve stepped forward far enough that his father's hands came into view. The knitting needles he held moved steadily, nowhere near as quickly as his mom or any of the aunts, but there was a respectable looking dishcloth hanging underneath the work surface.

"I can't cook, and I can't drive, because both those things make me feel like I'm ready to fall over." Randy let out a massive sigh. He lifted his head and his gaze met Steve's. "So instead of doing my work, I'm sitting here like a slacker and letting my sons work like dogs."

"I'd far prefer to have you bossing me around," Steve confessed.

Randy made a face and went back to finish the row. "I'm knitting up the washcloths Kate promised to donate to the church fair."

"Good for you for knowing how," Melody said. "That's a trick I've never learned."

"Mama Coleman insisted all her boys learn how to do everything, from splitting wood and fixing cars to cooking dinner and sewing on buttons. She always said there's no shame in getting the task done."

Kate stepped out of the kitchen, hands full with a dish of steaming hot food, Lee right behind her. "We're ready to go to the table. Randy, if you feel up to it, come join us."

He wrinkled his nose. "I think I'll stay here. I'm close enough I can give you what-for if the conversation starts to get boring."

Steve paused to greet Mitch with a firm handshake; the man's hands calloused from his hours of labour down at his family's garage.

"Good to see you again."

Mitch nodded in response before turning to rescue Anna and the heavy casserole she'd brought to the table.

"That one's mine, anyway," he claimed, taking a deep inhale and smiling contentedly. "Kate, you made meatloaf. You're spoiling me."

"You make my daughter smile. If meatloaf makes you happy, you get meatloaf," Kate teased easily.

Steve pulled back the chair beside his usual one and seated Melody at his side. Her blue eyes sparkled as the rest of the family joined them.

"Everything looks great, Kate," Melody offered.

"Thank you. In spite of Randy's comment about not being able to cook, he put most of this in the oven a couple of hours ago." Kate glanced at her husband, concern and affection written on her face. "I don't know what I'd do without him."

Trevor asked about Melody's work. Mitch shared a story from his day at the garage. Kate mentioned a couple extra chores for the following day. Good conversation and good food settled together, and again Steve felt the contrast between now and last year.

Why the *hell* had he not seen before how much he was missing?

Melody glowed brighter as the meal went on, her happiness clear as she shared with Kate her plans to train the new dog. Trevor joined in and even Randy offered a few suggestions.

She fit so well into their family, Steve wanted to jump up right then and there and point it out to her. Of course, that would be awkward as hell and probably get his foot stomped, but the thought did flit through his mind.

Trevor poked Lee in the arm. "How come you're not talking?"

Their little brother shrugged. "You're all talking enough without me."

"But tonight is different. You're quieter than usual." Trevor glanced down the table. "Ahhh, Melody is here. That's it. You're too shy to talk around girls."

"What am I, an elephant?" Anna demanded.

"And me?" Kate glared at her son.

Trevor didn't seem to know when to stop. "You're my sister and mom. You're not girls."

Laughter rang from behind them from where Randy was reclining in his chair. "You're digging yourself a deep, deep hole, son, and no one in this room is going to throw you a rope to save yourself if you keep it up."

"Hey, I was just pointing out Lee needs to find himself a lady friend. It sure improved Steve's mood." Trevor didn't have time to get out of the way before a spoonful of peas struck him straight on in the face. He blinked in surprise, his mouth opening in shock as he stared at his mother. "What was that for?"

Kate let him have it. "Number one, looks to me like you also don't have a *lady friend*, probably because there's no one willing to put up with your shenanigans full time. Number two, I'm not just your mother, I'm the one who's cutting the cake for dessert, and if you don't mind your manners, you'll find yourself eating the tiniest piece I can cut."

For once Trevor didn't open his mouth and continue chatting himself into more trouble. Steve reached under the table and caught Melody's fingers in his, her low laughter triggering his own.

"Actually, I think Trevor's the only one in the room without a lady friend," Anna said sweetly as she helped gather the plates.

"What?" Trevor glanced at Lee. "What's she talking about?"

Lee and his sister exchanged glances for a moment before his youngest brother broke eye contact, shuffling to his feet and picking up empty dishes. "Just because I like someone doesn't mean everything is going to go my way."

"Holy cow, Anna is right? You're sweet on someone?" Steve demanded.

He was given another one of Lee's patented younger-brother looks. The one that said "my, aren't you stupid" and "don't make me explain this all over again" at the same time.

"Drop it. It's nothing."

The temptation to keep poking was there, but so was the warning tug on his fingers from the amazing woman sitting beside him. One look into her eyes, and Steve promptly forgot about tormenting his youngest brother. The cool blue depths were so full of happiness he couldn't bear to do anything to upset her.

Instead he turned to his troublemaking middle sibling. "Some of your mail delivered to my house by accident," he announced.

"Yeah?" Trevor paused in the middle of pouring another drink.

"Your subscription with FarmersOnly.com is up for renewal, and they suggested you use a better picture this time. Seems the one you used last time, they weren't sure if it was you or one of the cows..."

Lee and Mitch were the first to chuckle, his father seconds behind them. All the women rolled their eyes, but Steve's point had been made as his brother offered him a glare of doom.

It was far more fun to torment Trevor than Lee anyway.

16

"Oh my God. What did he do then?"

Jaxi only grinned harder. "What do you think? Exactly what I wanted him to, of course."

The group of women gathered in Allison's recently expanded living room laughed, and Melody glanced around with a sense of awe and gratitude.

These women were her contemporaries. Not because they'd gone to school together or spent the last twenty years living in the same place. They all had different levels of education and hugely different backgrounds, but they were united by a love for the land and compassion for each other. Five women working in the middle of a male-centered society.

Allison's cheeks were rosy, and as she leaned back on the couch, the front of her shirt pressed to the small swell of her belly.

Melody couldn't resist. "You're showing."

Her friend's grin had become nearly permanent by this point. "It's the weirdest thing knowing someone's growing inside me. I can't wait until I can feel the kid move."

"It's very cool," Jaxi agreed. She held four-month-old Peter in her arms, and he nursed noisily as they visited. "At least until they get big enough to dance on your bladder. And poke knees and elbows into your ribs."

"Still looking forward to it," Allison said.

"Definitely." Jaxi offered her a hug and the two of them chatted for a moment as Melody sat back and relaxed.

Girls' night out. After the workload she'd been pulling, it was good to take a break. Steve had been...

Well, he'd been amazing. Not only in helping with Charlie, but in calling her when they couldn't get together. Dropping by for short visits when that's all the two of them could handle. And the sex?

Maybe Allison wasn't the only one with a perma-grin these days.

But tonight the call had been issued to spend time with the ladies, and Melody was glad to accept. Of course, as it turned out she was once again surrounded by the Coleman clan, but by now, she was used to it.

Along with Jaxi and Allison, Vicki and Ashley had joined them. Vicki wasn't as well known to Melody, but the young woman had a snappy way of responding that made everyone in the room smile. Ashley...

Ashley defied definition.

The blonde-haired woman returned from the kitchen with two pitchers of the icy-pink concoction she'd poured the instant Melody had arrived. One was plain lemonade, and the other lemonade with a serious attitude. "Who's ready for another round?"

Vicki pulled a face. "One is usually my limit. Plus, I have an online test I have to study for tomorrow. I don't know if I should drink any more of the spiked one."

"You're okay, honey," Jaxi assured her. "You know damn well

you're not going to get out of bed until noon anyway. I'll give you my hangover recipe, and you'll feel fine by the time you get up."

Allison frowned. "How do you know she doesn't get up until noon?"

Vicki's cheeks shot past a blush to bright red, and she refused to meet Melody's eyes, leaning instead toward her sister-in-law. "You said you weren't going to tell anyone about that," she complained.

"Oops." Jaxi muttered, holding out her hand for a refill of the virgin lemonade that Ashley cheerfully offered.

Secrets. Anytime a gathering occurred, there were bound to be some, but at the same time the gentle teasing and familiarity added an intimacy to their get-together.

And sometimes secrets were meant to be shared. Vicki folded her arms over her chest as if she was going to be stubborn before spilling the beans. "Jaxi stopped over the morning Joel had decided to go a little...bossy on me."

"A little?" Jaxi exclaimed. "Honey, he had you tied to the bed posts."

"Are you telling me you and Blake never play with ropes?" Vicki retorted. "Because if you are, I call Bull. Fucking. Shit."

"I never said that. I just think if you're going to play *kidnapped by the wicked cowboy* you should time it better so your poor sister-in-law-to-be doesn't get traumatized when she stops by to drop off a load of baking."

"Ha. The day you're traumatized by something the clan does, the national news will report it."

Ashley offered a top-up from the pitcher with no alcohol to Allison then plopped onto the couch next to Melody. "Okay, time for the most current gossip. I nominate Melody to start."

Melody hesitated. "Who, me?"

"Of course, you," Allison teased. "We're dying to know. You broke up with Steve, then went away for nearly a year. Now you're back, and I've never seen the man smile so much in his life."

"We know who's putting that smile there," Vicki agreed.

"But...exactly *what* is what we want to know." Jaxi waggled her brows suggestively before rearranging the baby against her shoulder to burp him.

"You want a play-by-play of our sex life?" Melody hesitated. "Is everyone going to share, because I don't know that's fair if it's only Vicki and I who end up on the hot seat."

"Sure, we'll share." Vicki snorted. "Everyone but Ashley, that is, because if she tells us what goes on at her place on a regular basis? We'll spend the rest of the evening with our jaws on the floor and a bad case of penis envy."

"I think that phrase is supposed to mean we wish we had penises," Allison pointed out.

Vicki shook her head. "You don't think Ashley has penises at her beck and call? Penees. Penises. Penii? Whatever."

Once the laughter faded, Ashley gloated. "I'll admit it, my cup runneth over."

Vicki only laughed harder, covering her mouth with her hand.

Ashley shook her head and a finger at the young woman. "I swear, you've got the dirtiest mind of anyone I've ever met."

"Why? You're the one who said it."

Melody sat back, sipping the fruity drink Ashley had put together for them. She popped another one of Vicki's jalapeno bites into her mouth and chewed happily, soaking in the atmosphere.

Across from her, the baby stared sleepily around the room for a moment, blinking his bright blue eyes hard before an enormous yawn stretched his little mouth. Allison cooed at him, then Jaxi laid him in the bassinet beside the couch, and suddenly four pairs of eyes were turned in Melody's direction and there was nowhere she could go to hide.

"You were serious? You want me to tell you how things are going?"

Four heads nodded like a dashboard of bobble heads on a bumpy road.

This time it was Melody's turn to laugh. "Bunch of snoopy old women."

Allison slid forward on her chair "You don't have to tell us specifics. But is it getting serious?"

Melody paused and considered. "Maybe? I don't know. It hasn't been long enough yet."

Jaxi was giving her one of those looks. The one that said the woman was older than her years. "It doesn't take long to figure out whether a guy's right for you or not."

"I agree with part of that—I like him a lot, and I'll say he's a different man than he was last year when I left. He's fun to be around, he seems a lot more responsible, and I find that sexy in a guy."

"Notice she's still not telling us what else she finds sexy," Allison said loudly enough to be overheard as she leaned across the couch to pretend to whisper to Ashley.

"I think the only way we're going to get some real answers is to play a game." Jaxi looked far too pleased with her own suggestion as she refilled her glass, settling in with a smile.

Ashley's hand flew up. "I'm game. I mean I'm game for any game."

Jaxi swirled the liquid in her glass. "All right, then, truth or dare."

"Good idea. I haven't played that since I was twelve," Vicki said.

"So, that means, like last year?" Ashley ducked the pillow Vicki threw at her head.

"I'll go first. Truth or dare—Jaxi," Vicki demanded.

Jaxi crooked one blonde eyebrow higher as she accepted the challenge. "Truth."

Vicki leaned forward. "In which room of your house have you *not* had sex?"

A ripple of laughter started low, progressing to full-out mirth the longer Jaxi hesitated, especially since it was clear she was trying hard to answer the question.

She gave up. "I don't think we've left anywhere untouched, to be honest."

"This is why you have four children," Allison said.

Jaxi nodded. "Probably, so it's a good thing making babies is a lot of fun."

Jaxi turned on Ashley. "What's the absolute—?"

"Hey," Ashley complained as she shot upright. "You're supposed to ask me to pick between sharing a truth or doing a dare."

"She figured you'd instantly take the dare. This is more fun," Vicki teased.

Ashley laid a hand over her chest. "I'm so misunderstood." But her eyes sparkled as she smiled at Jaxi. "Go on, what's your question?"

"What's the dirtiest—?"

"I can see this being impossible for her to answer," Vicki muttered.

Jaxi put on her most innocent face. "What's the dirtiest... you've ever gotten...while painting?"

They laughed again, and Ashley stuck out her tongue in response before confessing, "I've done body painting."

Melody tried to picture it. "How did that get you dirty, painting a body?"

"Well, you use your body to *do* the painting," Ashley

explained. "It tends to involve accidentally getting paint stuck places that take a long time to clean."

Ashley turned to Melody, her smile twisting as she posed the question, "Truth or dare?"

It was time to mix it up. "Dare."

Ashley clapped her hands with excitement, lifting her chin in challenge. "You're gonna make a prank phone call."

Oops.

"Don't get her into much trouble," Vicki warned.

Ashley shook her head. "I know, I know. We're models of discretion and pillars of the community. Yada, yada, yada."

Four gazes pinned Melody in place. "Be nice," she warned.

"Don't worry, I'm not telling you to phone the mayor or something."

Melody could guess where this was going. "I'm supposed to call who?"

As if they'd rehearsed it ahead of time, four voices went off in unison. "Steve."

"And you've gotta talk dirty to him," Ashley added. "Not just some 'hi honey how was your day?' bullshit."

Melody rolled her eyes. "You're so bad."

The longer she hesitated, the more expectation rose on the faces of her friends.

Fine. Like Vicki had said, this was just good clean fun.

Or maybe not *quite* so clean. There was a challenge in her friends' eyes as she grabbed her cell phone out of her pocket and hit Steve's number. Maybe they thought she couldn't talk dirty?

Time to rise to the occasion.

Only she sat back in her chair and focused on a spot near the ceiling as the call went through, because no way she could do this if she was watching their faces.

∼

Since Melody had declined his date, heading out to spend time with the girls, Steve sucked up his disappointment and drove over to the rental house to visit with Lee instead.

What he found was the semimonthly dishwashing expedition about to take place.

Lee held an armful of plates and bowls as he paused in the front hall. "Perfect timing," he said in greeting.

"If you think I'm washing anything, you've got another think coming. You made the mess, you clean up." Steve kicked off his boots, though, and grabbed the dishes teetering on the edge of the coffee table.

"You don't need to wash," Lee assured him. "But you do want to see this."

He tilted his head toward the kitchen, his grin widening, and Steve followed, curious to see what was going on.

The small room was filled with broad-shouldered men. Stacks of dirty pots, pans, glasses and everything else covered the side counter and spilled onto the table.

Jesse, Rafe and Lee were there, but so was Trevor, his sleeves rolled up and a look of disgust on his face as he eyed the sink full of soapy water.

Perfect.

"Dishpan hands look good on you," Steve taunted.

"Fuck off. They threatened to block my dinner privileges if I don't help." Trevor stuck his hands into the water to begin the herculean task, adjusting his expression to look like a long-suffering hero. "But, really, I agreed to help because I know it's the right thing to do."

Jesse snorted in disbelief. "Bullshit. It's because you heard my mom gave me a pile of steaks for us to barbeque tonight, and you can't stand the thought of missing out and having to eat ramen instead."

"Same thing."

"We should give up and buy paper plates," Lee grumbled as Rafe left the room.

Jesse shrugged. "Fine by me, but you know Rafe would give you hell. It's not environmentally friendly or some crap."

A call went out from the living room. "Hey, Steve? While you're here, can I get your help?"

"Hey, assholes," Trevor complained when they all turned to leave. "Someone needs to dry. Or at least make room for me to put the clean stuff."

Lee rolled his eyes as he picked up a hand towel. "Yes, Mom."

The joy of living with other guys. Steve was so glad those days were behind him, but they were entertaining to watch. He was still chuckling when he entered the living room. "What's up?"

Rafe pointed at the ceiling. "The light is out. We've changed the bulb, but the damned thing won't work. Did I remember right, and you fixed that before?"

"Yeah, the wiring is old and needs to be jimmied every now and then." Steve shoved the sturdy coffee table under the light then emptied his pockets looking for his knife. "Jesse? Turn off the power at the breaker."

Jesse spun on his heel and left for the basement. "Got it."

Steve gestured to Rafe. "You'll have to help hold the cover while I deal with the wiring. It's one of those stupid setups where the wires are too short to let you put things down."

They waited until Jesse's shout rang from the basement. "It's off. You're safe."

The two of them crawled on the table, arms extended awkwardly overhead as Steve removed the central screw that held the glass in place. "Hold this, but keep it close to the ceiling," he ordered.

Rafe shifted his weight to one side, balancing the large glass globe on his fingertips. No matter how much he tried, the cover created an obstacle for Steve to work around.

He'd disconnected the wires from the base and had the protective plastic covers between his fingers and three wires held in order when his phone went off on the table below him.

Melody's ringtone. He breathed out a low curse, but figured he'd call her back when he was done.

Jesse proved far too helpful. "Don't worry. I got it." His cousin not only answered the phone, he switched it to speaker and laid it back on the table.

Jeez. He supposed Jesse meant well.

"Hi, Melody," Steve spoke loudly as he worked to line up the wires. "I thought you were partying with the girls."

He'd expected laughter. What he got instead was a throaty rumble that set every nerve in his body tingling. "Hey, baby," she purred. "I couldn't wait to talk to you again."

Shit. He eyed his phone and the other guys in the room, both of whom had perked up to full attention at her sultry voice. "Melody, have you been drinking?"

"No. Well, not that much. Mostly, I've been thinking about you. Thinking about you and your big, strong hands. It's got me real wet."

A noise clattered from the kitchen, and Steve glanced over to see Trevor standing in the doorframe, Lee just behind him, the two of them grinning at him like fools.

Screw this. He dropped the wires and reached for his phone to shut off the speaker.

Jesse beat him to it, snatching it off the table and ducking behind the couch while Trevor blocked Steve's path.

Another throaty purr. "I'm so ready for you to do wicked things to me."

He was going to kill them, but first he had to stop her before it went any further. Steve called out a warning.

"Melody, as incredible as this is, you're on speakerphone. Stop, sweetheart."

There was a beat before she swore, her sexy come-hither vanishing as her voice changed to a far more embarrassed tone. "Tell me you're kidding."

"Hi, Melody," Jesse called. "Hi, girls."

"*Fuck*." She must've covered the phone because her voice was muffled, but all the guys heard her complain. "I hope you shits are happy. He had me on speakerphone, and I don't know how many people just heard me make a fool of myself."

Steve finally cornered Jesse and held out his hand. "Give it to me now, or I'll break your fingers as well as your pretty face."

"So testy," Jesse muttered as he passed the phone back to Steve with a wink. "Sounds like there's some fun in store for you for later, though."

Steve ignored the urge to throttle him and stabbed the phone controls. "Melody, you there? We're private again."

She cleared her throat. "Well, that didn't work out the way I hoped."

"It's okay. No one who heard you will survive the night," he promised.

That got a small laugh in response. "Hey, Steve. I just called to say hello."

"And quite the hello it was," he said as he made his way out the front door for a moment of privacy. "I take it you're having fun with the girls?"

"Well, if fun means I'm embarrassed half to death, and we're laughing far too much, and in a couple hours I'll need a designated driver—I'm having a blast," she confessed.

"I like the sound of that." Steve closed the door and lowered his voice. "And are you wet?"

She hesitated. "Yes."

"I like the sound of that, as well." He pictured her for a

moment, the way her lashes fluttered when she was on the edge of coming. "You have fun with the girls tonight, and I'll see what I can do about your other little problem later."

"She's gotta go now, Steve," a female voice said in the background, and the next thing he heard was a click.

He put his phone away, still chuckling to himself.

17

"We had another complaint today."

With one fell swoop, Tom knocked the shine off her day. It was getting to the point she hated to stop in at the clinic at the end of the day.

Things were off and on with the ranchers. It had been three weeks she'd been working on her own, which was long enough for some of them to stop whining and get over it. It was long enough some of them needed to step out of the way when she drove into their yards because she was tempted to run them over.

She hadn't expected everyone to fall in love with her. There were years of hero worship for Mathis involved—she got that, she really did. The man had done amazing things for so many of the locals; the fact she was a woman wasn't the biggest complaint. It was the fact she wasn't Mathis.

And then the *next* complaint was she was a woman.

Doing the job well should have been the most important criteria on everyone's mind. There could be no questioning her work, so the constant attempts by Tom to undermine her confidence by making comments about how upset and bitter people were? Was getting really old.

Enough. "Write it down and leave it on the desk. I'll look at it in the morning to see if there's any merit to it."

Tom made a rude noise. "That's not how it works. If someone complains, *you* don't get to decide whether they're right or wrong."

"Actually, in this case I do." She folded her arms and offered him the most deadly glare in her arsenal. The one that said *don't fuck with me, I'm on the edge.* "Mathis put me in charge. You know damn well some of these ranchers complain just to hear their own voices. If there's something seriously wrong, I have no problem trying to make it right. But it's not worth any more of our time to listen to them whine because they're upset Mathis isn't here for the first time in years."

Please, God, let him drop it.

No such luck. Tom was like a wall of annoying. "What if I happen to think some of them have merit? The complaints, that is?"

Jeez. This got more exciting all the time. "Well, I suppose we can discuss it. But again, Mathis put me in charge of the large-animal work, and you don't know what I've been doing in the field, so you can hardly judge if a complaint has merit or not. Unless you've got an issue with something else?"

Her determination to keep him in line seemed to shock him, and he paused.

Only to change topic.

"Yes, I have a complaint. Don't try to do my job as well as your own," Tom demanded. "Since it seems obvious you're not capable of completing the tasks required for the job Mathis gave you, I don't appreciate you butting in on the clinic work as well. You should focus on your own job and try to at least be semicompetent so that by the time Mathis gets back, he still has a clinic to come back to."

It was a hard challenge to not sputter in response. Melody took a deep breath and calmed herself best she could before responding. "Okay, tell me. What specifically was the complaint?"

"Number one complaint is you're late. It's a huge inconvenience to the ranchers when you're not there on time."

Good grief. The only time she knew for sure she'd been late was that first day with Dalton, and since then there'd been nothing but the usual small delays that were always a part of the routine. "I swear I have no idea what you're talking about."

"Simpson. Called and shared he didn't plan to pay the vet-visit fee since you put him out so badly. I assured him it wouldn't happen again."

Her blood pressure was rising rapidly. *Bullshit.* "What do you mean you *assured* him? I didn't do anything wrong. It might've taken me an additional ten minutes to get to the barn where he had his horses. He had them in the only barn on the property you can't get to even with a four-wheel-drive truck, and he didn't leave me an ATV—I had to wade through a damn stream. Plus, I waited for him for thirty minutes at the main barn before anyone bothered to tell me where he was. I can't get where I need to go unless I'm told. I'm not a mind reader."

Tom seemed to change the topic, but it was the same thing all over. "I'd appreciate it if you'd stop implying to the pet owners who use the clinic that I'm incompetent. You keep going on and on about how Mathis left you in charge of the large-animal work. Well, he left me in charge of the small animals, and it's very difficult to have clients confident with a treatment I suggest when they want to ask *your* opinion to double-check my diagnosis."

Melody's jaw must've been hanging loose in the wind. Okay,

maybe this was the root of the real problem. Tom was pissed that people didn't know he was in charge in the clinic?

"Who did that to you? That's not right—and if you have anyone who's been an issue, let me know and I'll talk to them."

He shot her yet another dirty look. "You're not listening. That's the biggest trouble in the first place. That, and the way you want to put your stamp of approval on anything I do. "

"I can see a few people whose animals I took care of as soon as I got back might want to speak with me." Melody was flabbergasted, and for once felt a touch of sympathy for the man. "Honest, Tom. I'm sorry you've had to put up with that, and I'll help however I can, but I guess it's like me having to deal with some crazy attitudes. We just have to do the best job possible, and in the end, they'll see we're competent."

Tom grunted then turned toward the door.

She attempted one final peace gesture. "Do you need me to—?"

"Nothing. I need nothing from you." He spoke quietly, the threat of fury in his voice. "I don't need some half-grown child telling me how to do my job, and I'll thank you to try and keep your nose out of trouble until Mathis gets back. Rest assured I'm going to make sure he knows exactly how rude and overbearing you are."

If her jaw had been hanging open before, Melody was sure it was now on the floor, along with the rest of her head that had burst free from her shoulders and exploded in response to the unwarranted attack.

Whoever said teenagers were angsty hadn't seen Tom on a bad day. *Christ.*

She gathered her things and escaped to her house at the back of the yard, wondering what had set Tom off this time that he wasn't sharing with her. Was it more than the clinic or his bad attitude? Maybe she needed to schedule a sit-down with him, maybe give him some of the large animal jobs...

And then she was mad at herself for trying to figure out a way to placate him because, dammit, *she* wasn't responsible for making Tom happy. She wasn't responsible for *anything* but herself and her job, and she was doing a good job. More than that, she'd been building a good life outside of work.

Worse than frustrating, it was infuriating as hell to discover that being tossed a bunch of shitty attitude was enough to make her start going back over the events of the past few days to see where she possibly could have gone wrong.

She hadn't trusted herself. She'd begun to search through her words and actions to see if there was any truth in what Tom had accused her of.

Agitation flared, and she paced the small kitchen area like her pants were on fire. She grabbed her keys and whistled for Charlie, heading out the door with a cloud of brimstone floating around her head.

She needed to burn off some energy, and she knew exactly where to go.

~

STEVE WAS SITTING on the front porch playing his guitar when Melody's truck appeared in the distance. The thick line of dust rising behind it warned him she was coming in hot, and he laid his guitar aside and approached the stairs.

The door slammed as she exited the vehicle and stomped toward him, fire in her cheeks that made her whole face come alive.

He hoped whatever had pissed her off wasn't him. "You okay?"

"Stupid, goddamn bastard, and the whole entire, freaking, insane, judgmental..." She stopped in front of him, passion blazing from her eyes as she jammed her fists against her hips. Her chin lifted high as she stood before him vibrating with energy.

That was part of an answer. "I take it someone pushed the wrong button."

She caught the front of his shirt and jerked him forward. Well, as much as she could jerk him forward considering he outweighed her by a lot.

"Fuck me," she demanded.

That was out of the blue. "What the hell?"

She narrowed her eyes as she stepped in close enough they touched, one leg jammed between his so she was riding his thigh. "I am so mad right now I want to shoot something, or punch someone, or just goddamn *rip* something apart with my bare hands. I'm not going to do any of those things, but if I don't burn up this energy, I'm going to explode."

"So you want to fuck." Steve thrust a hand into her hair to tilt her face toward him. "Sounds like you're using me, sweetheart."

"You want to argue about fucking me six ways to Sunday? I don't think so. Consider it an on-the-job perk. You're my therapist, and I need a really good bitch session."

She all but jumped up his body, wrapping her legs around his waist and clinging tight as she jammed their mouths together.

Hell, yeah.

He could work with her wild passion, but he had plans. She was on fire? He was going to direct the burn. In the end, both of them would be more satisfied than just falling into bed for a fast fuck to get her mad out. When he finally heard her call out in pleasure later, there would be nothing on her mind except him.

Nothing but *them*.

First he kissed her. He took her lips and accepted her response, and made it all about driving the flame higher. She was like a wild cat, scratching his shoulders with her nails as she nipped at his lip. Thrusting her fingers into his hair and keeping their mouths together.

He worked to slow her, stepping toward the house and spinning them until he could press her to the exterior wall. Trapping her between the solid wood and his body.

Her gasp of pleasure broke through his rising desire. The way she shuddered under his touch as he slipped a hand behind her head and directed her lips to meet his—her response caught his attention like a four-alarm siren.

Steve held her back when she would have rushed forward. Taking her lips for a brief, hard kiss before lowering his mouth to her neck and sucking. Leaving a mark as he rocked against her and let her feel exactly how turned on he was.

She dragged her lips free, words escaping in brief puffs. "You going to fuck me right here?"

"Nope."

She groaned in protest, squeezing her thighs in an attempt to rub them together. "Damn you."

"I'll fuck you," he promised. "But why rush? I owe you some orgasms."

Melody fisted her hands in his hair and tugged. "Don't patronize me, buddy."

Wow, she really was pissed. He jerked her from the wall and headed for the front door. "You think me offering to make you come is patronizing?"

"Settle down, little woman. It's all in your head..."

Steve laughed. "It's all going to be in your pussy. My tongue, my fingers. My cock. I'll use anything I need to fuck that attitude right out of you."

She clung to his neck, eyes wide as she stared at him. The edge of her fury was gone, replaced by rising desire. "Do it. Right now," she ordered.

Funny how she still thought she was the one in charge. "When I'm ready."

She swore at him. Dirty, filthy words that only made him smile as he carried her down the hall to his bedroom. He held her so she couldn't escape, and when he reached the door, he jerked to a stop to get her attention.

"You nearly done?"

"Fuck you," she muttered.

"Ah, no. I don't think we're quite there yet." He pulled her arms from around her neck and threw her toward the bed.

MELODY HADN'T FINISHING BOUNCING when he landed squarely on top of her. She tried to scramble away, but he was too heavy and he was too sneaky, sliding along her arm until he could wrap his fingers around her wrist.

He brought her arm above her head and pinned it to the mattress. A moment later he had her other hand in the same position, fixing her in place.

"I like that you want to burn off your energy without knocking someone's head off," he said, his voice gone low and husky. "And you're so fucking sexy when you're pissed off."

She rocked her body hard, slamming her torso into his. "I don't feel like your cock is inside me. Or am I missing something?"

Her insult hit the mark. His eyes flashed then he had her flipped over on the mattress, pinned in place with a hand at the back of her neck and his legs over her thighs. "I'd wash your mouth out with soap, but there's another punishment that suits foul-mouthed little girls."

She struggled briefly, but it was no use. She could've been

strapped down and had concrete poured over her for all the good wiggling did. "You gonna spank me?"

He lifted her hips in the air and reached under her to undo her jeans. "Damn right I am."

Suddenly the anger twisted, and the fire inside her turned to anticipation. "Shit."

He had her jeans peeled away in a flash, her underwear as well and then he was back over her. The coarse fabric of his jeans pressed against her naked skin as he laid his weight upon her and put his lips close to her ear. "You want me to stop?"

The question came out as a whisper. Gentle in comparison to how harsh and commanding he'd spoken a moment earlier. "Hell, no."

He caught hold of her earlobe and nipped, sending another shot of lust through her. "You tell me to stop, and I will, but if you want to burn for a while, I can take it."

Burn? She was on fire just thinking about it. "If I want you to stop what you're doing, I'll call you Stephen. Boring, old-fashioned, very *vanilla* Stephen."

He chuckled. "Damn, you are evil."

Then he wasn't laughing anymore. He was over her like an avenging angel, dragging her into the position he wanted, with her legs hanging from the bed, her butt balanced on the very edge.

His hands swept over her backside, shoving her T-shirt out of the way. She was about to offer to strip it off when his palm made contact with her ass and speaking became impossible. The sound and the pain hit at the same moment, and she gasped, centering on this new thing.

When he brought his hand down again, it wasn't necessarily the sensation on her ass that turned her on, but the fact he had her totally under his control. She tried to move and was blocked.

She tried to buck him off, wiggling her feet toward the floor in an attempt to rear upward.

Her endeavour earned another laugh and another series of hard, quick slaps against where her thigh and butt met. The sensitive place was so close to her pussy that the strike sent shock waves through her core.

Her butt tingled, and she found it difficult to draw a full breath of air when he moved behind her, his legs on either side of her thighs. His zipper opened, the rasp of the metal loud in the room, and she glanced over her shoulder to see him pull out his cock. The thick shaft thrust from his jeans, then she couldn't see anymore as he lifted her hips in the air. He caught her under the thighs and pushed her legs open as wide as they would go.

Precariously balanced on her arms with her hips in the air, she waited for the moment when he'd drive his cock into her pussy.

When it happened it was without preamble. No warm up. No harsh thrusts. Just a steady push as he entered her body and drove the remaining air from her lungs.

"Oh God, *yes.*"

Then dammit if the bastard didn't freeze. He sat there with her pinned in place like some freaky butterfly specimen. The thickness of his cock was impossible to ignore, spreading her wide, making her far too aware of his presence.

His grasp on her hips tightened as his fingers dug into her muscles. His thumbs like nails into her butt muscles. Melody squeezed around his cock, loving his reaction as she dragged a moan from his lips.

"Bad girl." He smacked his palm against her right ass cheek.

It wasn't just the way he held her immobile, but everything about the way he touched her. His fingers danced over her skin, the light brush a sharp contrast to a moment later when he scraped his nails over sensitized nerves. She wiggled, trying to get him to move, but it was impossible.

"Damn you, Steve. I said fuck me."

"You asked for it."

And finally, *finally*, he delivered.

He pulled back so every inch of her felt every inch of him. She expected him to drive forward in a rush, thrusting deep, but instead he moved like molasses twice, three times—four. He repeated the slow rocking motion until she thought she'd go mad.

Then he slid a finger between her cheeks, pausing to play with the sensitive spot.

Oh, damn.

"I want to take you here," he said.

It wasn't a confession, and it wasn't a question, and when he lowered her to the bed and stepped away for a moment, Melody debated snatching up her things and racing from the room.

The other part of her wanted to get right back into position and let him do his worst.

He returned while she was in the middle of rolling over, his dark gaze taking in her half-naked body, and the T-shirt now bunched around her chest.

"Going somewhere?" he asked, tossing a bottle of lube onto the bed beside her.

Melody scrambled back on the bed, and he went straight after her. Trapping her under his body and kissing her madly. His body connected with her naked skin from the waist down. It felt oddly humbling to be so vulnerable.

He pressed up on his hands to stare into her eyes. His breathing as erratic as hers. "Yes?"

She quivered under him. "I've never done that before," she admitted.

His nostrils flared as he took a deep breath. "Then I'll make it good for you, sweetheart. I'll make it really good."

He kissed her, this time a gentle touch like a morning breeze. While he caressed her lips, his fingers were busy at work, stripping away the shirt from her body, and undoing her bra until she was bare and vulnerable, completely at his mercy.

His shirt came off as well, flying into the corner of the room, but her eyes stayed pinned to his torso. To the beautiful muscles flexing as he rid himself of his jeans before leaning down to press a kiss over her heart.

The next ten minutes were all about sensation as he licked and sucked, his hands moving over her, pinching with his fingers until her nipples were rock solid and her breathing was ragged.

Farther down he moved, butterfly kisses flitting over her skin to her belly button. One hand skimmed over her until his fingers dipped between her folds to tease her clit.

And then his mouth was between her legs, his hands cupping the backs of her knees as he lifted her thighs apart and proceeded to blow her mind. Sensations built in one wicked rush until her entire body tightened with pleasure, and she called out his name.

But he didn't stop, driving her past the point where she might have been able to relax, her body sated with pleasure. He alternated tickling her clit with his clever tongue and sucking lightly as one finger stroked into her pussy. Then two fingers, easing in and out far too gently to make her come.

He was between her legs, her body twitching every time he hit the right spot, when his fingers moved lower. Circling, taunting. Out of nowhere extra moisture trickled between her cheeks, and the next time he put his mouth over her clit, he pressed one finger into her butt, spearing her on the thick digit.

It was the strangest sensation, not at all unpleasant. Especially not when combined with a rapidly approaching climax. Melody clutched her knees and held them out of the way, tilting her pelvis in a clear indication she enjoyed what he was doing.

And what he was doing was shoving her off the cliff. This orgasm hit hard and quick, her body pulsing, butt squeezing around his finger.

He groaned in approval. "You're going to be so damn tight."

She glanced down to see him staring at her, the fire she'd felt in her soul earlier transferred into his gaze.

Wicked hot, white hot.

He wiped his mouth with his hand as he continued to ease lube into her ass.

"Is it good?" he asked.

Melody took a moment to consider the new sensations, but she could honestly answer yes. "It feels weird. Not at all like when you go in my pussy, but it's good."

Every bit of her was warmed up and ready, and when he stood and stared down at her, she found it difficult to muster any embarrassment at the position she was in. She lay flat on her back with her knees held wide, offering a personal invitation for his incredible body to sink in deep.

He fisted his cock, moisture glistening over its length as he covered himself with lube. The entire time, though, his eyes never lost focus, never moved away from hers—as if she were the only thing in his world.

He knelt at the edge of the bed, staring into her soul. The tip of his cock pressed to her hole with enough steady pressure she knew he was there.

"Tell me," he said. "Tell me if you need anything."

Melody clutched her knees harder, breathing out as he pushed his hips forward. For the first moment she didn't think anything was going to happen, and then his cock broke through her resistance.

"Oh my *word*."

He froze. "Sweetheart?"

It sure the hell didn't feel like having his cock in her pussy, but she didn't want him to stop either. "Go really, *really* slow, okay?"

Steve nodded, dropping a hand between her legs and pressing his thumb over her clit. For a few minutes he didn't do anything except play with her, and the longer he teased, the less it felt as if she were being invaded, and more as if she was holding back from experiencing something incredible.

She caught his gaze and nodded, her breathing picking up again. "A little more."

The next couple minutes he showed so much control, using such small movements it had to be driving him mad. After half a dozen infinitely careful rocks, it was as if he'd flipped a switch inside her. No longer was she waiting for pleasure to arrive. It rushed over her, a cool, electrifying sensation that seemed out of place, and yet so perfect.

She slipped her fingers under his and took control of her clit. "I need more," she demanded.

He lowered his hands to her hips, and pulled back an inch before sinking all the way in, bumping their groins together.

His eyes rolled back in his head. "Fuck, that feels good."

Without any lying on her part, Melody could agree with him. More than agree—she was close to another orgasm. "It feels *really* good."

Slowly at first then faster, Steve pulled back before thrusting forward, opening her and controlling her. The only things she could do were dance her fingers over her clit with her right hand, and clutch the bed sheets with her left.

They were caught up in the moments before the end. The fire that had burned her earlier now centralized in her ass and pussy as he drove his cock into her. His finesse vanished as the grip on her hips tightened, and he hauled her back onto him, each motion harder.

Each more perfect.

Between breathing in to say his name and getting the word out, the orgasm surprised her. Stole her breath as everything tightened in her lower body. Steve shouted, and she could imagine why as her ass clamped down on his cock like a fist.

Then they were both shuddering with their release, her fingers falling away as she caught hold of his shoulders. He held himself over her. Cock buried in her body, intimately together.

Completely connected.

After the shaking was done, after Steve had taken her to the shower and they'd washed each other with soap bubbles until they couldn't stand it any longer... After he dried her off so tenderly her throat began to tighten with emotion...

After all that, he curled himself around her in the bed, their naked bodies spooned together as their breathing settled.

He brushed hair from her face as he nuzzled his chin against her neck. "You feel better?"

Melody had to think hard to remember what he was asking. And then it didn't matter what had brought her there. Not anymore.

"I feel great," she admitted.

She cupped the back of his head and offered her lips for a gentle good-night kiss.

18

Steve pushed through the door at the hardware store, the small bell overhead chiming softly and turning attention toward him. Conversation stalled among the three men at the counter as they glanced his way, one of them looking damn guilty before turning his back and pretending to make a big show of paying his bill.

His sister's words came to mind—Anna had said people were talking.

Good thing Steve's give-a-damn was broken. There was nothing going on between him and Melody to be ashamed of, and he certainly wasn't ashamed of *her*, either.

"Steve."

He faced Barry Ragan, offering the barest smile he could. The man rubbed him the wrong way, although he could never say why. "How're you doing?"

"I was doing great until I got my bill from your girlfriend."

Awesome. Money complaints were a common thing to bitch about, but no way was Steve going to step in the middle of it.

"That's always the toughest part," he offered sympathetically.

"We take care of our animals best we can, but when we need an expert, it costs."

"Oh, hell, I don't have any troubles paying for an expert. I have troubles paying for treatment that didn't work because some little girl likes to pretend she knows what she's doing." Barry gave him a stern look. "You need to take some control over that woman. Get her involved in raising puppies or something that doesn't interfere with our livelihoods."

For fucks' sake. Steve lost all patience with the man.

"Sure. How about I just get her pregnant? I could keep her barefoot and in the kitchen so she can spend the day chasing after my rug rats and not bother you any longer with her five years plus of veterinary training."

Steve's phone went off, buzzing with his mother's ring tone, and he stepped away from the idiot to answer her. *Jesus*, some people were assholes *and* stupid. "Hi, Mom. You need anything from town?"

Her normally upbeat tone was missing as she rattled back rapidly. "My sister broke her hip. I just got the phone call, so I'm headed to Edmonton to take care of the kids until she's out of the hospital."

"Damn, how the hell did that happen?" His aunt was far too young to be breaking bones unless she'd been in a huge accident. "Is everyone else okay?"

"She fell down the stairs. It sounds like she's lucky she didn't break her neck." In the background he could hear his father speaking, then rustling noises as his mom rushed to pack. "Sorry for taking off and—"

"Are you kidding? Of course you're going to take care of Auntie Deanna. Don't worry about us. We can handle everything at the ranch, and I'll make sure to keep an eye on Dad."

"I heard that," his father called. "I'm not a baby. I'll take care of myself, thank you very much."

"Yes, you're all grown up. Now be quiet while I talk to our son." His mom came back on the line. "I'll leave a list of everything that needs to be done around the house, and you can contact the Whiskey Creek girls to give you a hand if you need it."

"Don't worry about us," Steve assured her again. "Take care of your sister, and let us know if there's anything we can do."

He hung up and glanced around, but Barry had vanished—thank God. So maybe his sarcasm hadn't been the best response, but it was a stupid conversation in the first place.

Steve had just picked up the first of his shopping-list items when it hit. With his mom gone and his dad out of commission, it was down to the three boys running the ranch.

Strange how realizing that made the enormity of his responsibilities that much bigger. He knew the shifting of tasks from one generation to the next was natural. That was partly what he'd been preparing for over the last year, not only to impress Melody, but to do his damn job without being told. Just like a grown-up.

The trip back to the Moonshine spread seemed a little more significant than usual.

He'd barely finished carrying his purchases into the barn when his little brother appeared. Lee nodded a greeting, sauntering past with buckets in both hands. "I take it Mom told you the news?"

"Yeah, I heard." Steve glanced around to see if there were any emergencies to deal with in the barn. "We're going to need to plan ahead even more. You available tonight so we can talk? I'll contact Trevor and make sure we can all make it."

"Meeting here, right? Because if you leave Dad out, it'll make him feel worse."

That was one mistake Steve had no intention of making. "He might not be feeling well but his brain works fine, and he's got years of experience on us. There's no way I want to do this without him."

Lee grunted in approval, turning on his heel and heading toward the chicken coop.

Steve's mind turned back to the family dinner, and curiosity got the better of him. "Hey, Lee. Who are you interested in?"

"Not talking about this," Lee called over his shoulder as he continued on his path.

"Oh, come on." Steve jogged after him, not to tease but because he was honestly interested. "You can tell me. Maybe I can help you get together with her. You could double date sometime with me and Melody."

His little brother didn't answer, unlatching the gate to the coop and stepping inside. He dipped his hand into the bucket to scatter seed, silently watching as the chickens rushed in circles, pecking at the ground.

A striking image of the strong, silent type—the only problem with that was not talking didn't help anyone move forward. "I'm not being a shit. Is there someone you're interested in?"

Lee paused, resting the bucket on the railing outside the coop as he opened the sidewall to get at the laying racks. "Doesn't matter if I'm interested in her or not. It's not going to happen."

Oh boy. This was more mysterious than Steve had expected. "Why would you say something like that? There's no reason someone wouldn't want to get involved with you."

His brother was back to ignoring him, reaching carefully into the nests and placing the eggs in the empty bucket.

"Why is this an issue? Girls don't think you're hideous. Have you asked her out? Is there—?"

Lee turned on him. "Let's not do this. I don't need your help with my love life."

"I know I'm not the best example," Steve said, ignoring Lee's protests. "In fact, I'm the poster child for how to be a shitty boyfriend, at least if you look at how I treated Melody last year. But I can't think of any reason why a woman wouldn't want to get to know you better. You need to not give up so easy."

"She's married," Lee blurted out.

All Steve's encouraging gusto vanished into thin air. "Oh."

His brother snorted in derision. "Yes, *oh*. Which is why I told you to drop it. It's okay, it's not as if we were destined to be together. I'll get over it."

"Still sucks," Steve commiserated.

"That it does," Lee agreed, going back to his task. "I'll see you at supper. I already got things going for a spaghetti sauce, so it won't take long to pull together a meal. We can talk then."

Damn. Just another broken cog in the wheel. Maybe it was because he'd found out how good it was to have Melody in his life, but he felt doubly awful for his brother.

Steve made his way through the afternoon chores. Too many things to think about, too many things to deal with. But in the middle of all of it, his mind kept returning to Melody.

No matter how busy he got, he wasn't going to let their relationship suffer. She was too important. Somehow they'd work it out.

IT HAD BEEN DRIVING her crazy. Every time she passed Daltons' land she'd been in too much of a hurry to stop and check on the horses. Too much time had passed, and she'd had enough.

Today she was making time, even though it came at the end of a full day's work. Melody pulled to the side of the road closest to the nearest stile, grabbed a pair of work gloves and headed for the shed.

From the back of the truck, one loud bark rang out, and a sudden thrill of happiness struck. It was strange having a dog around, but also wonderful. Charlie had turned out to be a fabulous helper and a great companion.

Melody considered before lowering the tailgate and giving the command to come. "You need to listen," she warned. "I don't know what we're going to find."

Charlie bounced over the grass ahead of her, uncovering a game trail that led straight to the horse shed. Melody followed at a slower pace, her mind wandering through the different experiences of the past few days.

It was strange how life could be amazing and yet at the same time terrible. She slipped her hands into her pockets as she strolled forward, Charlie sniffed everywhere, running back and forth between Melody and the next interesting discovery on the path. Having an animal that was so well trained that she stayed close without being called. That? Was one of the good things. Having a dog in her life was amazing. It was something Melody had always longed for, and finally having it happen was like a miracle.

Ahead of her, two swayed-back horses lifted their heads at her approach, alert enough to notice her, but not wary enough to run away.

She edged toward the fence, trying to avoid the snarled barbed wire looped around itself in a clumsy repair job.

"Shit." Melody reached down to untangle herself from where she'd stepped into a concealed loop, hidden in the mess of weeds.

Charlie waited patiently at the end of the open trail, her tail wagging as she eyed the horses.

"No," Melody ordered. "Stay."

Charlie sat, but her eyes remained on the two equines in front of her.

Melody put her full attention to the mess she was in, attempting to escape without leaving herself battered and bruised. By the time she was free, though, her jeans were ripped and her new gloves had proved too thin to save her from multiple puncture wounds.

It meant when she finally made it into the pen she was already in a bad mood. But no matter if she'd walked in there singing like the bluebird of happiness, what she found would have been enough to send her temperature soaring.

The horses were nearly starved, boney ribs visible as they stared listlessly at her. As if all hope had been sucked from them and they didn't dare imagine she might be there for their sake.

Normally when Melody visited ranches, horses came forward to greet her. They'd nudge her pockets looking for treats or hoping to be scratched. If they weren't the social type she'd be ignored, the grass underfoot far more interesting than some human interloper.

These horses had eaten every blade of grass within the fenced area, and what they could reach on the other side of the wire. Melody poked her head inside the shelter, which was as close to four sticks and a shingle as any outbuilding she'd ever seen. It was barely any protection from the wind, and no protection from the rain they'd been experiencing over the past few days.

In the corner where a couple of boards were nailed together was a sodden pile of hay, mold growing in spots, so musty and decayed even the mice hadn't touched it.

Melody turned to the horses, shaking her head, furious on their behalf. "Don't you worry, I'm going to find out who did this and make it right."

Maybe she should have thought it through more, but she was far too upset to be rational. Steve had mentioned Sean's name before, so that's where she headed, pulling into the yard just as the Daltons were walking down the cobblestone path to their truck, the two of them dressed up as if they were headed to a fancy party.

Emily frowned for a moment before forcing a polite smile. "Melody. Is everything okay?"

Melody barely heard the question she was too focused on Sean who wore his typical sneer. "Stopped by to ask a question. I thought I saw a *For Sale* sign on the quarter to the south of your barn. Do you own that land?"

What she got was a far-from-polite response from Sean. "There are no signs posted anywhere in that area. What the hell are you talking about?"

"I could've sworn I saw one," Melody lied. "So, you don't know who owns the land?"

"We do," Emily answered. "But I assure you, it's not for sale. We don't have any—"

"What do you want," Sean interrupted his wife, brow furrowed as he focused on Melody.

That was all the information she needed. "You have horses on that land, and from their appearance, you've been neglecting their care. I suggest you change that immediately, or I'll put in a report to the authorities."

Emily's face registered her shock. Sean just looked more pissed off than usual, which was saying something. "You can't come on to my land and threaten me. I take good care of my animals, and there's no way you can prove otherwise."

Melody opened her mouth to give them the facts when he shouted at her before she could get a word in.

"Those horses have food and they've got water, and that's all I have to provide." He caught hold of his wife, leading them both around Melody as if she were a steaming pile of manure. "So I'll thank you to mind your own damn business. Now get off my land. I don't want to see you on it again. Not here, and not by the horses—not unless I phone you and ask you to come out, which isn't damn likely. If I see you or anyone associated with you poking around in my business, I'll call the RCMP and get you arrested for trespassing."

He put his wife in their vehicle then stood and glared until Melody reluctantly got in her truck and left, still vibrating with anger.

She tried calling Steve but got sent to his voicemail, so she headed home, desperate to figure out what to do. Normally she would have contacted Mathis, and right then she sorely missed the old man.

Her anger only got worse when she checked the regulations to discover Sean was right. While the animals' condition proved he'd been neglectful, there was legally nothing she could do. They had water, they had food—though the hay wasn't edible feed for any beast. Sean could claim the damage had happened in the "short time" since he'd dropped by last.

And with his final threat of trespassing in place, she couldn't even arrange to get food delivered.

Her hands were tied, which was frustrating beyond belief. And the longer she waited for Steve to call back, the more she wanted to scream.

Fuck this day.

She called Allison and hoped her friend was ready to be dumped on.

19

*I*t took until after eight p.m. before he and his brothers were happy with their plans. They might have finished sooner, but right in the middle of their meeting, Randy fielded a phone call from Kate, getting caught up on everything that was happening in Edmonton.

They were back to having far too many balls in the air, but at least Steve wasn't the only one trying to keep them there. "If we need help, we'll go to the cousins."

Thank goodness, everyone was in agreement.

"Mike has a good head on his shoulders. If you need any advice out in the field when I can't get to you, go to him first," Randy said. "Or ask George, or one of the crew over at the Whiskey Creek spread."

The unspoken comment was obvious. Uncle Ben was the only one of Randy's brothers he didn't want involved in the decision-making process. Steve had to agree, but he hoped they'd be able to get along without any help.

"If we're done, I need to give Melody a call."

"And I'm heading to town," Trevor said. "Lee? You want to come in with me?"

Their little brother shook his head. "I'm going to hang out with Dad for a while."

"Now, don't you go feeling like you have to babysit me," Randy grumbled. "I'm not scared of being alone in this big house by myself."

Lee raised a brow. "What makes you think I'm staying for your sake? You have no idea how many leftovers are in the refrigerator. I plan to raid the pantry and watch movies on your outrageously huge Blu-ray screen."

Their dad grinned. "I knew there was a reason why I liked you best."

Steve was still laughing when he got into his truck and put through his call to Melody. "Hi, sweetheart. Sorry I didn't get back to you sooner, but we had a family emergency to deal with."

Her response came softly, as if she was exhausted. "I'm over at your cousin's if you want to join us."

Steve assumed she meant Gabe and Allison's. Probably. "Limit my targets, please?"

"Oh, right. I'm a little distracted. I stopped by to visit with Allison, and they've been putting up with my mopey ass ever since."

"Sorry to hear that. How about I come over there and take care of your mopey ass for you?"

"If you feel like being a martyr, come on down."

He drove the extra ten minutes past his house to Gabe's place. Melody's truck was in the yard, and four of them were gathered around the small fire in the fire pit.

Rafe moved quickly out of the chair next to Melody. "I guess I'll head home now."

"See you tomorrow," Gabe said with a wave. "And don't worry. You didn't do anything wrong."

Steve gave his cousin a thump on the shoulder as they passed then sank to his knees beside Melody to offer her a kiss. She curled her hands around his shoulders, sighing as he pulled back to examine her face closer. "You okay?"

She shrugged. "Pissed off. Nothing new there, right?"

He moved into the chair Rafe had abandoned, watching as his cousin pulled himself up on his horse and headed over the dark fields toward the rental house. Steve glanced at Gabe and Allison. "Anything I need to know about what's going on with Rafe?"

Gabe shook his head. "Ben's being..."

"A butthead," Allison offered.

"I was going to say *difficult*, but your description works." Gabe stretched his legs in front of him, glancing at Steve and shaking his head. "You think it's something that comes with the territory? Do you think when *we* hit a certain age, we'll lose track of what's important to younger people?"

"What makes you think Ben ever gave a damn about what was important to you or Rafe, or anyone else for that matter?" Allison slapped her hands on her thighs, anger flashing in her eyes. "Same thing with the rest of the crew that's giving Melody grief. The issue isn't that they're older, it's that they've never had an original idea their entire life, so any kind of change just makes them crazy."

"Who was the bastard, today?" Steve asked Melody, hoping that Barry hadn't tracked her down.

She explained briefly, which made both her and Allison's comments all the more clear.

"Damn." There had to be a way to deal with this. "Maybe if they don't see us drop off the feed, no one will get in trouble."

"Right, because no one who knows that I gave him hell and that you and I are going out will *possibly* put it together."

"We could go and haul the horses out," Gabe suggested.

"Wouldn't take more than five minutes."

Allison laid a hand on his thigh. "I think that's called horse-rustling, and it's still frowned upon in these parts."

Even as Steve's frustration rose, Melody relaxed back in her chair. "We're not going to do anything illegal, because in the end, if something does happen, it's going to reflect on Mathis, and that's the last thing I want."

"We could—"

"Steve. Stop." Melody turned her big blue eyes on him and shook her head in regret. "I'm about three hours ahead of you. I know how you're feeling, but after having gone through the options, we have zero choices. Once Mathis is back he'll put the fear of God into Sean. I know he will."

She didn't look very happy about waiting, but as she said, it might be the only solution. He vowed to check with his father, though, before he gave up hope. "And the snarky comments you're getting?"

"Not important. I won't melt. The only way to deal with these shitheads is to ignore them. I refuse to comment when they say my skills are lackluster, or they suggest I should go play doctor with a My Little Pony set."

"Really? *Jerks.*" Allison poked the fire harder than needed, sparks flying skyward. "I agree with you in principle. There's nothing you can do, so ignoring them is the best bet. But you have to promise that every time someone is stupid, you give me their name. If they come into the restaurant, there's going to be a whole lot of nasty dinners served."

Laughter rippled for a moment amongst the group even though it was clear she was joking. "Don't put your business at risk," Melody warned. "Although that's a very entertaining thought."

"If I'd known sooner, I would've dropped Sean's dessert in his lap tonight."

"Just the offer makes me feel better." Melody chuckled. "What would I do without friends like you?"

She squeezed Steve's fingers as she spoke, and in spite of the increased workload he was facing, and his shared frustrations that life wasn't going smoothly for Melody, he couldn't help but feel things were pretty damn good.

It didn't seem as if a countdown clock was ticking ominously in the background. It sounded a lot more like two people finding a way to be together, no matter what.

He liked the change.

~

SOMEHOW SHE WAS GOING to make this day memorable. At least that's what Melody vowed as she hurried through breakfast. There was a lot going on in her life that was good—she needed to focus on that.

She opened the front door and headed down the steps, coffee mug in one hand and a treat for Charlie in the other. Her dog rose, trotting toward her from the small shelter Steve had dropped off a couple of days earlier.

"Good morning, Charlie. Have you been a good girl?"

Charlie stopped to stretch, wagging her tail even in the awkward position. The sight made Melody smile, and she knelt to offer her dog a quick scratch behind the ears.

"I need to get my work roster, but how about I take you to the park for a few minutes first? We may as well start the day right." The pause in routine made both of them happy, even though they didn't stay long.

Callie was already at the front desk, handing over the worksheets for the day with a smile lighting her face. "Nobody should be any trouble today." She spoke quietly, glancing toward Tom's office.

Well, that was a surprise. "How did you manage that? Did a whole bunch of people cancel appointments?"

The receptionist organized papers on her desk, her self-satisfied expression building. "I figured by now you'd need a break from the testosterone poisoning. Every time someone with a good attitude called last week, I tried to book them for today."

"You're an angel." Melody scanned her way down the list before grinning at Callie. "I'll come back at lunch to pick up what I need for the afternoon. No use in hauling it with me."

"I'll package everything up if I have time between patients," she offered.

Another thing to be grateful for—Callie had a heart of gold.

Most of the morning went by quickly, and the contrast was nearly heartbreaking. Walking onto a section of land where people smiled at her instead of scowling—that small gesture made a huge difference.

She hit the last stop before lunch, hoisting the heavy box she'd loaded her supplies into and making her way precariously toward the barn.

The farmer rushed forward, grabbing the box away. "Don't you be carrying things like that. It's not right."

Melody laughed before she could stop herself. "Roger, a lot of my work requires heavy lifting. Honest, I can do it."

He shook his head and headed to the barn, muttering over his shoulder. "You need to take better care of yourself. No use in overdoing it."

And for the next hour as she worked with the calves, he kept getting in her way, especially when she went to lift them. His unsolicited help made it difficult for her to do her job, but there wasn't much she could say. He honestly seemed to want to help, no matter how often she repeated she didn't need his assistance.

Strange? Yes. Awkward? Definitely, but when she compared his behaviour to the men who made nasty comments or outright insulted her, or those whose hands had a tendency to wander off the animals and onto her...

She'd put up with Roger's weird behaviour over those any day.

Still, it felt good to be done and head back to the clinic for some normal time.

She dropped the empty packaging and syringes in the back for Callie to deal with before making her way into the small staff room. Tom had the office door shut, a low rumble indicting he was probably on the phone.

Thank goodness. She didn't need to deal with him right now.

"Callie, someone's been dropping drugs into the water system, or something. I've never seen so many guys acting so strangely."

She'd just refilled her coffee cup from the urn when Callie snatched the cup away. "No more of that. It's not good for you."

Melody eyed her with suspicion and a touch of annoyance. "It's a good thing that wasn't my first cup of the day, or you'd be bleeding right now."

Callie shook her head. "You'll have to get used to doing without coffee. The caffeine isn't good for you."

"Getting between me and my coffee isn't good for you, either." What the heck was going on? She reached for the urn to fill another cup. "Did you find time to gather what I need for the afternoon?"

"Some of it. We'll have to change a few of the appointments. Maybe you and Tom should change some of your assignments. You shouldn't be involved in any contagious-disease situations. Not in your condition."

Not in her condition...

Melody caught hold of Callie's arms to force a face-to-face confrontation. "Honey, you're not making sense. What the *hell* are you talking about?"

"Well, I didn't want to say anything until you told me, but the news has been flying all around this morning. Are you planning on working your entire pregnancy? Because you'll have to consider—"

"What?" A loud whoosh rang in Melody's ears as the pieces fell into place. "I'm not pregnant."

Callie's mouth hung open. She frowned. "Are you sure?"

A laugh escaped as the ridiculousness of the situation struck her. "Yeah, I'm pretty damn sure. Who the heck said I was pregnant?"

The receptionist thought hard. "Tom came back from coffee at the café, so I assume he heard someone mentioned it this morning." Callie made a face. "Okay, now I feel like a fool. I set up the easy day for you before I heard anything, by the way. Just thought you needed a break. And then you were pregnant, but you're not... Yup, I feel like a fool."

"Don't worry about it—I don't blame you at all. But no wonder Roger was being stupid." Just another crazy thing to have to deal with. If someone at the café had announced she was pregnant, by now it would be all over the countryside. "*Jeez*. I'm going to have to walk onto every job and announce 'Hi, I'm not pregnant, so you don't have to treat me like glass.'"

"Annoying, but less annoying than actually being pregnant," Callie suggested. "I did think it was a little quick for you and Steve to be starting a family, but accidents happen."

Oh shit. *Steve*. She needed to get in touch with him a.s.a.p. Melody grabbed the work list from Callie. "I'm not pregnant, if anyone asks."

Her wonderful day had developed a nervous twitch. She headed back to her truck, hauling out her phone before she did anything else.

Hopefully she'd make contact with Steve before the rumour mill did.

20

Steve dug his way out from under the tractor, clicking on his phone one ring before it went to voicemail. "Hey, sweetheart, how's your day going?"

She hesitated before answering. "It's going strangely, but not because there's anything wrong with me. In fact it's not about me at all. I'm fine. I mean... Oh *fuck*, I don't know what I mean."

Steve pulled himself to a sitting position as he laughed. "If you want to talk about it, you'll have to be a little more coherent than that. I hope no one gave you grief this morning."

"Not in the old way. There's new trouble making the rounds, and I wanted to make sure you know it's a rumour and not the truth."

His amusement faded. "That sounds ominous. Has it been suggested we're gang leaders involved in the tearing down of the morals of our community?"

"That one I could see being fun. No, someone obviously decided my delicate female condition and bitchy attitude could only be caused because I had a bun in the oven."

It took a moment before what she'd said registered. "Someone started the rumour that you're pregnant? What the hell?"

"Exactly. But I wanted you to know it's not true, in case some good-natured Samaritan decided to drop that bomb on you. I am not pregnant, and while it makes no sense that anyone—"

"Oh, shit." Steve stared into space, desperately trying to remember the offhand comment he'd tossed at Barry the other day. "Oh, *fuck*."

"Steve?"

He felt like an idiot. "I'm not one hundred percent positive, but this might be my fault."

Her curse rang in his ear. "What the heck are you talking about? You told someone I was pregnant? Why would you do that?"

"I didn't say you were pregnant. I made a smartass comment to someone while at the same time pointing out you were far more educated than they were."

"Jeez. And then the rumour mill took that and twisted it into the crap I'm having to deal with now."

He didn't blame her for being pissed off. Not one bit.

"I'm so sorry. It was a casual comment to make my point, and then I forgot all about it dealing with my mom leaving, and you and the thing with Sean." She sat quietly on the other end of the line for long enough his nerves began to twitch. "Talk to me, sweetheart. What can I do to make this better?"

Melody let out a long sigh. "There's nothing to do. And I get it. I've said things in passing myself that could come back and bite me in the ass. I'm just frustrated I have something else shitty to deal with."

"I feel horrible," he confessed, bluntly honest. His gut was somewhere down around his toes.

"I know you do, but that doesn't change the situation." Another condemning pause rattled him before she spoke. "Give me some time to deal with it. I'm not really mad at you, I'm just—*mad*."

Steve understood. "I'll give you some room, but if you think of anything I can do to help, let me know. Please?"

"I will."

She sounded so sad and alone he was pissed off all over again at himself, and at the community that appeared to have the brains of a bat. "Come over for dinner tonight. I can't make it up to you, but I can take care of you. I'll rub your feet. Play your favourite songs..."

She laughed. "It's hard to stay upset when you're being adorable."

"Good to know. I'll keep adorable at the top of my arsenal just for you."

"Okay, dinner. And a back rub," she demanded.

"Anything you want," he promised, hanging up with a lump of dread settled at the base of his throat.

Fuck stupid mindless comments, and fuck small towns that thrived on gossip, and fuck...*everything*.

He powered through his day, hoping in passing that by the time his mom came back the rumour would be killed dead. He waited on the front porch for Melody to arrive, his feet on the railing, his hands crossed behind his head.

The evening had turned out to be beautiful and clear. The sound of cows grazing nearby and the occasional songbird were all that interrupted the whisper of wind in the trees at his back. To the west lay the only land in the area that didn't belong to the Colemans, and beyond that the Rocky Mountains rose to the skies on Alberta crown land. It was a glorious place to live, and in spite of his worries, Steve felt contentment roll through his soul.

They'd get through this stupid moment, him and Melody. They couldn't give up when they had so much to look forward to.

She turned into the yard, and he waited for her to join him. *Don't screw up again* that little voice in his head warned.

Melody seemed calm as she lowered the tailgate, and Charlie leapt down, heading off to greet Prince.

Steve watched her approach, her hips shifting rhythmically from side to side as she strolled forward, setting his blood boiling. She'd let her hair down around her shoulders, like golden strands of sunlight clinging to her.

He stood to greet her as she took the front steps two at a time, coming to a stop inches in front of him. She turned her pale-blue eyes up to meet his, a small smile curling the corner of her mouth.

She didn't look pissed off. This was a good thing.

"Hey."

Melody slipped her hands around his waist and eased their bodies together. "Hey, yourself. I hope you made a big supper, because I'm starving."

He placed his fingers under her chin and tilted her face up so he could press a tender kiss to her lips. Warmth passed between their bodies as they moved together.

Her eyes danced with mischief as she pulled away. "So you're planning on being extra good tonight?"

"Honest truth, I've been trying to be extra good ever since you said you'd go out with me." He linked his fingers with hers and guided her into the house. "Trust me to fuck it up with one ill-timed bit of sarcasm."

"After I had some time to think about it, it definitely got funnier."

She helped herself to a drink from the fridge, holding up a beer in his direction. He nodded then placed the rest of the food on the table.

"Can I hope you didn't get asked too many personal questions the rest of the day?"

Melody offered him a cocky grin. "I decided a strong offense was the best defense. Stopped off at the café and had a rather loud discussion with one of the waitresses about PMS and cramps."

"Evil."

She outright laughed. "You should've seen the morbid curiosity in that place. It was like they all wanted to listen to what we were talking about, but none of them wanted to *look* like they were listening. I think the café owes me commission for the extra pieces of pie that were ordered while people hung around hoping some juicy gossip would drop."

"So the rumours should die down?"

"I think so." She paused in the middle of scooping stew into her bowl. Laid her hand over his and looked him straight in the eye. "I'm not mad at you anymore, but like Allison and I pointed out last night, the best thing we can do right now is ignore the idiots."

"I can do that. Although in my defense, I did make the stupid comment *before* you told me to keep my mouth shut."

She shook her head. "People are crazy."

"They totally are," he agreed.

Dinner was quiet, peaceful and nearly perfect as they talked about nothing of consequence.

"There wasn't a single vehicle at Lee's place when I drove past. You hear what the rest of the boys are up to for the evening?" she asked.

"They're all over." Add another bizarre twist to his day. "It was strange—they all checked in with me before heading out."

She paused. "Maybe it's because with your mom gone, they want somebody to know how to get a hold of them, in case there's another emergency."

Maybe. The neat thing was Steve felt honoured to be included like that.

"Jesse and Lee decided to go tie one on somewhere south of

Calgary for the weekend—I didn't ask for any more details. Trevor is snooping around at the neighbours to see if it's worthwhile putting in an offer to rent the land. And Rafael is babysitting for Blake and Jaxi."

"You're kidding me."

He shook his head. "Nope. Stopped off here to see if I still had the box of Barbies my brothers gave me as a gag birthday gift once."

She took his empty plate and stacked it with hers, carrying them to the sink. "Is it terrible that I can picture him? Those three little girls demanding he help host a fashion show."

"He's good with kids."

She spotted his guitar leaning against the wall. "You want to serenade me a little?"

"Anytime, sweetheart."

Yet as he settled in the living room, he was torn between playing or putting her in his lap and playing with her.

Melody took the lead, passing the guitar over. "If you don't mind, I feel like singing tonight too. It's a good way to forget about everything else."

For the next half hour he led them through a medley of their favourites, the harmonies growing stronger the longer they sang until Steve thought they sounded pretty damn good.

She rested her elbows on her knees as she leaned forward and let him finish the final chorus on his own. "Well, that wasn't half-bad."

"We make beautiful music together," Steve insisted, which set her laughing even as she offered a smile.

"We're getting better, I'll give you that."

That was what he wanted to hear. He put the guitar aside and reached for her hand, pulling her between his knees. He slid his hands up her body, wrapping around her back until he could press them close, gazing up at her beautiful smile.

"I'm glad you're here," he confessed. "Not just here, in my place, but here, together. I'm glad we tried again."

Her fingers danced over his shoulders for a second before she dragged a hand through his hair, tilting her head as her smile grew more mischievous. "I'm glad I'm here too, especially since someone promised me a back rub."

He stood, giving her room to retreat. She didn't move, their bodies touching as if they couldn't get enough of each other. "Come on. You can lie on my bed," he suggested.

"That sounds like fun." Her voice had gone softer. Sultry. "Is this a clothing-optional massage?"

Steve laughed. "Is there some other way to get a really good massage?"

She paused at the entrance to his bedroom before stepping in, trailing a hand over the solid wood beams of his bedposts as she wandered past. "I suppose we could try with our clothes on, but that sounds complicated."

"Nah. Complicated is when I tie you to the bed before rubbing oil over every inch of your body."

Melody's breath skipped. "Is that one possible item on tonight's agenda?"

"Maybe." He took a step closer, the pulse beating rapidly at the base of her neck drawing him forward like he'd been lassoed. "I'm more interested right now in getting you naked. You need some help with that, or you okay on your own?"

Her gaze met his, and desire flashed. "I think I can do it on my own. But maybe you should watch me really closely—to make sure I do it right."

The evening slipped off *great* to *fucking great*. His body reacted to her teasing words, his cock thickening. Breath growing more rapid.

He pulled the chair from beside the wall and lowered himself into it. "It's your show, sweetheart. Let's see what you've got."

SHE STOOD beside the mattress and lifted her hands to her shirt, moving leisurely as she undid one button at a time. His eyes were fixed on her fingers as if he couldn't look away.

"You have any massage oil?" she asked, easing the shirt off her shoulders and letting it pool at her feet.

He didn't blink. Just pointed at the top of the dresser.

Melody sauntered over and picked it up, swinging her hips from side to side far more than necessary. She opened the lid and took a sniff. "Mmm, coconut. Makes me feel as if we're headed somewhere tropical."

"You and me, and a beach in Hawaii? I'm all over that."

His voice went rough at the end, probably because she'd tipped the container back and drizzled a line of oil across her shoulders and chest. The scent of summertime filled the room as she reached behind her and undid her bra.

"Oops. I forgot I needed to take this off first."

She leaned forward and shifted her shoulders, the soft material falling away as the oil she'd applied dripped lower in rivulets.

"Fuck."

Steve had a hand over his groin, rubbing briskly as he stared at her, mesmerized.

She brought her hands over her belly, cupping her breasts before moving high enough to get her fingers wet. As she massaged the oil over her upper body, she wasn't sure how much of the tingling was from touching herself, and how much was from the way his gaze burned her skin.

She was definitely having fun.

The button on her jeans slipped open under her fingers, then she eased the zipper down one tooth at a time, the rasp of metal on metal loud in the stillness. The only sounds were his breathing and the deafening pulse of her heartbeat in her ears.

She dropped her jeans to just off her hips, panties going with them until three quarters of her mound could be seen. She paused and placed one hand on her belly, sneaking her fingers under that final edge of material that had her blocked from his view. A moan escaped as she rubbed herself, dragging a curse from his lips.

"You need me to rub the oil on," he said.

"Soon. *Oh...*"

She arched her back and slipped her hand farther into her panties, closing her eyes as she enjoyed the tease.

She was flat out on the bed before she could blink.

Steve lay over her, staring down, his pupils gone dark. "No, I meant you *need* me to rub the oil on. It's in my job description, and I refuse to do a bad job."

Melody caught her hands around his neck and pulled him down for a deep lingering kiss, shivering as his clothes brushed her naked body, a wicked sensation that drove her desire that much higher.

"I suppose if you have to, go ahead."

She expected him to lose control and strip her bare. Hurry them together for what would undoubtedly end with another fabulous rush of physical pleasure.

What she didn't expect was for him to actually use the massage oil on her. He dribbled a line from her collarbone down the center of her body, past her bellybutton to stop just shy of her mound. Then he rubbed it in, so patient and thorough his touch sent her reeling the longer his fingers were in contact with her skin.

He eased along the side of her breast before sweeping inward, finger and thumb closing around her nipple for a brief, sharp pinch. He followed that with his palm, the even pressure of a liquid caress cascading her further into pleasure.

By the time he placed both hands on her hips to lift her to his mouth, she was ready to implode, arousal making every one of her senses more alert. More sensitive.

And then his lips were on her, his tongue dipping into her pussy. A tease and a promise, and oh-so-good she was on the edge of coming without ever feeling the build-up. Between one breath and the next she was gone. Her body responding like a well-trained instrument to his touch.

She was still spinning when he rose over her, pressing her legs apart with his broad hips and slipping his cock all the way in. The deep thrust that she was ready for, a connection and a promise.

There was no stopping this time. No teasing wait she needed to suffer through. Instead, with his gaze locked on hers, he continued to drive forward, rocking the bed with his thrusts.

Melody wrapped her legs around him, locking her ankles at his lower back. Keeping them as tightly together as she could. She placed her hands on his shoulders, clutching the strong muscles as he held himself on his elbows over her, avoiding crushing her with his weight even as he used her hard. No slowing down, no treating her as if she were delicate, and yet...

She felt precious.

The distinction turned something inside sweet and eager as the passion in his eyes deepened.

"This is all about us," Steve said softly, kissing her forehead. Kissing her cheek and the tip of her nose. "Whatever we want, whatever works for us, we do."

"Feels so good," she admitted.

He rocked his hips slower as they spoke, but never easing up completely. "Because it's us. Because it's what's right for you and me. Beautiful, strong, *amazing* Melody. So unique, so what I need."

As if he were serenading her, his words rang in her ears like the chorus of a song she'd been longing to hear. "We fit together."

"Always."

Another thrust, forcing a gasp from her. She held on tightly as he ground his hips against hers, providing the final bit of friction she needed to go off. He called her name as he came, still connected, their bodies one.

He never said it, but the words hovered between them. Like the perfect note at the end of the musical phrase, it *should* have been there, but neither of them was willing to risk it yet.

Always *and forever*.

Not yet, but soon.

21

*I*t was good to have familiar places to go.

In this case, *more* than familiar. Heck, Traders Pub should have renamed itself and kept the doors open strictly to entertain the Colemans.

He laughed at his own joke. It was obvious from the crowd that the place was growing in popularity with a lot of the locals. He slipped an arm around Melody, loving that he was able to hold her so intimately in public without any consequences. Loving the way she settled against him even tighter, as if there was nowhere else she'd rather be.

They'd abandoned the pool hall and pub side, slipping over to where dance music echoed off the walls. Steve led her forward, jostling past bodies to grab one of the tall standing-room-only tables that surrounded the open wooden floor.

His mom was still out of town, but his dad had insisted they join the rest of the clan at their regular Friday gathering. Nothing was on fire that needed to be taken care of, and Melody had actually completed work at a decent time.

He was looking forward to getting her on the dance floor, but in the meantime he slid to his left, opening space for his brothers to join them. He waved across the room to get Mitch Thompson's attention as he appeared through the crowd, Anna on his arm.

The family was changing, and Steve didn't mind one bit.

"You want me to grab you another drink?" Melody asked, her lips brushing his ear. "I have to go to the washroom anyway."

He nodded, slipping his wallet out of his back pocket to grab a couple twenties.

She laid a hand over his, tilting her head and giving him an evil look.

He shrugged. "Don't try and change me that much," he teased, the words coming out at a near shout to be heard over the blaring music.

"Don't pull that macho shit," she taunted back, giving him a wink before turning away.

Trevor put his empty beer bottle down on the table. "I hope you don't mind, but I see someone new. I better go make the moves on her before she is devastated at the lack of virile man in the room."

Steve and Lee exchanged a glance before bursting out laughing. Of course when Trevor walked up to a pretty redhead in the midst of a group of ladies and a moment later ended up with his arm around two of them, their laughter faded.

Steve shook his head. "Someday Casanova will strike out."

"When he does, I'm taking a video and putting it up on YouTube."

"It'll go viral."

"I'll make sure it's *extra* embarrassing. He deserves the best." Lee lifted his drink to his mouth as Anna and Mitch joined them.

"Does it seem exceptionally crazy in here tonight, or is it my imagination?" Anna asked.

"It's summer. Everybody's enjoying a weekend break. Next Friday if the weather holds we're meeting on the bluff," Steve informed them, making eye contact with Mitch. "Tell your brothers if they want to join us, they're welcome."

Mitch's dark gaze swept the room once before settling possessively on Anna. "We'll be there."

They chatted for a while, although Lee's attention drifted. His gaze had just passed over the far corner of the pub when he froze, his smile vanishing.

"What's wrong?" Steve demanded.

Lee blinked hard then refocused on Steve. "Nothing," he lied, because it was obvious something had caught his attention.

He wasn't about to drag it out of his brother though. He'd learned his lesson about that the hard way. "Let me know if you change your mind."

Joe and Vicki joined them as Lee took off. Steve waited for Melody to return, soaking in the pleasure of being surrounded by family.

The blissful mood lasted all of five minutes before a ruckus broke out in the corner of the room. They turned to see what was going on. Anna swore under her breath as she abandoned the table and headed toward the trouble.

A faint flash of a familiar face and swinging fists was enough to have Steve following hard on her heels.

"Lee. What the hell are you doing?" Anna caught their brother's arm in mid-swing and used his momentum to twist him into a pretzel, his arm jammed behind him as he glared at the man on the floor.

Steve glanced down in confusion. Since when did Lee have a beef with Gary Ricardo?

"Are you fucking crazy, asshole?" Gary shouted, scrabbling back as far as he could in the limited space. He caught hold of the edge of a stool and used it to bring himself back to vertical, the woman he was with hiding behind him in the dark corner. Gary gestured wildly at the people around them. "I didn't do anything. This lunatic attacked me out of nowhere."

Lee's fists were clenched, even as he was held immobile. But he didn't say anything. Not to Gary, not to Anna in defense.

Anna shook her head, shoving Lee toward the door. "Go home," she ordered.

She turned her glare on Gary. Steve expected the man to rant and rave, or demand Lee get more in punishment than a slap on the wrist.

Instead, he grabbed his coat and shuffled from the bar as fast as he could, his woman in tow as he headed out the door on the opposite side to where Lee had exited.

What the hell was that about?

"Anything I need to worry about?" Steve asked Anna as they made their way back to their table.

"I can't talk about it." Which meant it involved something that had been reported down at the police station.

How Lee was involved, Steve had no idea.

Melody was back at the table, waiting for them along with Mitch.

The man's cool composure confused Steve. "I thought for sure I'd see you go in there, guns blazing."

His future brother-in-law tilted his head toward Anna. "She's sat me down a few times and explained jurisdiction, and while I'll still beat the crap out of anyone who threatens to hurt her, she's got a pretty good handle on taking care of herself. And you guys."

"I swear I'm not coming into Traders anymore on the nights you boys are around." Anna shook her head. "It's bad enough I have to listen to people tell me to make the Colemans behave when I'm not out on the town."

Then the fight was forgotten, because Melody had him by the hand and out on the dance floor, wrapping herself around him.

She planted one leg on either side of his, casually bumping his thigh as they rocked together, their closeness explained by the crowded dance floor.

The honest truth was they couldn't keep their hands off each other.

The sexual energy between them was doing more than driving him crazy. With her so close, he could smell the scent of her skin. He got harder as the dance got hotter, the top button on her blouse coming loose to give him a perfect view of the top of her breasts.

The dancing ratcheted up a notch, and the music rang a little louder, and Steve thought he was just about in paradise. Especially since after they were done enjoying themselves on the dance floor, he was taking her home. That made all of this even better, like extended public foreplay.

He put his lips near her ear because it had to be said. "So, have we gotten kinky enough for you? Or are we still walking on the vanilla side?"

She answered by slipping her hands into his back pockets and digging in her nails, easing her hips against him in a move calculated to blow his mind.

It took every ounce of control he possessed to ignore the urge telling him to pick her up so they could go fuck each other blind in his truck. "Playing with fire, sweetheart. Because I have no objections to taking you in the parking lot."

She eased back, draping her hands around his neck and staring into his eyes with her most innocent expression. "Why, sir, what *ever* do you mean? Surely not something naughty?"

When she bit her bottom lip and fluttered her lashes, he couldn't stop the laugh that rocketed forth. Her *Little Miss Innocent* act was too perfect, especially when he contrasted it with what he knew to be true. "Don't tempt me..." he warned.

"I'm an angel," she insisted

An angel with a dirty mind. Just the way Steve liked her.

～

ONE MORE WEEK. Even as she and Steve drove each other crazy on the dance floor, an underlying beat rang with those words repeating themselves over and over.

Next Saturday Mathis would get home, and they would deal with all the issues that had come up during his time away.

She shouldn't waste time thinking about it, not when Steve was staring at her with those sexy eyes, but her worries were at the forefront of every waking thought.

Was Mathis going to be disappointed with her? She hoped not. God, she hoped not.

She took a deep breath and deliberately pushed her concerns aside, focusing on the man in front of her who'd discovered far too many ways to make her tingle with excitement.

Life wasn't perfect, and they still had things to learn, but right now she was feeling pretty pleased with their whole situation. In fact, she planned to tell him that.

Maybe even tonight.

They left the dance floor to cool off, sliding back into the group with Joel and Vicki, standing on the opposite side of the tall table from Anna and Mitch. Easy conversation and lots of laughter followed.

Steve gave her a kiss on the cheek before whispering in her ear. "I'll be right back."

He'd barely left when someone on the dance floor stumbled, sending people careening, struggling for balance. Joel stepped in front of her and Vicki. Another man appeared out of nowhere, he and Joel forming a rock solid wall between them and the tangled mess of bodies bouncing off their broad backs.

Melody lifted her head in time to see Jesse come face-to-face with Vicki, barely a hand span between them. For one second, Melody thought she saw something like longing in his eyes before a cocky grin twisted his lips.

As the floor cleared, and they regained room to move, Vicki curled against Joel, offering Jesse a hesitant smile. "Thanks. You want to have a drink with us?"

His response was far more arrogant than she'd expected. "Hell, no. I've got far more interesting plans for tonight than hanging out with you."

He stepped back, tipping an imaginary cowboy hat in Melody's direction before swinging on his heel and disappearing into the crowd.

Joel sighed, pressing a kiss to Vicki's forehead. "Sorry about that."

"Nothing to be sorry for," she insisted, laying her palm against his chest and looking intently up at him. "He was helpful *and* a jerk this time. I call that a win."

It wasn't the place to ask for more details, but Melody was curious what was going on. It seemed there were more changes to the Coleman family while she'd been away than she'd been aware of.

Once again, shouting broke out behind her, and they turned to see who was involved this time. Melody's stomach dropped as she spotted Steve in the middle of the loud discussion, fists rising. "Oh, shit."

"I swear I'm going to kill him. So much for my damn evening off," Anna muttered as she left the table for a second time, beelining it for the fight building by the door.

Mitch laid his hand on Melody's shoulder, holding her back. "I know it's tempting to interrupt, but let Anna do her thing. And deal with Steve in private later. No use in giving everyone in the room more ammunition."

The angry voices were getting louder, and Melody's name

was mentioned. Steve drove a fist forward, catching his opponent across the jaw. The other man cursed, swinging an arm wildly and knocking Steve's head back with the sickening sound of skin on skin. For a moment they scuffled harder, Steve getting in a jab that sent the other man reeling into his friends.

Then Anna was there, her law-and-order expression sending both of them looking for cover. Melody made her way to where Anna was for the second time that evening, ordering one of her brothers to leave the bar.

The other man wearing signs of battle was familiar, and suddenly Melody knew *exactly* what Steve had been fighting about. She dodged around Barry Ragan and caught Steve by the hand, hauling him toward the exit.

She didn't speak. Not then, not when they were inside his truck. She silently handed him a wad of Kleenex to deal with his bloody nose.

"Melody—"

She shot up a hand to stop him. "Take me home," she ordered.

For a small town, the drive seemed endless. Silence stretched uncomfortably between them until he pulled into her driveway.

"Can I talk now?"

"Depends. Are you going to say something I want to hear, or are you just going to piss me off more?"

"Fine, I should have let it go. I would have, but he wasn't talking about your work, he insulted *you*. Said the only way to get good service was to get between your legs. Bastard."

The fire burning through her veins made it hard to speak without letting him know how upset she was. "So what?"

He frowned, his face twisting with emotion. He stared at her, his dark eyes filled with confusion, a bruise rising on his cheek. "What are you talking about?"

Really? She was going to have to spell it out for him? "Do you think he's right? Or do you think he's like the rest of them, blowing wind up your ass?"

"Of course he's not right."

"They're a bunch of jackasses, Steve. This is why I said we were going to ignore them."

Steve damn near growled. "There's no way you should have to put up with that kind of crap talk."

"I agree, but you punching someone isn't helping me. It's a jerk move, I don't want it, and I *told* you that." From his lost expression, it appeared she could have been speaking Chinese and it would have registered as well. "Maybe not in those specific words. I mean, I didn't say 'Gee, Steve, don't beat anyone up for my sake', but I specifically said to ignore them."

She shoved open her door and headed for the front stairs, Steve breathing down her back as he followed.

"Don't tell me not to defend you," he growled.

"That wasn't defending me. That was you being macho and possessive, and along with that, *wrong*."

"They can't treat you like crap," he insisted.

"You're right, they can't. But you know why?" She twirled, standing at the top of the stairs with him on the bottom step so their eyes were level. "The reason they should shut their yaps and stop complaining isn't because they're afraid you'll punch their lights out. Or because they think they need to be more considerate of my frail womanly sensitivities. This isn't about hormones and who has a dick. It's about who is right and who is wrong, and *that's* why they can't treat me like anything but the competent vet that I am."

"I'm just saying—"

"That's the biggest trouble," she snapped. "You're talking when you should be listening, and I don't know why either of us is bothering."

He froze. "Melody? What are you telling me?"

"That I'm going to bed, and you're not invited. Take your sister's advice, Steve, and go home."

Before she could get to the door, he caught her by the hand, turning her gently to face him. The expression in his eyes was one step away from terrified. "That's it? Are you saying...*we're* over?"

She pinched the bridge of her nose between her fingers, fighting to keep from shouting something she would later regret. "I'm going to bed *alone* so I can get over being so mad at you that I want to scream. Am I calling us off? No, but that doesn't mean I want to look at you right now."

He stepped back, his feet stumbling on the porch decking. "I'm sorry."

She shook her head, not trusting herself to say anything else. "Me too."

Then she let herself into the house and crawled into bed, staring at the ceiling for the longest time before she could relax enough to cry in frustration.

22

Steve stared at her door in utter shock.

He'd screwed up. This was what he'd attempted to avoid all summer. Yet he'd still upset her enough that here he was, standing on one side of the door while she was on the other, and damned if he didn't want to bust it down so they could talk this out, and he could make it better.

Then again, he'd watched her do an autopsy once, and she had a mean hand with a knife blade. He wasn't sure he wanted to get near her when she was this spitting mad.

Heading home didn't seem like the solution, because all he'd do was look in the bottom of a bottle of Jack for answers, and that never solved anything.

He found himself cruising up his parents' driveway and parking beside Lee's truck—it appeared the Coleman boys were coming home for a dose of straight talk from their father.

He didn't have to go inside to find Lee. His little brother stood at the railing of the porch, staring at the distant mountains, his expression unreadable.

Steve wandered up, leaning on the railing beside him. He

wondered how long it would take before his brother acknowledged him, but for once Lee seemed to be in a talkative mood.

"It's Rachel."

With those two words, all the dominoes fell into line. Replaying the fight at the bar, the woman Gary Ricardo had grabbed before escaping had most definitely *not* been Rachel. "Oh, hell. Okay, now it makes a lot more sense why you took a shot at Gary."

"Still doesn't make sense." Lee paused for a beat, before looking Steve in the eye. "She said there were too many years between us. Any time I asked her out, she thought I was kidding around and turned me down. And then she started seeing Gary, and they had this whirlwind engagement, and the next thing I knew, they were married."

"They moved away, didn't they?" Steve asked. "I was surprised to see him at Traders tonight."

"They did move away. I thought that would make it easier, not having to see her all the time, but he's driving deliveries in the area. Which means every time I see him cheating on her, it's enough to make me blow my top."

The mess got even more tangled. "Does she know? That he's cheating?"

Lee hesitated. "I think so. I mean, word gets around. I can't imagine how she feels. So when I saw him fooling around with that girl tonight, I couldn't stop myself."

"I don't blame you." Steve laid a hand on his brother's back, not sure there were any words of wisdom he could offer.

"The good thing is Gary is scared shitless of me. Maybe at some point he'll be frightened enough to clean up his act. I hope so, for Rachel's sake."

His little brother had to be talking out his butt. "You don't want her to stay with him, do you?"

"If that's what she wants, of course. As long as he's doing right by her, why would I want anything less than what makes her happy?"

For a kid barely out of his teens, Lee was putting Steve to shame in the maturity department. "You're a better man than I am," Steve admitted.

"Then how come you're the one with the girl, and I'm the one over here singing the achy-breaky songs?"

Lee had no idea what happened after he'd left the bar. "I don't know about that. It seems you and I have something in common tonight."

"What?"

"We're both on Anna's shit-list for starting fights at Traders."

Lee glanced up, surprise streaking his face. "You?"

Steve checked out the distant mountains himself. "Even better, after I slammed my fist into Barry Ragan's face, and Anna read me the riot act, Melody gave me hell. She isn't talking to me."

"Ahhh. You did something she asked you not to."

His little brother was far too canny. "At the time, I didn't think so. After a moment's reflection, probably, though I still think I'm right."

"Listen to yourself. What a bunch of bull."

Their father's deep tones echoed from behind them, and they twisted to watch Randy make his way onto the deck, joining them at the railing.

"You eavesdropping?" Steve asked.

"Tonight, yeah. The windows are open, and I was sitting in the living room. But more than that, I've been listening to you two boys since you were born. You make your own decisions, but if you're willing to hear your old man out for a minute, maybe I can give you a thing or two to consider."

Lee waved a hand in welcoming. "Go on. You've never been

the type to interfere unless you had something worthwhile to say."

Randy rested an elbow on the railing as he glanced at them. "When I married your mother, Mike and Marion were already going together, and it was pretty clear Mike would be the one to take over control from our father when he passed on. I had no trouble with that—Mike's a good man, and between him and Marion, they set up a strong lead for us Coleman boys to follow."

Steve and Lee exchanged glances before Lee spoke. "You want to get to the part where this sweet family history has something to do with our particular problems, Dad?"

"Don't get cocky." Randy looked him in the eye. "They say those who don't know history are doomed to repeat it. The first six months Kate and I were together, we lived in the Peters' house right next door to Mike and Marion, and I thought everything was going grand until the night your mother walked down the stairs and plunked down a suitcase."

"She was taking a trip?"

Randy stared back, his face gone cold. "She was leaving me."

He definitely had their attention.

"How come we've never heard this story before?" Lee demanded.

"Because you never needed to hear it." Randy folded his arms over his chest, his breathing loud as they waited for him to continue. "Fortunately, before she left she gave me a straight talking to. Said she loved me, loved Mike and Marion, and loved being a Coleman. But there was no way in hell she was going to stop being Kate."

Lee was nodding, but Steve wasn't sure he'd gotten the message. "And had you asked her to? Stop being Kate?"

"I didn't think so, not at first. But when she left—and she did leave for a week—I sat down and thought it through and, hell yeah, there were a lot of things she'd had ideas about that I'd basically ignored. It wasn't that she wanted to run things, but she had a voice, and an opinion, and while she didn't care in the end whether we did things the way it had always been done or some newfangled way, she wanted to be heard."

Steve's problem had *always* been he hadn't listened. "Shit."

Randy stood up and patted the railing under his hands. "One of our solutions was to move a little farther apart—we built this house, and established the Moonshine spread so there'd be a bit of separation between us. It wasn't an earth-shattering change, but it proved I was listening, and valued her ideas."

And what Steve had done was the exact opposite. "I think I get it."

"Every day Kate proves she knows how to take care of us. The entire time I've been feeling poorly she's been a rock, and somehow found a way to get it done." He nodded at Steve. "That's why I called bullshit on you. It doesn't matter whether you think you're right or not. When you have a relationship, you make decisions together, and that means listening to each other."

Steve had enough to chew on. He slapped his father on the shoulder in appreciation.

"I understand what you're telling Steve, but maybe this time I'm the stupid fool," Lee said. "There's not much listening I can do when I don't have the right, and that just plain sucks."

"It does," Randy agreed. "But here's the other thing. Sometimes the people who listen the best are our friends."

Lee shook his head. "I don't see Gary approving of Rachel and I being friends."

"And it's so much more helpful when you punch her husband out?" Randy's condemning glare had Lee squirming. "Maybe you should leave it up to Rachel if she needs a friend or not, instead of Gary."

Lee didn't answer, just got a far-off look.

The three of them stood in silence, listening to the owls debating territory from the nearby trees.

"When did life get this complicated?" Steve asked.

Randy's chuckle echoed off the wall of the house and wrapped around them. "Wait until you have kids. Then you'll know complicated."

"Save us all," Lee intoned. He tilted his head toward the house. "Come on. If anyone wants a drink, I'll see what I can find."

"I might have discovered something I can eat," Randy added with a grin. "So far the more grease, the more fat and the more calories, the better."

"That doesn't make sense," Steve offered as he held the door open and let them go in ahead of him. "I thought that stuff was what made you feel worse, not better."

"Hush. Don't mess with my brain. I don't care if it's that placebo effect kicking in, I'm happy."

For the first time since Melody had closed the door on him, Steve didn't feel like all hope was lost. He had a lot of work to make up, and it definitely came down to following Melody's timing, but somehow they'd get through this.

He wanted to be able to share this story with his own stupid son someday.

SUNDAY MORNING DAWNED bright and clear, and Allison sat quietly, her hands folded on the table between them. "Now that you've had a hug, let me find something heavy to knock some sense into Steve."

Melody stirred the spoon in her cup even though the sugar had to have long since dissolved. "I don't know how else I can possibly make him understand."

"How long until Mathis gets back?"

"This is the last week of work without him." Melody eased back in her chair and looked around the comfy cabin Allison and Gabe had turned into a home. "He should be back in town by Saturday, but dumping everything on him the instant he walks into the office is a crappy way to end his holiday."

It was Allison's turn to give her a stern look. "This is not about inconveniencing him, it's about you doing the best job you can. And if it takes him stepping on a few of his contemporaries to get things straightened out, you know Mathis will stand up for you."

Melody was pretty sure of it, but the part that made her sad was she didn't want *only* Mathis's support —

I want Steve's.

She put her head down on her hands and sighed. "Steve called this morning and left a voicemail, but I can't deal with him yet."

"Any idea when you might be ready?" Allison reached across the table and grabbed her hand. "Honey, I know he messed up, but I really don't think he meant any harm."

"He didn't," Melody agreed. "That's what made it worse. You should have seen his face, Allison. He had *no* idea what he'd done wrong. And maybe I overreacted a little, but I was so upset."

"Hey, I don't think you overreacted. There were no pitchers of beer involved this time," Allison teased.

The reminder was enough to make her smile. "Go me."

Allison winked. "He knows you care. I think..." She paused and examined Melody. "How much do you care? Maybe that's the question."

Melody dragged her gaze off the picture on the wall. The one with Gabe and Allison sitting on the hillside, smiling at each other like they were the only people in the world.

She wanted that. She wanted a home...

With Steve.

"I care enough to want us to work this out before I confess anything about rainbows and puppies and..." Melody met her friend's gaze. "When I tell that man that I love him I've got to love *all* of him, and right now, I don't."

Understanding lit her friend's face. "Although, you know even after you say *I love you?* Chances are you'll both make mistakes and do things the other person won't like." Her expression grew more serious. "And that's when you realize they need you to love them all the harder."

Melody breathed out slowly to stop the tears in her throat from making it up to her eyes and escaping. "I'm scared."

"I know." Allison stood and offered another hug, and it was everything that Melody needed at that moment. Acceptance, giving...

Everything except it wasn't from Steve.

Allison patted her back. "There's nothing wrong with you taking a few days. Once Mathis is back, that will change so many of the stresses you've been under—think about it."

"Even though you'll probably have one or the other of us over here every night until we do make up?"

"Not a problem," her friend insisted. "And after you make up, you'll be over here together, and that's fine as well. The door is always open, honey. For both of you, because we love you."

"I'm going to be bawling in a minute if you don't watch it," Melody warned.

"Got it covered." Allison grabbed the tissue box strategically placed on the nearby counter and held it out. "Pregnancy hormones. You ain't got nothing on me."

23

*H*alf the town might think she was incompetent, but she still had a job to do. Melody set a new box of supplies on the counter in the clinic storage room as guilt and amusement hit at the same time.

Melodramatic much?

Even as she gave herself grief, she went to work unpacking the order. After a couple cancellations that morning, she'd ended up finished far before five—and while she wasn't sure if the jobs were cancelled because the farmers were making a point, or something had simply come up, she might as well put her energy toward being productive.

Tom was blessedly busy. Far too busy to do more than toss her disapproving glances when he caught sight of her. And every time it reminded her how unfair the entire situation was.

At some point she would get over her mad, but it would not be today. Not with the thoughts running through her mind, most of which involved impaling certain customers on blunt objects and listening to them beg for mercy.

Not a day to be out and about providing customer service—nope, not at all.

Her cell phone rang. She took a deep breath and focused so she didn't take her bad mood out on some innocent person.

"Melody Langley."

"Hi, Melody. Marion Coleman calling."

Great. Now his relatives were getting involved. "What can I help you with?"

The older woman offered a chuckle. "Well, first off, I wanted to tell you Kate and I agree that Steve was one hundred percent wrong, but we're also sure you guys can work this out."

Ummm. "We'll see."

Marion hurried on. "Don't worry, we'll stay out of it. You go on and teach that boy to mind his manners. That's the best way for him to remember it for the rest of his life. That's not why I called."

"It's not?"

"No. Unfortunately, I need to talk to you about Ian Mailer."

Melody thought back, focusing on the old man. "Yes, ma'am?"

"He passed away today. I'm sorry if that's blunt, but he was in town having dinner at the café, and after his meal he just leaned back in the booth, closed his eyes and never got up. We don't think he suffered."

Sounded like a good way to go when it was your time. "I'm sorry to hear that. He was a nice man."

Marion agreed. "He was, but he was also a bit of an eccentric. I don't think anyone's been up to his place in years. He was always nice to folks in town, but got completely ornery when anyone went near his place."

Melody clued in where this was going. "Bear. Did he have his dog with him when he came to town today?"

"No. That's why I'm calling you. Would you be willing to go to his place and check if Bear is there, or if he has any other animals that need to be cared for?" Marion clicked her tongue. "Ian had no next of kin, so the community is going to look after his things."

That was only right. It was also a wonderful distraction from the continuing pity party that was her other option for the afternoon. "I don't mind. Is there anyone I need to talk to about getting into the house? I don't want to cause any trouble with the police."

"I just finished talking to them, and they were thrilled to have the help. There's a ruckus happening a county over, and all the constables are being called out. Anna said to tell you the key they found in Ian's pocket is waiting for you at the RCMP building. When you're done, you can either drop it off here or back at the station. Jaxi and I will be sending out a group of ladies to clean up the place before it gets sold."

Melody reached for her coat. "I'm on my way."

She stopped in the back of the clinic and picked up an assortment of things she might need. It only took a couple minutes to check the records for what animals Ian had brought in over the years, searching her memory for any animal-related questions he'd asked.

Melody loaded a number of cages in the back of her truck, just in case, along with a backpack full of treats for both dogs and cats. Most of the cats would be fine, but she wanted to be ready.

She also took the tranquilizer gun with her, and the shotgun. It hadn't even been a day, so there shouldn't be any wild animals moving in yet, but Ian's cabin was set in a pretty remote area of the community. She hoped her truck could make it all the way to the door, because she didn't look forward to hauling cages any distance.

STEVE'S CELL phone went off, and for a split second he was tempted to ignore it. He didn't need another woman telling him he was a jackass, he'd already gotten the message. And rumbling along in the tractor with his music blasting was a good enough excuse for having missed the call.

Only...it was his mother on the line, and he couldn't ignore her.

He turned down the music before he answered. "If you called to lecture me, don't bother."

"Not everything is about you," his mother drawled. "Gee, maybe that was a lecture all in itself."

Steve groaned. "You couldn't resist, could you?"

"Miss an opportunity when it's handed to me on a silver platter? Never."

Now he wished he'd gone with his first instinct and let the call go to voicemail. Still... "Mom, I hate to rush you, but I'm busy. What's up?"

"I called to ask a favour. Marion just let me know Ian Mailer passed away. I'm not going to be able to get back in time to help them deal with things. I want you to go and do all the heavy lifting, you and your brothers. You understand me?"

Loud and clear on this one. "That's too bad. Ian was a decent guy."

"He was." His mother paused. "Are you sure I can't lecture you just a little?"

He laughed, the sound harsh even in his own ears. "I've spent the last five days lecturing myself more than enough for the two of us."

"Steve. I really hope you figure this out before you lose that amazing woman."

"I thought every man was supposed to want someone just like their mother?" he teased.

"Don't go getting Freudian on me, young man. But yes, you should want someone like me. Or at least someone like me in terms of what I give to your father, which might be something entirely different when it comes to Melody and you. We're not cookie cutters, son. We're individuals, with our own hopes and dreams. Our own strengths and weaknesses. But don't you go on being a fool and thinking the fact that she's a woman is a weakness."

"Honest. I have been figuring that out."

"Good boy."

He stared out the window. "How is Auntie Deanna doing? Will you be home soon?"

"By the end of the week. Do you miss me?" she teased.

"Not me. I have my own woman troubles, if you haven't heard. But Dad? He's missing you something awful." Steve grinned. "Well, except for the part where he's had bacon every single day since you left."

"You mean the stuff in the downstairs freezer in the container labeled 'spinach'?" his mother asked.

"Yes." He paused. "You know it's really freaky when you do that."

"Come on, I'm a mother. We have eyes in the back of our heads." Kate laughed. "Don't tell your father, but that's turkey bacon. He can have it every single day if he wants. Heck, he can have it three times a day until he's got it coming out of his ears if it makes him happy. I cooked it up a few weeks ago in the hopes he'd find it and start sneaking bites. He needs a few more calories to fatten him up for winter, and if he can keep it down, that's wonderful."

The entire race of women was far too tricky for him. "You scare me, Mom."

"But you love me, right?"

He chuckled. "Of course I do. Because you're my mom, and you're always willing to teach me new things."

"I love you too. And don't forget, talk to Marion and find out when she needs your help."

He got off the phone, tempted to postpone calling his aunt until the next day. He had enough on his plate, and once he was done work that day, he desperately needed to get in touch with Melody.

But ignoring his responsibilities didn't sit right. Steve sighed. Damn behaving like an adult, anyway. He turned the corner on the edge of the field, got headed back on the next pass, then punched in the number to the Six Pack ranch.

Five minutes later he was offering up thanks for having given in and done the right thing. Sometime during the past year, he had to have built up enough good karma that for once everything worked in his favour.

Auntie Marion got in a dig suggesting he needed to apologize a lot harder, but *then* she told him about Melody's task.

The receptionist at the Rocky Mountain Animal Clinic offered the cheerful opinion that he was a fool, followed immediately by telling him Melody had left town fifteen minutes earlier, headed to Ian's cabin.

The temptation was too great to ignore. She'd avoided his phone calls, disregarded his emails—it was damn near impossible to make things right between them when she wouldn't let him get close enough to do the job.

Steve shut down the tractor right there and then, abandoning it in the middle of the field. He headed at a jog for the side of the road where he'd left his truck, phone in hand to make one final call.

"Trevor, I'm taking off early. I've got something I need to do."

While the rumble of the other tractor working the far

section of the field faintly reached his ears, his brother's dismay was crystal clear over the phone. "What? What the hell are you doing? You can't stop now, you're only halfway through the job."

"And I'll finish it tomorrow, but today I've got something more important that needs to be taken care of."

Even as he hung up on Trevor's curse of protest, he knew this was exactly what he had to do. He'd backed off for a few days as requested. But it was time to make sure Melody knew he'd understood what she'd said, and that couldn't happen without them being in the same space.

She needed him to listen better? He would give her both ears and his entire, focused attention. Right smack dab in the middle of the wilderness where there would be nothing, and no one, to interrupt them.

MELODY REACHED Ian's cabin after a long hour's drive, her whole body vibrating from the trip down the washboard dirt road. He hadn't built like most settlers in Alberta, placing his cabin in the middle of a clearing. He'd picked a spot right up against a rocky bluff, the cabin looking like it popped out from the mountain.

It had probably helped with passive heating, the rocks acting as natural insulation. She admired his handiwork as she pulled into the parking space between the house and a small barn. Building smart had been the only way to go with Ian's generation, far before *Going Green* had become buzzwords.

She glanced at Charlie who was being spoiled rotten, riding in the passenger seat. "The man was definitely trying to discourage visitors."

Charlie's tail thumped into the seat the instant Melody

started talking, and in spite of the sad task ahead of them, she had to smile as well. "Yes, I'm glad you're with me too."

Melody opened her door and stepped into the neat yard, Charlie pouring out of the cab on her heels.

She eyed the cabin as she considered the most logical way to go about this. "Check the outbuildings first, or the house?"

Charlie was already sniffing at the front door, whining softly as she explored.

"House it is. Thanks, girl." She went around to the back of her truck, rummaging through her med-kit for supplies, as well as stuffing a few treats into her pockets. "Now I understand why people have dogs. It means I can talk to myself and no one can consider me crazy."

She slipped a knock-out injection vial into her breast pocket for safekeeping then took the shotgun in hand, just in case.

The key slipped in easily, turning a well-maintained lock.

She cracked the door open an inch in case there were animals looking to escape—it would be far easier to cage them from inside the house than chasing them all over the wilderness.

"Charlie. Stay," she ordered.

She got instant obedience as the dog settled her hindquarters on the porch, although she did look up with pleading in her eyes. "You can help in a bit," Melody promised.

Bear was a good-natured animal. He'd probably enjoy a little company, but first she had to find him.

She closed the door and leaned her back on it, looking around the room to get her bearings. A musty scent hung in the air, the aroma of wood smoke and dust and ancient furniture. The living room held an old couch and an easy chair, a pillow and blanket piled on top of the desk shoved along one wall under the window. Toward the back of the room, she caught a glimpse of a kitchen, and off to the right, a hall that must lead to the rest of the house.

A cat stuck its black head out from behind the couch,

vanishing before she could do more than see it was there. Melody ignored the feline for now—if Ian had one, chances were he'd have more than one.

She'd just stepped into the kitchen when Bear wandered up, limping on one leg, his tail wagging.

"Hello, old-timer." She knelt to caress a hand over his head, sadness striking her in a rush. "Sorry, boy. I've got news, and it's not good. You're walking the trail without your master, now."

She spoke past a throat gone tight as Bear tilted his head, his tail beating a steady rhythm on the floorboards, oblivious to her words.

Another cat appeared from behind Bear's dog bed, shooting around them both to disappear into the living room. Melody added one to her count then headed to the back of the house.

Bathroom—nothing. Closet—nothing. The next room confused her until she realized it was tucked up against the mountainside, so it had no windows and not much else than shelves. Another couple cats shot past her, and now she was beginning to worry about getting them into crates. Bear wouldn't be a problem, but the cats could have minds of their own when it came to being transported.

She leaned her shoulder against the final door and turned the knob, pushing against the stubborn wood panel. It refused to budge more than a few inches, and she peeked her head around the corner to discover discarded clothing blocking the way.

Strange, considering how neat the rest of the cabin was.

Melody leaned the gun against the wall, then squatted to stick her hands around the door and pull the clothing free. The door opened easier and she stepped in, freezing as a loud *hiss* sang at her from across the room. She raised her gaze to the top of the dresser and fought to keep from bolting.

A cougar glared back.

Even as her heart rate skyrocketed, stories flooded her mind.

People would find wild animals and raise them from kits to full-grown adults. The trouble was the creatures weren't domesticated, no matter how long Ian had had the beast.

The cougar pulled itself onto its haunches and pounced.

Melody stumbled backwards, desperate to get out the door. She tripped over more clothing, making it into the hallway as a set of razors slashed her leg.

Everything slowed. Pain and fear tangled together, blurring her vision, clouding her thoughts.

A large furry body barreled past her and crashed into the cougar. The moment she was free Melody scrambled through the doorway on the opposite side of the hall and slammed the door closed, adding her body weight to keep it pinned in place.

Low-pitched barks joined the cougar's complaints, and Melody swore. "Bear. Oh *no*."

A heavy body smashed against the opposite side of the door, along with a furious scream of disappointment that fit the horror setting perfectly. She was trapped in near pitch-black, her thigh throbbed, and outside, there was a large animal with teeth and claws creating havoc.

She scrambled for a weapon as the fight on the opposite side of the door grew louder. Outside the cabin, Charlie had picked up the cry as well, her high-pitched yelps echoing through the walls.

Why the *hell* had she put the shotgun down?

The only way out of the windowless storage area was through the lone door, the other side guarded by a creature with a set of teeth and very sharp nails.

Melody pressed a hand over her thigh, her fingers sticky with blood, and for a moment her head spun. The barking and hissing continued to rage as she ripped part of her T-shirt away to create a makeshift bandage.

If she had to shoot her way out, she could. It would be risky, but it was possible, as long as she could get to the gun.

And then she heard the *beep beep* of a horn, and her heart sank.

Somebody else was out there. Someone who could, at any moment, open the front door and come face to face with an enraged cougar.

24

Steve had spent the past hour while driving the road from hell trying to figure the best way to handle this golden opportunity—time alone with Melody. Should he apologize first then help her, or help her and then apologize? Or start with apologizing and not stop?

He'd just decided to open with a sincere "I've missed you" and see what happened when Charlie's hijinks drove his planning from his mind. The dog stood at the door to the cabin, barking her fool head off as she clawed at the wood. Not typical behaviour from what he'd seen during the time he'd cared for her, not even if she was annoyed Melody had gone into the house without her.

"Charlie. What's up?"

She broke off barking, racing to his side for a moment before heading back to the door as if frantic to get in.

Something wasn't right—not at all, and the closer he got to the cabin the more certain he grew as a strange din rang behind the closed front door. He pushed on it carefully, sticking his head inside to try shouting.

"Melody, it's Steve—"

Charlie took total advantage, sneaking past him into the house, growling violently, the angry sound increasing in volume.

From the back of the house, Melody's voice echoed faintly, her words jumbled and incoherent. The tone in her voice wasn't anger, it was fear.

He was already moving, headed toward her when a massive bundle of tawny fur stalked around the corner and looked him in the eye.

Ten feet, no more, stood between them as Steve jerked to a halt.

A couple house cats made a break out the open door behind him, but he was far more focused on the cougar eyeing him as if deciding how to serve him for dinner. Between him and the cougar, Charlie had planted all four feet, put her head down, and was in the process of barking herself hoarse.

And Melody? No sign, and no word either.

"Melody?" Steve tried again, keeping his feet immobile as his hands curled into fists in a useless response to his fight-or-flight instinct.

The cougar tensed, but didn't do anything except lower its head and snarl at Charlie.

"Steve, if you're there, don't move."

Talk about damned if he did, damned if he didn't. "Melody, there's a cougar—"

"I have a gun. I need three more inches. Keep it looking at—"

The cougar twisted its head toward the hallway, and Steve spoke louder, fighting to be heard over Charlie, who was at least not attacking. "Need me to be the target?"

"Oh, God, I hope not. I have this. Trust me. One sec..."

The cougar snarled, trapped between three unknowns—two humans and a noisy dog. It had to be at its breaking point, and Steve didn't want that break to be toward Melody.

Only, she was the animal expert, and he was the scared-as-shit boyfriend, jumping out of his skin as two shots rang in succession, and the cat jerked in front of him.

Too late, the cougar leapt for the door, and Steve had nowhere to go to get out of its way. The animal slammed into him, knocking him to the ground as Charlie rushed to his defense.

For a moment it seemed there were claws and teeth everywhere, pain shooting through his arm as momentum carried the creature forward, and then death left it immobile, a literal dead weight crushing down on him.

"Don't move," Melody ordered again, the echo of her footsteps rushing toward him.

"Trust me, sweetheart, I'm not moving," he confessed. "I'm doing my best imitation of a pancake."

He pushed as she pulled, and somehow they rolled what had to be a full-grown female cougar off him. Melody checked quickly before giving a brisk nod. "She's dead."

She swung her attention to him, clasping her hand over his arm where pinpoints of blood had begun to seep through his shirt. "Don't think she hit too deep, but I want you to keep pressure on this."

And then damn if she didn't leave him to run back down the hallway.

"What the hell you doing?" Steve demanded. "And why the heck did we get attacked by a cougar?"

He followed her farther into the house, jerking to a halt as he discovered her working over the prone body of Ian's dog. Charlie had run ahead as well and stood beside them, licking the old dog's muzzle.

Bear whimpered, his back limbs twitching as Melody checked him over. She petted his head. "Such a good boy. Thank you for protecting me."

His tail thumped once, but other than that, the dog lay motionless except for his breathing as a faint rumbly noise escaped him. He was obviously in pain, yet still pleased by Melody's praise.

She reached into her shirt pocket and pulled out a syringe, staring at it for a moment.

Steve didn't know what had happened, but from the look on Melody's face, this was going to break her. The driving need to make everything better ramped up, and he dropped to his knees beside her. Draped an arm around her shoulders as if he could will his strength into her. "We can take him back to the clinic," Steve offered. "I'll pay whatever it costs to get him fixed up."

"He's in a lot of pain, Steve." Melody's hand shook as she filled the syringe with liquid.

He wasn't going to argue with her. This was her area of expertise, and he knew damn well that at some point animals came to the end of their life. But as he watched her, tears welling up in her eyes as she stoically moved forward, he wanted all over again to fix things.

He couldn't. There was no fixing this.

What he could do was be there for her.

Steve moved to cradle the dog's head in his lap, petting the old-timer's muzzle. "If you're sure. But if you can fix him up, I mean it. He can live out his days with me."

Melody swallowed hard and put the needle to the dog's skin, depressing the plunger halfway until the whimpering and shivering stopped. "We need to get him to the clinic as soon as possible."

Steve moved before he thought it through, pressing a kiss to her temple and holding her close for a moment. "Thank you. For saving him. And for saving me."

She leaned into him briefly, waiting until he'd lifted the dog in the air to struggle to her feet.

That's when he noticed. "Jesus, woman. You didn't tell me the cougar got you too."

"I'm fine." She swayed, slamming a hand against the wall to catch her balance. When he would've put Bear back down to help her, she glared hard enough to set his feet tromping toward the door. "I'll grab his bed and be there in a minute. Put him in my backseat. The ride will be smoother than in the truck bed."

It took a few minutes to follow her directions so they could settle Bear into the backseat, Charlie next to him. Only when she would have handed him her keys, Steve came to a full stop.

"What are those for?"

"You drive my truck—I didn't want you to get blood in yours. Phone the clinic as soon as you've got a signal and tell Tom you've got an emergency—"

"And what do you think you'll be doing instead of heading into town with me?" Steve dropped to his knees in front of her and reached for the shirt tied over the bloodstained section of her pants.

"What're you doing?" she complained, attempting to push away his hands. "I'll stay here and deal with the cougar. I can't leave that in the middle of the house for Marion and the others to face." She hissed in pain as he pulled the bandage free to examine her leg. "Steve, stop."

"You stop being a martyr," he ordered. He grimaced at the slashes, long but shallow grooves, the bleeding slowing already. He retied the makeshift bandage firmly as he glanced upward, putting on the most commanding face he knew. "It's not being irresponsible to change your plans when you face a crisis. And no one is going to complain you didn't do your damn job, and if they do, I will personally see they get on the receiving end of the wrath of the Coleman women."

"But—"

"The only butt I'm seeing is *your* butt in the truck, because I will fucking tie you up if I have to so I can get your ass to a hospital."

All her bluster faded and she drooped as she nodded in agreement. Steve caught an arm around her waist, bringing her with him into the truck cab and letting her curl up beside him the best she could.

The road seemed even more impossible now than thirty minutes earlier—and he couldn't believe everything that had happened in that short of a time.

"Are you okay?" he asked. "I mean, relatively? Not too much pain?"

They rocked together as he guided the truck over an extra bad section. "It hurts, but I can handle it. You?"

"Felt worse getting caught walking through a patch of thistles." He glanced over his shoulder, but the two dogs were doing fine in the back. Bear wasn't moving, and Charlie had put her head on the edge of the dog bed, swaying as she responded to the uneven road.

Melody eased out her leg, moaning as she stretched into a new position. "Never expected that."

"A cougar? Did she break into the house?"

"No, she'd been left in the back room, and didn't like someone new in her territory."

Jeez. "Ian had a cougar in the house?"

"It happens. Happens more often than you'd think. Someone finds an abandoned den with kits or wolf cubs, and for whatever reason decides to keep one and raise it as a pet."

"Bet that doesn't work out well in the end."

"No. Usually we find these after the 'pet' turns on their owner. You can only train a wild animal so far. They're not domesticated, and it shows."

Steve slipped his fingers over her shoulder, needing that extra assurance she was safe. "I'm sorry you got hurt."

"Thanks." She snorted. "At least it wasn't totally outrageous to find a cougar in our neck of the woods. Imagine walking into a house in Calgary to discover a full-grown lion staring you down—I've heard of that as well."

He wasn't interested in letting this time with her vanish in inane small talk. "I came after you to tell you I was sorry about being an idiot the other day."

"Steve—"

"Because I was an idiot. You were right, you'd made it very clear what you wanted, and I still went around you, and I'm sorry."

"I know you are."

God. His apology wasn't enough. She wasn't looking at him with those eyes of mesmerizing blue. She wasn't slipping her hand into his. She wasn't *his*...not in all the ways he desperately needed her to be.

He reached for where she had her fingers linked, hands resting in her lap. "What do I need to do to prove I've learned my lesson?"

All he could spare was a second's glance off the road—just long enough to read her face as she examined him. There was hope written there, and his heart rate accelerated.

She spoke softly but clearly. "Back at Ian's. You were pretty damn bossy about me leaving."

"Damn right."

"Even though it means I didn't finish my job? You don't think that shows you're still trying to run the show?"

He shook his head. "Not the same thing, sweetheart. You've got Bear to get to town and take care of, and you've been hurt. I'm not letting you put yourself in harm's way. You bet I'm going to be bossy if you try that nonsense."

She hesitated. "And that's different than you taking a swing at someone who insulted me because you don't want my feelings hurt?"

Night and day different. He opened his mouth to explain that, and got hit by another two by four.

He glanced at her. "You're sly. And you're brilliant, and you're so damn beautiful *because* you're sly and brilliant. Yes, those things are totally different, and I promise I'll only be an asshole when it comes to protecting you from real dangers. Although, it was all you protecting me at the cabin."

She snuggled against his side and breathed out slowly. "I already forgave you, by the way. Before you came up to the cabin."

Another ray of hope struck. "You're okay with us being together?"

"Yes, only..."

The silence went on for far longer than it should have.

"I don't like sentences that end with 'only'. Tell me what you're thinking." He squeezed her fingers. "Tell me how I can be there for you."

This was about so much more than sex, or liking how he felt around her. How much he admired her, and wanted to be with her all the time. It was everything at the same time, and so much *more* than everything added together.

Somehow falling in love had taken all those bits that were enjoyable by themselves—very enjoyable, he would admit—and churned them to create an entirely new sensation. Something as vital to him as air.

There was no denying it any longer. He'd fallen in love.

She twisted in her seat, grimacing as she adjusted position. With one elbow resting on the dashboard, she hung onto his good arm with her other hand so she could look at him, and he could peek glances without driving them off the mountainside.

"I need to deal with the ranchers. I need to have that put behind me, and the only way it's going to be solved is when Mathis gets back. He had enough faith in me to put me in charge, and whether I screwed up like the men think—"

"You didn't."

His insistence dragged a reluctant smile from her as she finished her thought. "—or if they're a bunch of idiots, I have an obligation to Mathis to finish the job and see how he wants to handle it."

That made sense. But... "What does that have to do with us?"

"It's just a few more days. He'll be back by Saturday, and until then, I don't want to give anyone anymore ammunition against me."

"Dating me isn't a crime," Steve drawled.

"No, but you are a distraction, and I..." She sighed. "Maybe this is mixed up and wrong, but I need to finish the damn job before I start anything new, even if the new is being with you."

The words *horse hockey* sprang to mind, but what he said was, "I get it."

Melody wrinkled her nose. "Then you're smarter than I am, because part of me thinks I'm crazy. But—"

"No, I hear you. You want a fresh start. Put the things behind you that weren't good and move forward."

He was bullshitting one hundred percent right then because the longer they talked, the whiter her face grew, the pain in her leg obviously hitting hard.

This wasn't the time to berate her and tell her no bloody way would he sit back and let her mope through the next few days without him to hold her hand.

But his comment did the trick. Quieted her enough that she curled up, her head on his shoulder in spite of the bumpy road carrying them back to town. Silence filled the cab, but Steve

didn't mind. He had a pretty good idea of what he wanted to say
—when the time was right.

He put his arm around her and hung on tight, the way he
intended to hold on for the rest of their lives.

25

"*W*ake up, sweetheart."

Cool, comfortable sheets surrounded her, along with a cloud of fog in her brain, which didn't feel as good. "Steve?"

"I hope so. There shouldn't be any other men in your bedroom while you're scantily clad."

The mattress shifted, and she looked up into his blue-grey eyes, concern creasing the corners. "Am I scantily clad?"

One brow cocked higher. "There's only one way to find out..."

Melody stretched cautiously, a smile rising to her lips. She had aches and pains in parts of her body she hadn't expected, yet a blissfully numb sensation on her right thigh. She sat up, Steve reaching to help her, his arm curling around her shoulders.

She glanced at what she wore. "That looks an awful lot like your T-shirt."

He shrugged. "I was all for naked, but you were insistent. You had to have something on in case there was an emergency at the clinic."

"You're making that up."

His head shifted from side to side. "You also had a very strong opinion about what kind of ice cream we should stop for—one guess what type you didn't want?"

Okay. She thought she'd woken in a fog, but it wasn't getting any clearer. She glanced around the room, gaze settling on the alarm clock beside her bed. Two a.m.? But light was streaming in the window. She hesitated. "What time is it?"

Steve traced a finger down her shoulder and over her biceps. "Two in the afternoon."

That made no sense. "We went out to Ian's past three..."

She figured out the solution the same time he offered it. "You've slept for nearly twenty-four hours."

The hospital. She twisted away and threw back the quilt to discover her right thigh wrapped in a crisp white bandage. She pressed lightly. The limb felt bruised, but nowhere near as painful as she'd expected.

"You can check mine too," Steve offered. He lifted his left arm, showcasing the shiny packaging of his own. "I take it you don't remember?"

Melody racked her memory. "We dropped off Bear at the clinic, and you took me to emergency." She paused, pretty sure she hadn't imagined this. "You were going to drop me off, but I made you come in with me."

"Thus the matching bandages," Steve agreed. His smile twisted. "We're also going to have matching scars from the sound of it, but the scratches weren't serious. Neither of us needed stitches—they used that tape stuff."

She was still missing details. "How come it's the middle of the afternoon, and how come you're here?"

He pointed to the top of her dresser where she spotted a prescription bottle. "Painkiller. Between the post-adrenaline-rush crash, and whatever is in that prescription, you've been out like a light."

She swung her legs off the edge of the bed, pulling his arm toward her to examine it closer. "Doesn't explain why you're here and not working."

Then his hand cupped her face and turned her toward him, his expression gone serious. "There's nowhere else I'm supposed to be when my girlfriend needs me."

She wanted to complain. Protest that he wasn't listening, because she was pretty certain they'd talked about waiting until Mathis got home.

The other part of her, the part that was being brutally honest, was damn glad he was there. She was tired of being alone and tired of being strong.

Steve traced his thumb over her cheekbone, his gaze fixed on her as if she were precious. "I'm glad you're okay."

"I'm glad we're both okay." She leaned her cheek into his caress. "You don't need to baby me."

"Ah, there's where you're mistaken. This isn't about what you need, not really." He gazed intently at her. "This is all about me, sweetheart, because the sight of that cougar just about killed me. Not being able to protect you—*brutal*."

She caught his hand in hers, pulling his knuckles toward her lips and giving him a kiss. "You don't mind that I saved you?"

"Hell no. Crack shot as well as everything else you bring to the table?" He gave her a lecherous grin, and she had to fight to keep from laughing. "I'm a happy man, except I feel a little uneven on the playing field. So for the next twenty-four hours you get to just be you. Not Ms. Langley, large-animal veterinarian, taking names and kicking butt. Not the woman who had to teach a slightly stupid cowboy how to mind his Ps and Qs. Just Melody, who had a bit of a run-in with a cougar and needs some TLC."

"I think, maybe, I can go along with that."

He helped her up, steadying her as she wavered on spaghetti-like legs. "They said you shouldn't operate any heavy machinery for a couple of days," he teased.

"Drat, there goes the test drive on the earth mover I had scheduled for this weekend."

He grinned as he led her to the bathroom. "You're definitely waking up."

He gave her some privacy, and by the time she'd made herself feel human again, there were amazing smells drifting from the kitchen.

She settled at the table. "Chicken noodle soup?"

"From Allison." He stirred slowly, gesturing toward the fridge. "Of course, if you'd like something different we also have tomato, mushroom, beef barley, Mexican taco, Italian—"

"Did you raid the kitchen at the restaurant?"

"That's only what you got from the Coleman side of the family."

He lowered a bowl in front of her, slipping a package of saltines beside it before catching her eye. "Everybody's been worried about you, including Emily Dalton, who sent a casserole."

"You're kidding."

"Check the freezer. I think I'm going to get attacked by a cougar more often—it's a great way to stock the pantry."

Well, it was good to know that half of the Dalton family was willing to give her another chance. Melody savoured the soup, grilling Steve for details. "Bear. Did Tom do the surgery?"

"He did, and he did a great job—Callie told me that. Bear is under surveillance in the clinic. If you feel up to it after you eat, we can check up on him." He urged her spoon toward the bowl. "My brothers went out to Ian's to deal with the cougar, and while they were there they gathered up the cats that were hovering around the house. They've been relocated to a bunch of Coleman barns."

"Thank you." She placed her left hand over his fingers, holding him while she ate, more of her worries sliding away. "I can't believe I slept that long."

"You've been under a lot of stress—it makes sense." He cleared his throat. "And I promise I'll take you to see Bear, but then you need to rest. One more good sleep, and you'll be back up to speed."

The idea of crawling into bed should have been terrible, but it was actually quite appealing. "I won't even argue with you."

"Melody?" His expression had gone serious. "I'm telling you this now so you can try to put it aside, and I didn't think it was my place to keep it from you. Mathis phoned. He returns tonight, and some of the locals have been in contact with him. They want to hold a meeting first thing tomorrow morning."

"Damn. He's home early." She put her spoon down on the table and deliberately relaxed as she exhaled. "I figured that would happen, I just didn't expect it to happen that soon."

"Sooner the better," he insisted. "Once we get the meeting out of the way, everyone can move on."

It was one thing to nod in agreement, but there was still an edge of uncertainty twisting her gut. She tried her best to shove it aside, laughing as Steve helped her pull on sweatpants and escorted her across to check on Bear.

He was awake but groggy, his furry black tail moving slowly as he lay on his side and stared up at her. She stroked his fur, careful to stay away from the fresh stiches that seemed to cover far too much of his body. "You're a survivor, aren't you, boy? Such a good dog."

Another thump from his tail, then he closed his eyes, his chest rising and falling in waves as his breathing settled.

Melody looked around for his paperwork. "Did he have any internal injuries? How long until he—"

"Slow down, sweetheart." Steve helped her to her feet, guiding her out of the clinic even as he soothed her. "Tom said everything went well, and he'll give you a full report tomorrow. Let Bear rest. You need to go give Charlie a hug as well. She's been worried about you."

Thoughtful, caring. Melody held on to Steve, grateful for everything that had changed between them as he led her to Charlie's doghouse and waited for her to pet and soothe another animal.

When he slipped a treat into her fingers for her to share with Charlie, she was seconds away from tears all over again.

This man? She could trust him with her heart. With everything.

By the time they were back in the house, she was exhausted and sweaty.

Steve ixnayed her request for a shower. "One more day with dry bandages. That's what the doctor ordered."

"I'm not going to sleep feeling like I just ran a marathon," she complained.

"Of course you're not."

She was too tired to ask any questions as he led her to her bedroom. She was too tired to lodge a protest when he stripped off her clothes and laid her on the quilt. The second dose of painkiller she'd taken after eating hit her system, and she wasn't complaining about *anything* when he put a warm cloth to her skin and proceeded to give her a sponge bath.

"I think this is turning me on," she commented, the words dripping lazily off her tongue.

He ran the sponge over her breast. "I know this is turning me on, but that's not the goal."

"Oh." She dragged her fingers through his hair, pulling him

toward her until his smiling lips met hers. Such a soft, tender kiss, combined with his touch, and she was completely relaxed. On the verge of falling asleep. "I *like* when the goal is to turn me on."

"Soon. Right now we're doing something else that's special."

"What's that?" She closed her eyes, caressing her fingers over his biceps and upper body. "Those are good drugs," she commented.

Steve laughed. "And on that note, it's time for you to go to sleep."

Maybe she shouldn't have said it, but there was no stopping the honest truth from escaping. "I want you to stay with me."

Steve pulled off his shirt, his pants hitting the floor a moment later. Then he was under the covers and curling himself around her like the best human blanket in the world. "There's nowhere I'd rather be."

He slipped one arm over her, hand resting across her belly. His hard, muscular body was pressed against her, his legs carefully arranged to cradle her bandaged thigh.

Melody laid her hand over his, linking their fingers. "You said we were doing something special," she reminded him.

Behind her, his chest moved in rhythmic waves, slow and even, the timing urging her to join him. "This is another way to make love."

She fought to stay awake. It didn't seem as if they were about to have sex, and she highly doubted *that's* what he was talking about considering she was higher than a kite. "Making love?"

"Everything we do together, every time we touch. Every time I get to care for you, or you care for me—it's part of love."

She wasn't far enough gone to miss that Really Big Clue. "Are you saying you love me?"

"Hell, yeah."

Huh. "I hope you plan to say that sometime when I'm wide awake."

"Hell, yeah," he repeated. "Now, go to sleep, and when you wake up, we'll deal with the next thing. Together."

That sounded like a great plan, and even if it had been a terrible one, she was all out of energy to protest. She cuddled against him and let sleep take her.

26

*M*athis stood at the side of the room, his expression serious in spite of the tan and casual clothing. Melody felt horrid that the first thing he had to deal with upon returning from vacation was controversy.

He was never going to go away again.

Her mentor had brushed off her attempts to explain when she'd walked in and found them setting up. Instead, he led her to a chair, smiling as he seated her. He dipped his head toward her ear, speaking quietly as the first of the ranchers joined them. "I put you in charge for a good reason—I trusted you. Now, trust *me*."

Cryptic words. Ones that effectively tied her hands. She sat and watched as the room filled.

The growing crowd was quiet as a good two-dozen local ranchers gathered in the large-animal surgery at the back of the clinic, settling into folding chairs that had been gathered for the occasion.

The dread in Melody's stomach was a solid brick, and she

took a deep breath, fighting to keep from twitching with nervous energy.

There were more than just the men who'd complained about her. Steve was there, his dark gaze offering support from where he sat.

He'd been gone when she'd woken. A note on the table giving her details of the meeting time, and a promise he'd watch her back. He'd signed it with Xs and Os, and she wasn't sure if the giggles that escaped were hysteria-based, or just what she'd needed to break the tension so she could get ready.

There were other Colemans present as well—Gabe and Blake, Travis and Lee, and Jaxi, who sat with baby Peter in her lap, a stern, unwavering glare aimed pointedly at Sean Dalton.

"I have to admit I'm surprised by your complaints," Mathis said, opening the discussion. "These are some serious charges you're considering."

"Nothing against you, Mathis," Sean Dalton insisted. "We just want you to know what kind of trouble you've got under your roof."

"And you really think she's incompetent?"

The question made Melody cringe, another shot shaking her when Sean responded instantly, "Incompetent and insolent—the girl is plain, outright rude for no reason. Think the power you gave her went to her head."

Melody itched to respond, but Mathis had asked her to wait until the men had a chance to voice their concerns.

Steve rose to his feet. "I disagree. She's competent. More than that, she cares. *We* trust her skills completely. I speak for all of the Coleman families when I say Melody is our choice when it comes to having someone work with our animals."

Her throat tightened at his words. Then someone in the back shouted, "Of course you'd support her. You're sleeping with her."

His grin should have seemed out of place, except as Steve

faced down the heckler, his easy shrug was so reminiscent of a typical, laid-back ranching attitude, it made his words hit with more impact. "Don't know that has anything to do with her work skills. As far as I'm concerned it just shows I've got better luck than I deserve."

Steve paced forward a couple steps, looking the other ranchers in the eye as he spoke.

"At the end of the day, we want strong work animals and strong breeding animals. We need healthy herds to deliver for sale. She's more than capable of helping us met that goal. Fact is, between the four Coleman ranches, we pretty much pay her salary." Another shrug lifted his shoulders as he focused on Sean. "Anyone who doesn't want to work with her can call some other vet to come out. Drayton Valley is closest—although your visitation fees will go up. I hear he charges by the mile."

Mathis chuckled. "I should've known when you asked to be a part of the meeting you weren't going to play nice."

Steve's grin was back as he tilted his head toward Melody. "I'm not here to defend her. Her work speaks for itself, and any fool who is too bigoted or blind to see that doesn't deserve to have her work with their animals."

"Agreed," Mathis said.

"What?" Sean was on his feet, glaring at Melody for a moment as if she'd somehow forced Mathis to say the words. "You mean she can waltz in and charge whatever the hell she wants? You're okay with her coming on our land and making rash accusations?"

Melody held her breath. She hadn't had a chance to tell Mathis about the horses yet.

"Sometimes rash accusations look a whole lot different to an experienced eye, Sean. Maybe you want to let that one go for now." Mathis advised.

Mathis knew about the horses—Steve had to have told him.

She glanced across the room at him and the flicker of hope inside her chest grew a little brighter.

Especially since Sean was now so mad he was sputtering. "You're going to believe the word of one person, when all of us don't feel comfortable working with her?"

Mathis took a deep breath, his shoulders shifting wearily as he shook his head. "Sean, it always comes down to a choice. You don't have to have Melody out to your place. Like Steve said, she's got enough people who will work with her. I believe she's a better vet than I am, and the time is coming when I plan to retire. At that point, you can either hire her, or get yourself another vet for the job."

"Tom is talking about putting out his own shingle," one of the other ranchers mentioned.

A low rumble washed over the gathered crowd.

That was enough. It was great to discover she had the support of the people who meant the most to her, but at this point what Melody wanted was to honour her mentor. He didn't deserve to have to wade through anymore of this crap.

She rose to her feet.

The angry voices and murmuring didn't die away until she hauled her chair from the wall and stepped up on it so she could be seen.

"I stand by all the treatments I gave, and the bills I delivered. If any of you want to file a formal complaint, I will help you fill out the forms so you can get in contact with the proper authorities."

Her offer sent a ripple of consternation through the crowd, this time at a much lower level.

Melody focused on the worst of the lot, and it was Sean's turn to squirm in his seat like a kid being held in at recess. "If you don't believe that I have you and your animals' best interests in mind, then we *should* part ways. But I'll tell you right now, you won't succeed in suing me for breach of skill or for trying to cheat you financially. I can guarantee that, so put that idea out of your head right now."

Sean sat back in his chair, his arms folded over his chest as he deliberately broke eye contact to stare at the front wall.

So be it. She looked into the crowd instead, examining the faces of people she'd worked alongside, some of them during situations where she knew she'd saved their animals' lives. She'd given her all, and damn it, they had to know that as well.

If the ringleaders were quelled, the others might see reason.

"When you call us, you're trusting us to work alongside you as you care for your animals, for your livelihood. It's not a trust I take lightly. Every time I'm in the field I fight to do what's best for today and for your future. You matter to me, and your animals do too. Hell, it's why I became a vet in the first place."

Here and there in the room heads bobbed as the men who had come to the meeting out of curiosity acknowledged her passion and skill.

Maybe she should have left well enough alone, but it had to be said. The *other* issue she'd dealt with far too often. Since she was blabbing her head off.

"This job works two ways, gentlemen. While I don't expect to be treated with kid gloves, I expect to be treated with dignity and respect while doing my job. It seems that's too hard for some of you, so there are a few locations where I won't be the attending vet any longer." She glanced at her boss, guilt rushing in for not warning him. "If that's an issue with you, Mathis, you can let me go, but otherwise they'll have to wait until you or Tom can fit them into your schedules."

A protest rose from the back of the room. "Typical woman. Comment about her work, and suddenly it's all about how she's a lady, and we aren't allowed to complain."

Steve's hands curled into fists. Melody gave him a quick frown as she took a deep breath to regain control as well.

"I don't mind the shit talk and jokes. Take Mark Mason." She swung a hand toward the far corner of the room. All attention turned toward him as she continued. "Mark, you have a way with words. Some of your jokes are so damn funny I'm chuckling about them hours after I leave your ranch. Dirty talk can be just fine, and you, sir, have a gift."

Mark eased back in his chair, obviously surprised to be picked out of the crowd to be praised. He wasn't one of the instigators—probably had shown up when he'd heard there would be a meeting.

She held herself in tight control as she went on. "But some of you need to consider this—if you wouldn't put your hand between Mathis's legs and check his balls, then I expect you to keep your damn hands to yourself when I'm around, or in the future you'll find out how quickly I can apply a castrator when motivated."

The murmur in response was louder than before.

"I've heard enough." Mathis walked over and offered Melody his hand, which was a good thing because she was about at the end of her rope. He lowered his voice as he helped her down from her perch. "You're not fired, and if you'd told me earlier someone was getting out of line, I would have hogtied them myself."

He turned back to the crowd. "If any of you want to discuss things with me privately, we'll deal with complaints one on one, but the bottom line is if you want to work with Rocky Mountain Animal Clinic, Melody is my top assistant. If you have an issue with that, contact the front desk and Callie will give you a list of neighbouring vets you can work with."

And that was it.

She was shocked by the abruptness of the conclusion, reeling slightly as men got up and left without another word. Jaxi offered her a wink before passing the baby to Blake then beelining for Lee, comments regarding his fresh black eye audible as they left.

"Sean," Mathis called before the man could stomp from the room. "You might want to consider checking those horses on your south forty. I hear animal services are planning a visit to the area in the next while, and I have the paperwork from when you bought the animals not three months ago. I'd hate to have to do a report up for neglect."

The man glared angrily at Melody before leaving without another word.

Finally it was down to Mathis, her and Steve.

She turned to her mentor. "There are a million things I need to say, but they all come down to *thank you*."

He smiled. "Wait until we announce you've bought in as a full partner. You know, down the road when I'm prepping for retirement. We'll have them screaming bloody murder."

His confidence was unshakeable, and she lifted her head, prouder than ever to be able to work with a man like him. "Hey, I hope you took some pictures during your holiday."

"Over six hundred shots. Steve here already invited me out for a barbecue tomorrow afternoon. Promised I could show you every single one."

She was going to be crying in a minute if she didn't watch herself. "Thank you," she repeated.

He squeezed her fingers then let her go, pacing out of the room. "Heads up. You're on first shift Monday morning. I've gotten used to sleeping late, so you'll be doing a heck of lot more early tasks." He grinned over his shoulder. "Perk of being the boss, you know."

The room grew quiet as Steve stepped toward her, and she stepped toward him, and they met somewhere in the middle of the room.

She took another deep breath. "You stood up for me."

"Not soon enough. I told you I was done being stupid, but obviously not." Steve narrowed his eyes. "I want to know who was getting fresh with you."

Melody gave him a dirty look. "What part of *I can take care of myself* did you miss hearing?"

He shook his head. "No, this is entirely different. This is about teaching them some manners. Their mothers would be ashamed."

But he'd kept his cool, he'd listened to what was important, and all that meant more than she could explain in a few words. "I'm proud of you," she said, catching his fingers in hers.

"I'm even more proud of you." He glanced around the room. "Come on, let's get out of here."

Absolutely. "You have somewhere in mind?"

"Nowhere in particular. Just not here." He pushed open the door for her. "Somewhere private."

She knew just the place. Melody held out her hand. "Give me your keys. I'm driving."

27

*T*raders Pub wasn't officially open. Steve had no idea how she'd got them through the locked doors and into the dance section of the pub, but somehow she did it. Ten seconds after she'd led him onto the dance floor, the muted lighting clicked on overhead.

He glanced at her, so glad that tension haunting her for so long had vanished. "Do I want to know?"

"Know what?"

Music started playing, and he laughed, pulling her to him and swaying to the beat. "You seem to have gremlins working for you."

She rested her head against his chest, fingers tangled in his belt loops as she let him lead. "Gremlins whose pet pig had colic last week. I phoned ahead and asked for a few favours. Now shut up and dance. I like this song."

He shut up, wrapped his arms around her and enjoyed having the place to themselves as the country singer serenaded them. Words about forever and a night that never ended—everything he longed for with Melody.

"Good song," he commented, the tickle of butterfly wings rising in his stomach as he considered what he was about to do.

"He's got a sexy voice." She slid a hand up his chest, stopping with her fingers resting over his heart. "But yours is sexier."

"I'm glad to hear that." He sang along, echoing the words. Feeling emotion building all the way down to his toes until he was ready to burst with it.

Before he could speak, though, she broke in. "This part of the song is wrong."

He paused, running through the lyrics. "You're looking hot—that can't be the part."

"We *know* what roads we've been down." Melody tangled her fingers in his hair, teasing the back of his neck. "You were partly right, back at the start of summer when you said what we had before wasn't important because what mattered more was the future. But when I think about us, here and now, our relationship is *so* much richer because I have our past to compare to. And there's no doubt in my mind what kind of a man I have."

Anticipation and hope surrounded him, and his feet stopped moving to the music because she was all he could concentrate on. "I'm your man?"

"I sure hope so. Unless there was someone else who crawled into my bed last night and told me they loved me."

He tucked his fingers under her chin and tilted her head back. "Nope. That was all me, in my favourite place in the entire world. Right by your side."

Melody's eyes sparkled. She lowered her voice. "This would be a good time for you to say it again, since I was kind of loopy the last time."

"Hey, I thought since I said it already, it was your turn."

"I'll say it." She brushed their lips together. "I'll say it a whole bunch of different ways, until you're drunk on me."

Nice one. "You're quoting songs at me. Now I know it's love."

He wrapped his arms around her and lifted her in the air, bringing their heads in line. "I'm more than drunk on you. I'm flying because when you look at me that way, I can do anything. Anything, especially love you for the rest of our lives."

She cupped his face in her hands, her soft smile blooming until it lit up the entire dance floor. "I love you too. So much."

They stood there in the middle of the room, not moving, not doing *anything* except grinning at each other like fools. Then Steve came to his senses and kissed her, taking her lips like he'd wanted for days. With everything in him because she meant everything *to him*.

Somehow they ended up with both feet on the ground, swaying to another song.

"Oh, I forgot." Melody broke them apart, stepping to the edge of the stage. "I have to apologize."

He paused a beat. "Okay."

She shifted on her feet, but she still wore a smile—the one that said she couldn't believe he was there with her. "I did something that wasn't very nice, and I've been trying to think of a way to make it up to you."

He grew more intrigued by the moment. "I don't know that you've done anything bad."

"See, that's the problem. You don't even think it was wrong, but it was. I got away with it because I'm a woman." She tilted her head to the side and pulled a face. "And that's why I want to apologize. It's one thing for me to get mad at you, or for you to get mad at me. That's a part of a relationship and part of learning to get along. Obviously, we're going to do a lot of that—the fighting —since we're both so easygoing."

She looked so glum for a moment he laughed.

Her smile reappeared. "But as everyone likes to remind me, I dumped a pitcher of beer on you, and that was inappropriate in so many ways."

Steve shrugged. "It's forgotten."

A burst of laughter escaped her. "That's the one thing it'll never be—*forgotten*. That incident gets mentioned all over town, and I'm so sorry that I did it in the first place."

He paused for a moment and considered. "You're right, I couldn't have gotten away with dumping beer on you."

"But you can." Melody pulled a plastic pitcher from behind the speaker, turning back as Steve's amusement grew. "I thought about giving this to you in the middle of a Friday-night crowd, but I don't want to wait until then." She stepped forward and offered him the pitcher. "So I hope you'll accept my apology in private. Go ahead, Steve, take your revenge."

"You're not serious."

She pressed the pitcher into his hands. "Very serious. Do your worst."

Steve glanced over his shoulder, but they were still alone. The music in the background changed as Melody stood before him, a contrite expression on her face, her body swaying to the upbeat tune.

What a difference a year had made. A year ago if she'd offered him this? He would've had no idea how to deal with it. But now he knew exactly what to do.

"You really want me to do this?"

Melody nodded.

He shrugged then picked her up with one arm, lifting her in the air at his side. "Okay."

"Wait, what are you doing?" She shoved at his shoulders in an attempt to get free. "You're not supposed to do that. Wait—stop! Not on you too—"

"Your choice, sweetheart." He held the pitcher over both their heads, meeting her gaze straight on. "I love you, and that means we're in this together. We're in *everything* together. So, do I pour, or not?"

She was laughing so hard she could barely speak. "I love you. Oh, damn, I love you so much."

He placed the pitcher on the nearest table and carried her with him toward the exit door. "I love you too. Now, instead of wasting a pitcher of good beer, you and I are going back to my place so we can find some other way to get you good and wet."

Melody cupped his face in hands. "Vanilla ice cream first?"

He laughed. "Anything, as long as I'm with you."

It had been a long road, but worth the journey. Steve took her by the hand and headed toward forever.

~

New York Times Bestselling Author Vivian Arend
invites you to meet the Coleman's. These contemporary cowboys
ranch the foothills of the Alberta Rockies. Enjoy the ride as they
each find their happily-ever-afters.

~

Six Pack Ranch
Rocky Mountain Heat
Rocky Mountain Haven
Rocky Mountain Desire
Rocky Mountain Angel
Rocky Mountain Rebel
Rocky Mountain Freedom
Rocky Mountain Romance
Rocky Mountain Retreat
Rocky Mountain Shelter
Rocky Mountain Devil
Rocky Mountain Home

~

ABOUT THE AUTHOR

With over 2 million books sold, Vivian Arend is a New York Times and USA Today bestselling author of over 50 contemporary and paranormal romance books, including the Six Pack Ranch and Granite Lake Wolves.

Her books are all standalone reads with no cliffhangers. They're humorous yet emotional, with sexy-times and happily-ever-afters. Vivian pretty much thinks she's got the best job in the world, and she's looking forward to giving readers more HEAs. She lives in B.C. Canada with her husband of many years and a fluffy attack Shih-tzu named Luna who ignores everyone except when treats are deployed.